P9-CBG-376

The Address Book

Also by Anne Bernays

The School Book

Growing Up Rich

The First to Know

Prudence, Indeed

The New York Ride

Short Pleasures

The Address Book

A NOVEL BY

ANNE BERNAYS

Little, Brown and Company Boston–Toronto

FIRST EDITION

Library of Congress Cataloging in Publication Data

Bernays, Anne.
The address book.

I. Title.
PS3552.E728A64 1983 813'.54 83-12030
ISBN 0-316-09195-2

BP

Designed by Susan Windheim

Published simultaneously in Canada
by Little, Brown & Company (Canada) Limited

PRINTED IN THE UNITED STATES OF AMERICA

To Arthur

Acknowledgments

I would like to thank Patricia Berens, Justin Kaplan, Edith Luray, Pamela Painter, Betsy Pitha, and my inspired editor, William Phillips.

The Address Book

CHAPTER

One

SOMETHING odd happened; the light was exploding. It threw itself against the pale surface of the wall opposite Alicia's desk where it was chopped into trapezoids by the window's wooden elements. The light seemed unreliable and fierce.

"No, not again," Alicia said. She watched to see if it would do anything spectacular, such as sparkle suddenly or go out altogether, leaving her in shadow. The phone on her desk buzzed.

"Davida Franklin is here to see you," the receptionist said.

"Ask her to come up, please." Alicia swiveled back and forth in her chair. Above her, behind her, lay piles of manuscripts, pages and pages of them, in binders, in boxes, hundreds and thousands of words, most of them extruded by people whose work would never see the light of day, but who continued to write, against all logic, all sense. These words Alicia would have to read, or at the very least skim, to make certain no diamonds were there, buried in the mud. She should not be going to lunch with Davida, she should be here, searching for diamonds.

Davida Franklin breezed in, bringing with her clouds of Opium as seductive as hope. She was wearing a bright blue nubbly wool coat, a dashing purple scarf and high-heeled boots. Her black bangs shone as if polished.

"There's a decapitated squirrel out there by the gate," she

said, whipping off the scarf and making herself comfortable in Alicia's one armchair. "It's revolting, *dégoûtant.* You'd think the blood would be dark red and arterial but it isn't, it's a sort of baby pink. The body's still intact. I don't quite understand . . ."

"You don't have to convince me you have the eye. I'm your editor, remember? Spare me the details." Alicia smiled.

"I thought you thrived on that sort of thing," Davida said. She withdrew her kid gloves, one slim finger at a time.

"One of my authors phoned me this morning just to tell me I was lovable. I must say, it was unexpected and it unnerved me."

"Well you are, you know," Davida said, reaching over and patting Alicia's arm. "I've told you that often enough. You wouldn't be fishing, would you?"

"Hardly," Alicia said. She knew something about Davida that she didn't want to talk about, nasty news. When she let her secret go, it would be in her role as Editor, not Friend. Friend would have to go sneak off somewhere out of sight and out of hearing.

"That other author—whoever he is—must have finished his book or he wouldn't have called you lovable."

"It was a woman," Alicia said, "and yes, her manuscript went off to Production yesterday." Alicia's attention was trapped by a novel she had promised an agent to have finished an hour earlier, vowed, crossed her heart to have read by eleven-thirty; she was only ten pages into it. "Ah," she said, "I really shouldn't leave, I have so much to do, I'm buried under my work."

"Do you good to get away for an hour or so, *chérie.* Besides, you can't send me home hungry. And I need a small editorial transfusion, feeling somewhat shaky . . ." Davida's eyes were older than her skin, her smile. They were the eyes of a woman to whom choice no longer seemed a reasonable plot device in her own life.

"Would you like to hear what happened at the Editorial

Board Meeting this morning? Only you mustn't repeat this," Alicia said.

"You're speaking to the woman of a thousand secrets."

"Well, we were discussing this novel that came in last month and Peter Fairchild, you know Peter, always ready with the salient analysis, he said, 'The trouble with this novel is there's too much talking and not enough fucking.' Everyone broke up, of course, except Phyllis, you should have seen Phyllis's eyes clamp shut; she looked as if she were about to pass out. Myself, I thought Peter had put his finger neatly on the trouble. I believe Peter's looking for a job in New York."

"You'd miss his wit, wouldn't you?" Davida said. There were clouds in her voice; Alicia heard them.

"You sound down, Davey. Is it that stupid lawsuit?"

"That's part of it," Davida said.

At that moment, Alicia, in a flash of transcendence, saw down through flights of stairs, through floors, down three stories and into the reception area, where the man everyone in Griffin House called Celestial Sam was delivering his annual manuscript in a decomposing box, a manuscript all but indistinguishable from the others. The title blazed, the letters typed in red, conveniently enlarged so she could read them in her mind clearly: *UFO and FBI—An Intergalactic Conspiracy.* Things like this had happened to Alicia before; she could no more account for it than she could the fact that her marriage had changed, that distance was as much a part of it now as sex was and being parents. She loved Barney, but where was he? Her prescience frightened her: it wasn't natural; she did not enjoy seeing through plaster and wood. I am a freak of nature, she thought, this is not a gift, it's a curse.

"How could anyone have guessed that a man I hadn't slept with in ten years would sue me for libel? I mean, it isn't the least like him, you know that, my character's a teacher, not a copywriter."

"Davey, we've been over this, you don't have to defend

yourself to me, it was *our* mistake. We should have had it read by our lawyer. I should have asked you if there was anybody 'real' in your novel."

"Yes, and now look," Davida said. She jumped up from where she was sitting and began poking around in Alicia's Out box. Alicia let her. "We've got to get through this whole legal mess and I can't prove a negative. I can't prove I didn't mean to libel Archie Tanner."

"And you had to go and make him a bisexual sodomist . . ."

"You'd think the man would have too much pride," Davida said. Alicia saw the parody of a smile. They would both think it funny, but it would take ten years for the grimness to give way entirely. Her boss Phyllis Vance, Griffin's Managing Editor, on the other hand, didn't think it was funny now and never would.

When Phyllis had hired Alicia Baer eight years earlier, she had warned her: "Don't get too chummy with your authors, it leads invariably to the sort of trouble we can all do without. Don't marry 'em, don't even go to bed with them. Keep 'em at a long arm's length." Alicia thought Phyllis hopelessly rigid, locked into categories. The kind of trouble they could all do without, Alicia felt, was sweet cream over strawberries. They were not alike, she and Phyllis, Phyllis with her caveats and her categories. . . .

Each time her phone buzzed, Alicia thought it was Phyllis about Davida; statistically speaking, it almost never was.

"The money he wants takes care of the pride," Alicia said. Her phone buzzed. It was an agent in New York. Davida pulled out a compact and studied her right eye in its mirror. Alicia didn't want to do business with Davida in the room, obviously pretending not to listen. She tried to be cryptic, giving the agent one-word answers. He must think she was crazy. The lovely Davida grew fangs and claws over Alicia's other authors. It was amazing. Sibling rivalry rampant, breathing fire, weeping buckets, sulking, spitting. Davida snapped the compact shut.

"Thanks, Frank. 'Bye," Alicia said.

"What was that all about?" Davida asked.

"Do you really want to know?" Alicia said, getting up. "Come on, if we're going, let's get out of here now before the phone rings again."

As Alicia and Davida left the building, Alicia caught sight of Celestial Sam shuffling off toward Tremont Street, then dissolving into the crowd. It did not surprise her to see him, but the verification of her second sight, the look of his bare head with its ashy scalp, made her feel faint. She tucked her arm in Davida's, grabbing on. There was a connection between her and Davida that Alicia relied on as on a lifeline. Davida was a giver, not of objects especially (the presents they exchanged were more amusing than precious), but of the things Alicia most needed: a faithful ear, a response untainted by morality, a style that slid easily into satire. She came up close, breathed on your face, batted her pretty hazel eyes, smiled, shrugged and lapsed into Frenchisms. Davida looked more like a Thirties movie princess than a serious writer, but serious writer she was; she spent most of each day in her apartment on Marlborough Street working on her novels, each one better than the last. A reviewer had recently said of Davida that she "skins her characters while they are living but, miraculously, leaves them more alive than when she began to peel them." Davida's reaction to this was, "He made me sound like a cook."

Davida said, "You knew I was going to call you at the last minute for lunch today, didn't you?" And when Alicia said nothing in response, she went on, "And I knew you'd be free. Right?"

"Wrong," Alicia said, "I didn't know. And neither did you, Davida, please don't start on that E.S.P. stuff again. It's gaga."

"You *were* free, weren't you?"

"I'm mostly free." Alicia tried to laugh it off but there it was again. First Celestial Sam and now Davida, claiming prescience for both of them. Flickers of thought coming out as whole entities. Seeing through walls and through time. When, occasionally, she reported these things to Barney, he told her in a not unkindly voice that she should not bother him with her E.S.P.P., meant to be a joke but more like a knife.

"I feel like pizza," Davida was saying. "How about it, Alicia?"

"Pizza," Alicia repeated. "That's on my proscribed list."

"Oh, for Pete's sake," Davida said. "You're not going to worry about a few calories at your age, are you? Come on, don't worry so much, you look fine, you look heroic, look at the way people eye you, they think you're spectacular!"

Was Davida angry? Alicia couldn't be sure; but this vehemence was unusual. She looked at her friend and realized that Davida would have to be vain herself to look the way she did at thirty-nine or forty or forty-one (odd, she couldn't remember how old Davida was). She was a knockout, her eyes alone sent men into frenzies. And as for her elongated figure and madcap face . . . well, even Barney admitted that she was sexy and warm. A sport almost, among women and certainly among serious writers.

They walked, no longer arm and arm, down Washington Street. All Boston and suburbs seemed to have gathered there as if summoned by a gigantic give-away. "Who *are* these people?" Davida said.

"God's children," Alicia told her, doubting it herself but determined not to let Davida's mood infect her. "I thought you liked crowds," she added.

"Not today," Davida said. "I'm sorry I suggested this."

"You really are in a trough, aren't you?" Alicia said as she swerved to keep a massive youth from crashing into her. He'd done it on purpose, she saw this in his eyes.

Davida was saying, "More people seems to mean more ugliness. Beauty is a recessive trait, it must be, everybody looks deformed, I swear it, they all have the wrong heads."

Davida guided them into a restaurant on a curving street near the North End, where they slipped into a booth. The place smelled of herbs and beer stains. "You've never taken an author to a pizza joint for lunch, have you?" Davida said. Alicia shook her head. She watched an old man bite into a hero sandwich and chew, with downcast eyes, in sad, rhythmic chews.

They ordered a large pizza and a carafe of red wine. "I promise to cheer up," Davida said. "And I've got a new one for you." She opened her purse and pulled out a small notebook from which she read: "Enormity," she said, with a smile. "That's today's word."

"That's easy," Alicia said.

"I should have known," Davida said. "Up until yesterday I thought it meant very big. *Mais, pas du tout,* it means wickedness, moral outrage. The enormity of her crime—she scalded her child to teach her a lesson or something like that."

"There *is* nothing like that. Scalding your own child is unique."

Davida shut up her notebook and laid it on the table by her paper doily, which pictured a large pizza piled high with everything. "He doesn't have a leg to stand on," she said.

"Perhaps not, but that's why there are courts and lawyers, judges and juries. By the way, in cases like this, the jury usually finds for the plaintiff. Doc Gurney told me, he's the lawyer we deal with. He doesn't want it to be a jury trial."

"Even when the plaintiff's lying?"

"The way he put it was juries think all writers are rich and immoral. Ergo, they find for the plaintiff."

"Oh, God," Davida said. The waiter, a mere kid, wearing an apron that looked blood-stained but was probably tomato, brought their meal on a huge chrome tray. "You ladies want plates?" he said. They nodded.

It was worse than Davida knew. Phyllis Vance was fed up. Davida Franklin's books never sold more than eleven thousand copies; the lawsuit, as Phyllis said, obliged them to put down the camel, poor broken thing. "The last straw," Phyllis said on the morning papers were served her by a sheriff's deputy, reeking of beer and smiling lewdly as he handed them over. "Have a good day," he said, exiting.

"The goddamn last straw. That author of yours is jinxed. Maybe this person, this sodomist who's suing her, is some nut out in left field but he's hired himself the fanciest law firm in New York. Yes, I know we've given her an advance on the next book but I say, it's time to cut bait. She's losing us big money and now this legal mess, that's the last straw, or have I said that?"

Alicia vowed to fight. The Davida Franklin sales profile was unfortunate; twenty years before she might have made it to the *Boston Globe*'s best-seller list. Today you had to write a book forty thousand people were willing to pay thirteen-fifty for, a book that Jane Fonda wanted to turn into a movie, a book for a quickie read on the flight to Chicago. Or else . . . or else go into the catering business. Alicia stared into her author's elegant face and wanted to make everything better for her, as for a vulnerable young sister. Davida bit into a triangle of pizza. A thick spider's web of cheese pulled off and stuck to her chin. She smiled. "Good," she said.

They both concentrated on the food.

"Everything seems to come at me at once," Davida said, taking Alicia by surprise.

"Meaning?" Alicia knew this to be true for almost everybody. But right now she had to be as neutral as a therapist, someone for Davida to bounce off; later she might turn the tables, knowing it wasn't in her job description but doing it nevertheless because she needed Davida almost as much as Davida needed her.

"Meaning first the lawsuit, and now Craig. Why doesn't it ever work out? How is it you've managed to stay married to the same man for seventeen years and I can't keep a relationship going seventeen months? Apart from my so-called marriage, that's my record—seventeen months."

"Why do you assume you and marriage were made for each other?"

"I'd just like to see if I can live with a man without one of us wanting to kill the other at the end of a quiet Sunday at home." She looked down, uncharacteristically limp. "Look what Craig's gone and done now," she said. She hooked a finger into a heavy, braided gold chain and pulled it up from under her shirt. Hanging off the chain was a pendant shaped like a crescent moon with a human profile etched onto its surface. "See this eye? It's a real sapphire. The rest of it's eighteen-carat gold. Too much. *De trop.*"

"It's Nixon," Alicia said. "The nose—it looks just like him."

"No, it's not, it isn't anybody."

"Nixon or not, why are you wearing it inside?"

"It's ostentatious, wouldn't you say? Also, it's much too attractive to those maniacs who ride the subway."

"That only happens in New York," Alicia said. "It'll be another twenty years before chain-snatching catches on in Boston."

Davida smiled. "You're so funny," she said. "I don't quite know what's wrong but I keep getting strange vibrations from this man. Let's not even talk about the fact that I think he makes far too much money for an acoustical engineer. I don't know, he's got this marvelous polish but he's such a sneaky sort of bastard. I never quite know where he's been before I see him or where he's going afterwards. He never lets me meet him at his office—we have to meet in a bar. Charlie's or somewhere like that. Lots of swinging singles. I'm too old."

"Too old to swing or to be single?" Alicia said.

"Both, I guess."

It was an old story, the story of Davida and men. She was fine with women and not so fine with men. Alicia suspected that Davida was getting only what she thought she deserved. She called it "my lousy luck," but it didn't have much to do with luck. Davida's former husband, a nuclear physicist with a heavily compensating social conscience, was a rotter. According to Davida, he slept with whatever happened to appeal to his fancy and sulked when at home. Since her divorce, Davida had run through a series of men, many of whom Alicia found attractive simply because they were so openly—and casually—rotten. As she said to Barney, "Isn't a pineapple about to go rotten the sweetest fruit there is?" Barney agreed and added that Davida was "self-destructive. Sexy, but self-destructive."

Davida flushed when she talked about Craig; there was something undeniably powerful there, working against common sense. He continued to bemuse her, with his Italian suits, his laid-back mannerisms, his sandy mustache and manicured beard. It was obvious to Alicia that Davida concentrated on the physical and then let the rest of Craig touch her more slowly and with greater risk. The serious writer clung to the romance of a girl. In one way, then, Davida was lucky; life was simple for her: she was in love or out, working on a book or stuck, having a good time or bored. A binary life, a primitive existence outside the work; while inside the work lay a world of ambiguities.

Alicia was aware she was floating off when Davida said, "I'm talking about myself again."

"That's all right," Alicia said.

"No, it isn't. I'm so selfish! Your eyes are funny; you're not telling me something."

"You're imagining things," Alicia said.

"You lie easily but not well, if you don't mind my saying so," Davida said. "You've got to learn to leave your mouth alone when you're fibbing. Don't touch it, don't put your hand up to your mouth."

"Good God," Alicia said. "Isn't there *any*thing you don't see?"

"My own future," Davida said.

Davida's books did not sell the most copies but her language was the one she most enjoyed reading; she was also sure that Davida's best book was going to be an important one. Compared with many of Alicia's books—dry cereal crammed with vitamins but essentially tasteless—Davida's work was rich, rum custardy stuff. Sweet but not cloying. Alicia loved Davida as author, as friend; more, she cared about what happened to her. "Okay," she said in a rush, "you'll find out soon enough if I do it. If I don't, it won't make any difference." A young man and woman took the booth in back of Davida and put a quarter into the juke box. Loud rock music swept through the place. Alicia smiled ruefully. "My overture." She took a sip of wine. "I may go to New York," she said.

"Alicia!" Davida cried. "Why didn't you tell me this before?" She looked stricken. "Are you going with Peter?"

"Oh, Lord," Alicia said. She began to laugh, felt the laughter start to get out of control.

Davida looked uncomfortable. "I guess I'm wrong," she said.

Alicia nodded. "Wrong," she said. "Peter's got a girlfriend in New York. He's crazy about her. She's married to a TV producer who ties her to the bed or something before he fucks her."

"*Tiens,*" Davida said. "What I'm not learning today." Her face turned sober. "What about you? Why are *you* going?"

"I didn't say I *was* going," Alicia said. "I said I *might* be going."

"Okay then, why *might* you be going?"

"Tolland and Lutwidge just offered me a job as Executive Editor. That means editorial autonomy, big office with window overlooking skating rink, a hefty raise in salary, stock options in the company, no Phyllis, all kinds of things I'm not getting here. No Phyllis, just imagine. Pure bliss."

"You're going to take it, aren't you?"

"I haven't decided." Alicia said.

"But why not, it sounds dreamy. Bliss, you said."

"There's an obstacle," Alicia said, wondering why Davida didn't see it.

"Toby's portable, so you must mean Barney."

Alicia nodded. "Barney."

"Can't he cut people up in New York? Why can't Barney go to P and S or Cornell or just Park Avenue?"

"Would you leave Boston if you were Barney?"

"That would depend on what *you* did." Davida grabbed hold, scraping Alicia along the bottom. "What does your old man have to say about all this?"

"He doesn't know." The music stopped. This slack was taken up by the sound of running water in the kitchen and then a word spoken loudly in Italian from behind the swinging doors. It sounded as if someone were about to do something violent. A second voice, equally angry, responded. There was a thudding. Alicia cringed.

"He doesn't know?" Davida said. "I thought you two shared everything. How is it possible to be wooed by a publishing house in New York without your husband knowing? I think it would be harder to manage than an affair." She stopped. "Listen, Allie, if this is all getting too close to the bone, I'll shut up."

Alicia shook her head. "It's all right. I might as well talk about it. The affair, so to speak, was carried on mostly long distance except when I made my usual trips to New York. The rest of it was done from my office—though that got sticky once when Jenny opened a letter she shouldn't have. And of course I never brought any of this home, I never left any lipstick-stained handkerchiefs or love notes around. And Barney doesn't know. He's so busy with his committees and his teaching and his conferences and his microsurgery seminars and God knows what all, that he sometimes even forgets to ask where I've been. Professionally speaking, we have the ultimate open marriage."

Davida smiled. "And I'll bet you thought if you didn't bring it up, it would go away."

"That's terribly stupid, isn't it?" Alicia said. "And I was afraid of bringing him into it because I listen to him too carefully, I give him points for wisdom that I don't have, never did have . . ."

"That's not true, Allie," Davida said sharply. "You sound as if you had Barney confused with your father. He's not your father. And you're not a child."

"He's not? I'm not?" The laughter punched her again. Alicia was astonished by her frailty, something she thought she had banished years before. And here it was returned suddenly, with no message preceding it—make the beds, put out more towels, provide—but stood on her doorstep, waiting to be taken in again.

Davida laughed. "I don't know how you manage to keep your nutty sense of humor," she said, misunderstanding Alicia's laughter. So then, Davida saw a lot but did not always comprehend what it was she was seeing.

"I have to tell him," Alicia said as her laughter deflated. "I can't put it off much longer . . ."

"He'll understand. He's a nice man," Davida said. "As men go." She wiped her fingers on the flimsy paper napkin. Then she took out her compact and looked at her right eye.

"He may understand," Alicia said, "but this may be a problem with no solution. Either I stay here in Boston or I go to New York. If I go, either he stays here—bad—or he comes along with me. Equally bad."

"How so?" Davida said. "I don't see that."

"Because of the guilt I'll feel about uprooting him from his practice, his colleagues, his students, his beloved nurses, his Harvard."

"*Mon dieu,*" Davida said, "his Harvard. You know, Allie," she continued, "I don't see why this has to be an either-or thing. You could commute. And so could he. He makes a bundle, that's no secret. So there's no reason why you shouldn't have one place here and another in New York. It could be the ideal solution."

"Except," said Alicia, breaking in, "that it's neither here nor there. It's neither one thing or the other."

"So what?"

"So, it wouldn't meet the needs of any marriage I ever heard of and it wouldn't be a separation either."

"But it *is* a solution, isn't it?" Davida said. It struck Alicia as interesting that this woman could suggest an orchestration as basically equivocal as this one and yet fail to provide herself with the same kind of answers.

"I'll think about it," Alicia said.

They took the long way back, skirting the ocean of shoppers. Alicia tried to think of a way of asking Davida to go with her to New York—if she went—without telling her outright that she might soon be finding herself up for grabs. It was too hard, too complicated. Instead, she said, "If I take this job in New York I hope some of my authors will eventually want to join me."

"That's stealing, isn't it?"

"Depends on the way you look at it. Some writers can't live without their editors. They think we're the ultimate muse. It's all in their heads, of course, but then so is infatuation. Anyway, Davey, it's done all the time. Editor moves from one house to another, simply scoops up his or her authors and off they swim together into the sunset."

"Should I buy a new bathing suit?" Davida asked.

As Alicia entered her office at two o'clock, her phone was ringing. The phone these days so rarely delivered anything heartening that Alicia had begun to hate it; it was a miserable creature sitting there on her desk, dressed in plastic, waiting to harass her. This time it was Dick Freyburg, calling from Tolland and Lutwidge. Dick asked Alicia how she was. They compared weather in Boston and New York. They shared a piece of publishing gossip about which each had a slightly different version.

Then Dick said, "Did you get my letter?"

"Yes, I did," Alicia said. The room was growing hot; she couldn't reach the window from her desk.

"I don't want to pressure you," he said. She figured he was saying the opposite of what he meant.

"I realize that," she said. "And I appreciate it."

"You're a prize," he said. "We want you here. That's about it."

A prize. If Alicia suspected that T & L, in offering her this plum of a job, was going to pay her less than a man doing the same editorial tasks, she had no way of proving it; these private matters were kept under lock and key. Perhaps, she thought, I don't want to know. "You flatter me," she said. She hoped he too wasn't going to call her lovable.

"Is end of April enough time?"

"I think so," she said, knowing she couldn't stall Dick Freyburg forever. He seemed to fade; Alicia could hear him saying something muffled to someone in his office. Then he returned. "Look, sweetie, I'll let you go now. One of us will get back to the other by the end of April, right?"

"Right," she said. They hung up and she opened the window, pulling in chilled air which pricked her throat as it went down. She knew Dick Freyburg wanted her badly but not quite why. There was something in all this that wasn't clear: her numbers were not *that* good. The notion that she had so much professional charm for Freyburg pleased her immensely, made her proud but clouded her image of herself. "Why?" she said aloud. And then: "And why not? You're as good as anyone in this business who still cares about language more than residuals."

CHAPTER
Two

ALICIA Baer had worked out an arrangement with Griffin House whereby she left work an hour and a half earlier than the other employees and rode the subway home so that her fourteen-year-old daughter, Toby, would not have to come home to an empty house. This meant not that Alicia had less work than her fellows but that she did it at home in the bedroom, where she had installed a desk, a typewriter, a blue filing cabinet and two large olive-drab metal wastebaskets. On the one hand, she was spared the constant interruptions of office life, but on the other, her husband sometimes did not seem to realize that she was really *working* when she was working, seemed to believe she was engaged in an interesting hobby. As for Toby, she always remembered to knock when the bedroom door was closed and appeared (unlike the children of Alicia's friends) to be somewhat awed by her mother's professional life. While this was gratifying, it made Alicia a little uneasy. "She acts like my apprentice," Alicia complained to Barney. "Why doesn't she shriek at me once in a while?"

"Be grateful, honey, what would you like? Would you rather she was on 'Ludes?"

"I'd like to be worried once in a while about her school work or what she does on the way home from school. Like Bunny Roberts down the street. Bunny Roberts eats angel dust."

"You're putting me on, aren't you?" Barney said. He did not recognize how straight his daughter was compared with most girls her age. "Besides, you *are* worried about her. You always think she's been run over or raped or something if she's five minutes late coming home."

"I admit it, I admit it," Alicia said. "But that's my problem, isn't it? Not *hers.*"

When Alicia got home on Friday afternoon, the house in Brookline was empty, the lights were off, the cat was napping on a neatly stacked pile of *Boston Globe*s and *New York Times*es on the kitchen table.

Alicia changed from her Boston clothes—the suit that was too mannish for her taste, she was sorry she'd bought it, and a tailored silk blouse—into a pair of jeans, the heavy blue Irish sweater Barney had brought back for her the last time he was in London, and a pair of beat-up rubber-soled shoes from L. L. Bean. She referred to them as her girl scout shoes.

Alicia looked at herself in the mirror to see if she was noticeably fatter or more wrinkled than during the last inspection. "It's only a matter of time, honey pie," she told her image, "you'd better get ready." Then she repeated to herself in a kind of chant: "You've got to tell him, you've got to tell him," until the words lost meaning and became a mantra. He's a good person, no malice, he's just busy and distracted, he'll understand. This "understanding" that she counted on might, of course, be meaningless in the long run. Understanding didn't change the enormity of her choice.

She climbed down the back stairs into the kitchen, where residual heat from the stove surrounded her. May had been there, letting herself in and out of the house while its occupants were away. The floor was clean and glossy, the counters cleared, the drying rack by the sink empty. An odor of chocolate hung over the stove. May was a ghost; Alicia rarely saw her but felt her presence every weekday; May's ghostly hands had touched and altered almost everything in the house.

Toby walked in through the back door, wearing faded jeans and a yellow sweat shirt, her slight body just beginning to swell in interesting places. Who could tell at this moment whether her breasts would be ladylike little things or great big embarrassing globes, whether she would be hippy or slim, whether her skin would erupt or stay silky? Toby could go any of a number of ways and it was all there waiting; she was programmed, ready. The sight of her in her round glasses thus poised made Alicia swallow to keep from crying.

There was something different about Toby now, a kind of covered look. She said hello to her mother and then made for the back stairs.

"Aren't you going to have a snack?" Alicia said. "I think May left some brownies. I can smell them."

"No, thanks," Toby said.

"How come? Not feeling well?"

"I'm on a diet," the child said, pulling her mouth together in a tight round wrinkle.

"You're on a *what*? That's nuts. You're not fat, who's been telling you to lose weight?"

"No one's been telling me anything, Mom. Please don't bug me, I only want to lose five pounds. I'll eat dinner, I promise."

"Toby dear, I can't let you do this. You're growing, you can't starve yourself!"

"I'm not starving myself, Mom. Please. Please don't give me a hard time. I'm not eating brownies anymore, that's all. Now may I go, please, I have to study."

"Oh, Lord," Alicia breathed as her daughter disappeared up the spine of the house. "This is crazy." Her impeccable daughter was showing signs of independence but was taking a route Alicia was totally unprepared for. A diet, a slim child-girl like that not eating in order to look different? But hadn't Alicia done the same thing herself—many times, accompanied by sighs and groans? I can't eat bread, it's fattening, I won't have any dessert, I don't eat crackers, no, thank you—sometimes with tears of desire in her eyes. Alicia passed up the urge to blame herself entirely for what was happening to her daughter, and wandered into the living room for her moment of rest. Dusk had settled over the house, turning the air a grayish purple, throwing a dusky light against the white walls of the room. She kept the lamps off during the few tinted minutes of dusk because she loved the glow of the light. But now it seemed more a bringer of gloom than of reprieve.

What kind of a wife was it who dreaded the return home of her husband? A bad wife, a selfish woman, a lackluster heart, a flawed spirit, a woman greedy for change, fed up with routine and longing for risks, ready to stretch, absurdly and unreasonably ambitious, a greedy bitch . . . the list lengthened and deepened. Finally she cut it off: you're not a monster, she told the gloom. And you're not fat either, and your daughter's going to be okay and you've got a pretty good life here, you can afford to buy your sheets in Bloomingdale's even though you wait for the White Sale and you have a disposal and, as your mother's Aunt Eva used to say, "Darling, if you've got your health, you don't need nothing else." She had her health.

Dinner was generally something of a problem, as Alicia had little time for shopping, save on Saturday, when the market was jammed with other people who could shop only on Saturday, and because the part of her head used to organize and make lists was the head she took with her to her office and applied to her work. Sometimes she asked Barney to help out with her lists but there were strange lesions in him too: he forgot crucial items like sugar and milk; and if he went to the market instead of her he came back with things like Crispie Critters and the minuscule size of vinegar and peanut butter. On purpose? Surely not, he wanted to help, he said so himself, over and over, "I want to help you, Allie, you're busy, why shouldn't we *both* do these things?"

When Barney came home on Friday evening, Alicia had their dinner under control. He came into the kitchen and kissed her face straight off. "Hello, honeylips," he said. "Had a good day?"

"Yes," she said. "Fine. Peter Fairchild said something funny at the editorial meeting." She repeated what Peter had said. Barney laughed out loud. "Pity he's leaving Griffin," Barney said. "You'll miss him."

"What did *you* do?" Alicia said, turning back to her lettuce washing.

"The usual scissors and paste jobs," he said.

Alicia watched Barney twist three ice cubes out of the tray and drop them into a glass, then pour in the makings of a Scotch sour. "You?" he said, nodding at the drink. "A little wine please," she said. His fingers' joints were articulated like a wooden toy's, and worked perfectly; there was no hesitation or stiffness. She could never look at Barney's hands without thinking of blood. He poured her a glass of wine and sat in the kitchen while she put the chicken on a platter and ringed it with potatoes and vegetables. They began a conversation, then Barney picked up the *Globe* and began to read. Alicia sighed and went off to tell Toby her dinner was ready.

She recalled that at breakfast he'd mentioned a "possible double mastectomy"; she was grateful not to hear the outcome of this particular story. During dinner she kept an eye on Toby; the child ate normally, if somewhat slowly. Alicia kept up a nervous kind of chatter and Barney ate somewhat grimly, like a patient instructed to "feed up" for the big operation. Alicia surprised herself by searching his face. After all these years it still looked thoughtful and kind; it was the sort of face other women sized up quickly and then told her how lucky she was to be married to a man like Barney. They were not mistaken.

After dinner Toby cleared her plate, helped with the dishes and then went upstairs to her room. As usual, Barney headed for his study. Alicia stopped him. "Can I come with you to your room for a few minutes? There's something we have to talk about."

A cloud passed across Barney's features. "There's an article I have to finish, a deadline. Can it possibly wait?"

"Not really," she said, biting down. "When was the last time I asked you to give me some time like this?"

"You're right," he said, reaching his arm out for a touch of her. The skin on his hand was polished from so many scrubbings. She had bought him extra-strength skin cream but suspected he forgot to use it. "Come on, Allie, I can tell it's important."

He put her in his visitor's chair; in fact, she felt like a visitor.

"You look nice in that sweater," he said. "Did I give it to you? It goes with your eyes." He sat himself down on the other side of his desk. She wasn't his visitor now, she was his patient, consulting. The reflection from the lamp on his desk got caught in the disks of his granny glasses; he had two new eyes, flaming in front of the other ones. She tried to move to reduce the number of eyes. "Well, now," he said. "What's up?"

She shut her eyes, took a breath of air, held it briefly down there among the alveoli, and as she let it out, said in a rush: "I've been offered a job with another publisher in New York, Tolland and Lutwidge."

"Well," he said, "you must feel very good about that." It was an unexpected response. He took out his pipe and began to load it with honey-flavored tobacco. "It's always flattering to be asked to move to a competitor. Even in business."

"I *do* feel good," Alicia said.

"Well, what can I say? Is there a problem?" She thought he might be growing impatient but he said, "Come on, Allie, open up, we can talk about anything . . ."

"I haven't decided whether to accept it or not."

His head jerked. For the first time, Barney seemed to be really hearing her.

"What?" he said. The pipe died. He took it from his mouth and placed it carefully in front of him on the enormous glass ashtray she had bought him some years back.

"I said, Barney, I haven't decided whether to accept the offer or not."

"You mean leave your job at Griffin, leave Boston?" He took off his glasses and stared at her, disbelieving. "What would happen to our family? What would Toby do?"

"I know, I know," Alicia said. "But Griffin House is a dead end. I'll never be able to do what I should be doing at Griffin. Unless Phyllis disappears. And she won't, people like Phyllis go on forever. Tolland and Lutwidge is a different world, it's New York, it's where everything comes together. You should see their furniture, Barney! I just can't work with Phyllis Vance anymore. I know I'm saying a lot of different things but it's really *her*."

"You can't mean that," Barney told her. His face looked tired.

She was aware that she and Barney had not held what Toby would have called a "heavy dialogue" in a long time. It wasn't easy for him; she could tell from the way his hands kept fidgeting with things on his desk, and the way his forehead began to glow. Poor Barney, he hadn't been properly prepared for the news she was laying on him suddenly; this was too much all at once.

"I mean it, Barney, I realize it sounds paranoid but aren't there some people you can't work with, that Dr. Bacon you told me about, the hypomanic chap who never shuts up? Well, Phyllis and I exist in separate places. We're like those little magnetic dogs. No, it's much worse, I can't sustain that joke, it's gone beyond that."

Barney's face registered surprise, then he took some of her pain and registered it as a lowering of the eyes, a frown. It had gone, as she said, far beyond the joke stage. It wasn't simply a matter of husband versus career, it was a question of the rest of her life, where it was, what it was. If she stayed in Boston, she would be rejecting the chance to go to New York—where everyone *knew* the tangible action was, ninety percent of the agents, the cozy lunches where deals were hatched if not actually inked, the cocktail parties where agent and editor did a little business as they dumped their coats on the bed in the master bedroom, the telephone conversations permitted to come to full term, rather than aborted because of long-distance rates. The motor of publishing throbbed comfortably on the island of Manhattan, ignoring most of what went on in Boston, Chicago, the West Coast. An editor in Boston, Alicia figured, had to be twice as noisy in order to make her voice heard in New York. Alicia began to feel she too, like the mimeograph machine they still used at Griffin House for interoffice memoranda, was obsolete. "Barney," she said, "maybe I'm sticking all my grievances on Phyllis, maybe I'm just blaming her for my failures, but I can't turn this offer down without some serious thought. You understand, don't you?" Barney looked up, his eyes misty. She saw he did not understand. She sighed and took up her pursuit of Phyllis again. "Maybe it's just that I'm the other top woman editor. Phyllis has some weird ideas about women," she continued. "Whatever it is, she throws ice water on every idea I come up with. I can have the most beautiful manuscript and Phyllis will try to find a reason why we can't publish it."

Barney rubbed his face with both hands. "I didn't know it was that bad," he said.

"I don't like to talk about it," Alicia said.

"It helps to talk," Barney said. "You know that. I don't have to tell you that."

"I guess so," Alicia said.

"Why don't you go over to Houghton Mifflin? They'd love to get their hands on you."

"You mean Ancient House? It's nice of you to think they'd want me, I'm flattered. I'm not sure you're right. In fact, I'm sure you're wrong." She would not go to Ancient House or any other place in Boston; she wanted to expand like one of those doughy muffins on television, swelling. . . . "We could commute. I could commute?"

"I don't know . . ."

"It could work," she said, flinching at the lack of conviction in her own voice. "It's not ideal, but there's no reason why it shouldn't work. After all, marriage consists of a series of compromises, doesn't it?"

"And how about Toby? Does she go to two schools?" The words were sharp but his tone remained soft. Alicia looked at her husband and realized how stunned he was, and hurt, more than angry. "Speak of the devil," Barney said as Toby walked into his study, wearing pajamas and looking doleful.

"What's the matter, pet?" Alicia said.

"I couldn't go to sleep." Alicia wondered if Toby were having bad dreams, perhaps even Alicia's dreams which, when they had done with her, wrung her out, had moved on to her daughter and were now busy frightening the child. "And I was hungry."

"Well, go ahead and get something to eat, then go back to bed."

"Tomorrow's Saturday," she told her mother. "What were you talking about?" Her face seemed to Alicia to be accusing them of something awful, but she wanted to kiss the face anyway. She touched Toby whenever she could; she touched her to convince herself her lovely daughter was real. The sister or brother they had wanted for Toby had never put in an appearance.

"Your mom and I were talking about her job offer."

"What job offer?" Toby's boy's pajamas were too short in the pants; the ankles stood out like knobs on a dead branch. As Alicia looked at her, she saw a shadow move across the wall of bookshelves, a shadow with no apparent source. It was so pale it was almost invisible. Neither Barney nor Toby appeared to notice it, but Alicia heard a soft rustling noise like silk against silk. It brushed her arm, then moved off. She felt a familiar prickling along her skin and thought: *Toby's doomed.*

"I've been offered a job in New York," Alicia said, bypassing her fear. "The same sort of thing I'm doing now, only with a lot more say on my part. No one looking over my shoulder."

"More money?" Toby asked.

"Yes, more money, but that's not so important."

"You gonna take it?" Toby said. She had her feelings so marvelously under wraps that Alicia hadn't the faintest notion what was going on inside her head.

"She doesn't know yet, Toots," Barney said.

"I like New York," Toby said. "Would you go too, Daddy?"

"How do you know whether you like New York or not, you've never been there," Barney said.

"That's not true," Toby said. "I went down last spring vacation, don't you remember? I went to visit Joanna from camp. Don't you remember, Daddy?"

"Of course I do, Toots, now that you remind me. You went by bus. And you got lost in the Port Authority terminal." Toby nodded.

"I like New York, there's lots to do."

"There's a lot to do here too," her father said. "Now how about going on back to bed? Mom and I want to talk."

"And you don't want me to hear!" The heat of Toby's accusation baffled them both.

"Oh, hell," Barney said. "What are we going to do with you?"

Toby said, "I've *been* to the aquarium. A million times," and she bolted from the room, left so fast it took several seconds for her core to follow her.

"What's got into her?" Barney said.

"All of a sudden she's getting uppity," Alicia said. "We didn't flog her enough." She tried to coax a smile from her husband.

He obliged, but faintly. "We have to talk about you," he said. "It's more important right now."

"If it's a problem, then we have to solve it together," Alicia said.

"Of course it's a problem, unless there's something else going on that I don't know about." He gave her such a searching look she cast her eyes down and avoided him. And yet there was nothing to feel guilty about.

"Listen, Allie," Barney said, and unable to remain seated, he got up and walked back and forth in back of his desk, touching this object and that, straightening a book, a pile of papers, touching, as if to maintain his hold on the real world while his real world threatened to take off. "Listen, here's an analogy for you. A couple, a married couple. One of them, it doesn't matter which, wants a baby, the other doesn't; how do they compromise, how can they possibly reconcile their differences?"

"Why, they have half a baby," Alicia said. After saying this, she began to laugh, the laugh started a pain in her stomach, her eyes squeezed shut and tears dripped out. Barney stood with his fingertips resting on the edge of his desk. She thought he wanted to laugh too.

"Allie," he said, "maybe we shouldn't try to do any more problem-solving tonight. I don't know, maybe it wouldn't hurt for you to see someone, a third party, someone who's disinterested . . ."

"A shrink?" Alicia had a coppery taste in her mouth. Barney was a believer in history. They sent their daughter to a school where they made sure you knew your dates and the sequence of human events. If he believed in history, then it followed that he would believe in psychiatry. What was therapy, after all, but a history lesson pared down for one?

"It might help," Barney said.

She knew it wouldn't help. The problem was there, no amount of analyzing would make it go away. He took off his glasses and, without looking at her, said, "Don't you love me anymore, Alicia?"

Anger would have been easier. The word "love" had not

escaped him since the day he had got his appointment at the hospital and the money and the Harvard chair and the secretary and the lab assistants. He had told her that day he loved her.

"Of course I love you," she said. "You're my husband and of course I love you. But what am I going to do with the rest of my life?"

The phone's ringing interrupted them. Barney picked it up. "It's Davida," he said, his palm over the receiver. "Do you want to talk to her?"

She nodded and reached for the phone. "Hi, Davey," she said.

"Is Barney okay?" Davida asked Alicia. "He sounds weird."

"He's okay, Davey," she said. The copper in her mouth began to make her queasy. "What's up?"

"I forgot to take down the number of your eye doctor. Could I have it, please? This thing on my eye is getting bigger. It hurts like fuck."

"I'll get my book," Alicia said. She looked at her husband, who had sat down again and was shuffling papers, his Cross pencil in his right hand. He looked up at her briefly and smiled halfheartedly. She fetched her purse from the front hall and scrambled through it for her address book. She couldn't find it. She felt dizzy and leaned against the doorway, her head light again, panic thudding in her ears. She raced back to Barney's study.

"Have you seen my address book?" she demanded.

"No," he said, and his head went down again like a mechanical chicken's.

She spoke into the phone, trying to keep her voice neutral. "Look, Davey," she said, "I can't seem to find my book right now. But his name is Blond, Stephen Blond, and his office is in Kenmore Square. It's in the phone book."

"Right," Davida said. "*Merci bien* and tell Barney to have a good day, I mean night." She chuckled.

"I will," Alicia said. "And you too. I'll call you tomorrow."

She began, then, to babble, telling Barney about how she had gone to lunch with Davida and how she had not removed her address book from her bag even though Davida had asked for the doctor's name and how she couldn't understand because the address book was *always* in her purse, it was a charm, her talisman.

"If you didn't take it out of your bag," Barney said, "then it must still be there."

"But it isn't!"

"Then just call the restaurant in the morning."

"Some of those addresses are irreplaceable," she said. "From Europe, from school. It goes back longer than our marriage, it goes back twenty-five years!"

"Look, honey, you'll find it. You always find things you're dead certain you've lost. They always turn up."

"Not always," she murmured.

"Poor thing," he said. "By the way, where did you say you ate today?"

"Oh, an Italian place in the North End. One of Davida's discoveries. The pizza was very good, I'll take you there . . ."

"Pizza," he said. "I thought you were on a diet."

"If I'm not careful, I'll grow so big and fat my body will be hanging off flesh, fold upon fold of soft, pliant flesh. Flesh you can grab by the handful and squeeze like a sponge. I'll be so fat and ugly you'll need a compass to find my clit!"

"Alicia!" Barney looked as if he were about to burst into tears. "Don't, please don't."

"Okay, then, my pussy."

"You need a shrink, you *do* need a shrink," he said.

"I'm sorry," she said. "I don't know what made me say that. I'm really sorry, Barney." She hated hurting him; she did it anyway.

"I'm going to bed," Barney said, without acknowledging her apology. "You coming up?"

"Aren't you going to work?"

"I don't think I can now."

"I'll be right up, I want to check out the lights and the locks. I'll be right up."

Alicia hung back. She knew he would be asleep within ten minutes and that was what she gave herself: ten minutes of grace, while she turned off the lights and tried the back door and fingered the jowls of Martin, the cat.

Upstairs she opened the door to Toby's room, saw black, except for the radio, which glowed and emitted soft music. She left the door ajar and went into their bedroom. Barney was asleep on his back, with the light on across the room. He was snoring. He sounded like a faraway train. She would have to poke his shoulder to get him to turn over. Alicia took a quick shower, so distracted by the loss of her book that she forgot to put on her shower cap and realized it only when the water reached her scalp. Cursing, she got out of the shower, threw a towel over her head and moaned, "Where *is* it?" She looked at her body in the mirror: it looked bloated, her breasts round and stretched, the nipples the size of infant thumbs. She closed her eyes and prayed for three things, three wishes, please God. The address book back, change without catastrophe, love without pain.

Before she got into bed she held her purse—it was the size of a small satchel—upside down and shook it over the bed. Things in profusion fell onto the quilt in a mound: two lipsticks, a compact, several pencils, a couple without points, many slips of paper: Visa and other receipts, grocery lists going back three months, rubber bands, a memo from Phyllis to the editorial departments reminding them that subsidiary rights had accounted for 11.7 percent of industry profits over the past year and they had better keep this in mind when considering properties (when had a *manuscript* become a property?), a letter from her widowed mother in Florida, full of woe and thinly veiled recriminations, a tapestry-type glasses case, some balled-up Kleenexes, the last three peppermints in a roll, the top one covered with strings of crud, a crumpled recipe in four colors she had ripped from a magazine in her gynecologist's waiting room and never used, a tiny tin box she did not recognize, a postcard from a friend showing an Italian woman in what appeared to be heavy mourning, sitting vacant-eyed on a backless chair, a chrome Cross pen, retracted. No address book. She unzipped the side pocket: one Super-plus Tampax for emergencies.

Even now she could not understand why losing the book hit her with such force. Had she tried, she could probably have reconstructed all but one or two of the names and addresses. The others were the ones she had not consulted for perhaps twenty years and were obviously expendable. It was the *idea* of losing it and having to start all over again that frightened her. The book itself was half an inch thick and brown and fit easily into her palm. It was made of calfskin, which had softened over the years to a silkiness she would run her fingers over for the pure tactile pleasure of it. Inside the covers were marbled papers, each a flowing abstract in blues, pinks and browns. The paper was thin but very tough. Her handwriting had changed and she liked the look of that too: from her college friends, to her newest author, from under twenty to over forty, a hand becoming more itself, more unlike any others. The top front corner was ragged, it looked as if a tiny animal had been gnawing at it. Altogether there were probably over a hundred and fifty names in the address book—friends, teachers, colleagues, acquaintances she thought she might sometime call and sometimes had. Whenever she met anyone she liked she would whip out the book and write down their name and address. The tabs along the right-hand margin still read clearly, the letters in groups of two. Doctors, dentists, vets, several of her mother's friends, *her* doctor, *her* lawyer.

Alicia wanted to sleep, but her body felt as if it were being stretched and twisted. She turned the radio on low to her favorite all-night madness, a talk show out of Washington, and heard the host, Larry King, attempting to make sense of a caller's tearful story about her two daughters, both of whom had married the same man. "Not at the same time?" he asked. "No, one after the other," she said, her mouth gluey with grief. "Is either of them still married to him?" King asked. "No, both of them got divorced. He was a devil. They don't talk to me anymore." King said something meant to convey sympathy and hung up on her. The next caller was a woman who claimed to be able to see things when her eyes were shut. The host said, "Well, folks, it's a full moon tonight." After this, Alicia fell asleep, with the radio still going, then dreamed about menace in a number of guises: sleeping through a botany exam, standing up in front of the Griffin sales force and forgetting everything she had prepared on behalf of one of her books and breaking down in tears, Celestial Sam in a burning house, his bed on fire, herself being chased through the streets of New York by a huge black man with a whip like a huge gold chain, coming closer and closer. . . . When she woke up she was exhausted, anxious, jumpy.

At nine she called Garibaldi's and got no answer. At eleven she tried again. "Doesn't anyone eat pizza in the morning?" she said. Barney, who was wrestling with a storm window in their bedroom, grunted. "You'll find it," he said. "You always do."

At twelve someone at the pizza place answered.

"Did you by any chance find a small brown address book?" she asked.

He didn't seem to understand what she was saying; she had to repeat herself. He was stuck on the word "address," for which there was no easy synonym.

"No," he said, having gone to look under tables and chairs. "No book, nothing."

This didn't surprise her. "I'd like to give you my name and phone number in case someone picked it up by mistake," Alicia said, pushing probability to the brink.

"Okay," he said, "what you name?" He had trouble with her phone number.

"Useless," she said, hanging up.

Barney turned and said, "I'll help you look, Allie, I don't like the way this is upsetting you. It's not a catastrophe."

"Not for you," she whispered, then realized how unfair this was. Neither of them had mentioned—not while in bed, not at breakfast, nor in the hours that came after this—neither had alluded to the subject that preoccupied her and must surely be troubling him. In fact, they both behaved as if her threat to alter their lives had never been uttered at all. They were cowards, both of them. Could it be that Barney too hoped to avoid the inevitable by denying its existence? This idea caught her by surprise; she felt sorry for him. She went over to where he was wiping his million-dollar hands on a rag, put her arms around his middle and hugged him. He looked down at her and smiled, "You'll find it," he said for the third time.

"No," she said. "But it's all right," she added, lying now. "I'll get another book and start all over."

Barney was wearing his Saturday clothes, chinos, blue oxford shirt rolled up at the sleeves, loafers. He had most of his hair, and his granny glasses made him look both intelligent (he was) and sexy (he was, off and on, but it didn't seem to have much to do with her). He was attractive—where had their intensity gone?

Toby came into the bedroom and Alicia told her to practice her clarinet. As she spoke, she heard her own mother's voice. It chilled her, that voice; her inflections were not her own. Toby never wanted to practice but she said nothing; she was a brave child.

"What's the matter with you, Mom?" Toby said. "You look funny."

Alicia sat at her desk, trying to read a manuscript, one of three she had been grappling with for several days. Toby practiced and left the house quietly. Barney shut himself into his study where he worked on his paper. Alicia was restless. The phone rang. She stuck her pencil in the spine of the manuscript to mark her place and answered. It was Davida again.

For the second day in a row Davida was awash in gloom. "Craig and I have hit an all-time low," she said. "He was just over here. I invited him to leave."

"What happened?"

"Oh, I don't know."

"He didn't hit you, did he?" Alicia asked.

"I wouldn't let *any* man lay *any* hand on *any* part of my body, not in anger, that is."

"Do you want to tell me about it?" Alicia said. "I'm trying to read a manuscript but I can't seem to concentrate."

"That's nice of you, but you're working. I'll tell you about it when you've got more time. What are you reading, by the way?"

"It's a mystery, Davey, set in Guatemala. With murderous natives and stolen idols. Not your sort of thing at all."

"Any good?"

"It's okay." Actually, Alicia was loving it, but she wasn't going to tell Davida; Davida would want her to fashion an immediate comparison between her and this author. She had to plan her strategy carefully, in order to slip this book by Phyllis and get it safely on the Griffin list. First she would ask her co-editors Jane Templer and Peter Fairchild to read it. She knew they would like it; they almost invariably responded, with Alicia, to the same things in the same way. Then she would ask the author's agent to supply her with anything that would help push her across the goal line: previous sales figures, supportive quotes from other writers, future plans, the backfield manuscripts needed in order to score. Phyllis might argue but, in the end, if the team showed sufficient strength, sharp enough knees, she'd buckle. But rarely did Alicia feel triumph after one of these victories; they would exhaust her, she hated the waste of time and energy, she hated the feeling that Phyllis was more adversary than friend.

After hanging up the phone Alicia went back to her reading. It was during the sacrifice scene, as the old man picked up a two-headed ax preparatory to chopping off the head of the deaf-mute twelve-year-old girl, that the phone rang again. "Damn," she said, getting up to answer. The caller was a man who identified himself as Buddy, at Garibaldi's.

"You call this morning, lady?"

"Yes, I did," she said, her heart hopping.

"We fown your address book. My girlfriend fown it in the ladies' restroom." Alicia had not used the restroom, nor had Davida.

"Thank you. Thank you," Alicia said. "I'll be right there. Don't go away; I'll be there in less than half an hour." She went into Barney's study. "They found my address book," she said.

"That's a relief," he said.

"Oh, come on, Barney, aren't you glad?"

"Of course I am, honey. Go on, then, what are you waiting for?"

She was so happy in the car driving toward Boston that she started singing Cole Porter—"It Was Just One of Those Things"—and nearly hit a small girl who darted out from between two cars on Hanover Street. She parked in a tow zone and ran into the restaurant. The waiter, the same one who had waited on her the day before, handed over the address book. She took it and thanked him, pressing a dollar bill into his hand.

"Thanks, lady," he said.

"Thank *you,*" she said.

She got back into the Volvo and looked at her old friend the address book, then she put it to her mouth, brushing it across her lips.

"I told you you'd find it," Barney said.

"It was really strange, he swore they found it in the ladies' room. I didn't go in there."

"Well, the important thing is you've got it back. How about you and me going down to the Puritan for lunch? I need a half sour pickle and a liverwurst sandwich right away."

CHAPTER
Three

BARNEY and Alicia left the Puritan Deli and walked back to their car. Barney said, "What are you going to do this afternoon?"

"I've got some reading. What are you going to do?"

"Finish my paper," he said. "You wouldn't like to go over it for me, would you?"

"If you promise not to get angry," she said. "Or cry."

Barney promised but she didn't trust him. She wondered where Toby was; the sky was gray and low, the horizon almost purple, she could feel snow beyond the clouds.

Her relief at recovering her address book soon gave way to physical uneasiness. Alicia felt as if she were being stared at from behind by eyes, which when she turned to meet them, would not blink but go right on staring. This odd impression she could only blame on her prescience, that incipient faculty which came and went as quixotically as a teenager. The strange thing about this faculty was that whenever Alicia was anxious it sharpened, which went against what made sense. When things went well, when she was not distracted, it often lay low for weeks.

On the ride home, with Barney driving, Alicia fixed on Phyllis. She thought of wicked things she would say to Phyllis if she found the nerve, if Phyllis were not her boss, if she was drunk enough to dismiss caution. Send her a telegram: "Fuck you, Phyllis—insulting letter follows," which wasn't all that witty but what the hay. If you knew what was good for you you didn't mess around with Phyllis. Phyllis picked things up out of the air, Phyllis rememberd words the size of fleas.

As for Alicia, she held the reins on herself tightly, did not say the wicked and witty things that occurred to her, except to Davida and Mickey Eversharp, head of Promotion, and one or two friends who had nothing to do with writing. Not to Barney anymore; he was too busy or distracted, somehow had stopped focusing on her. She thought, as she glanced at his profile going soft around the chin line, that she might have gradually shut down her comedy and stopped trying to amuse her husband. Whose fault would *that* be?

Alicia's authors could say anything they damn pleased, that was the understanding, and authors were invariably difficult—they were everything from vaguely dissatisfied to pains in the ass or rampantly paranoid. The rare happy author made no noise, the unhappy, cyclones. Some years earlier, Alicia had found their excitement intolerable and wanted to unlist her telephone. Barney and Toby said no. Toby had started to cry. Barney said, "Absolutely not. A doctor can't have an unlisted number." Alicia did not see it his way; he could get a beeper, which was as good as a telephone, better in many ways. Her author at that time, Edward Beal, called once a week for a month and a half to ask her how his sales were coming along. It got so that Alicia began inventing figures, throwing him imaginary numbers in order to appease him, a ploy that did not make her proud of herself and nearly landed her in hot water. Beal had called her at three in the morning, smashed, from a bar opposite South Station and wept that she was his guardian angel. She nominated him for the Worst Author of the Year, a running contest between Griffin and Panther Press. However, Beal had been beaten out by sex therapist Elsa Kronkheit, whose manual for the sexually dysfunctional, illustrated with easy-on-the-eyes sepia graphics, had sold 60,000 copies. The young man in charge of Kronkheit's publicity quit publishing and opened a scuba-diving school on Tortola, B.V.I.

The job offer from Tolland and Lutwidge was turning into a curse, for it was directly tied to separation. Alicia loved Barney and Toby and she loved the unit created by the three of them when they were together. A Family. There was no getting around the fact that if she left Boston for New York, Alicia would alter her family forever. But the idea of her going to T & L. God, she would really take off, do what she wanted, no more exhausting battles to get her books accepted by Phyllis, the covert lining up of Griffin allies, the watered-down terms, the humiliations she visited on her authors—"I know you've won a National Book Award, but would you mind very much submitting three chapters and a twenty-page outline? Phyllis wants it . . ."—the nights spent wrestling with Phyllis instead of giving in to sleep, which God knows she needed, the dark beneath her eyes looked like hell. If she stayed in Boston she would never be sure whether she had done everything—or anything. In New York, the real Alicia Gordon Baer would once more give birth to herself. Alicia was forty-three and not holding.

The sky radiated menace, shoots of gray climbed to the stratosphere, shavings of snow hit the window. Barney turned the wipers on; the flakes began to smear across the glass. "Damn," he said, "another storm."

"It's not supposed to amount to much," Alicia said. It didn't matter to her one way or another.

Back home the three manuscripts in their boxes sat on her desk in the bedroom, waiting for her to read them and pass judgment, while their authors, like anxious parents waiting for the doctor's diagnosis, were pacing up and down or sitting catatonically in rooms all over America, paralyzed by suspense. Was what they had written good—or at least commercial—

enough to be published by Griffin House? Alicia saw every last one of them each morning as they scrambled through the pile of mail. An envelope was good news, anything bulkier bad, bad. Or, if the poor soul had an agent working for him or her, an intermediary who helped cushion the shock of rejection, they would read the following: "Dear Henry, Those idiots at Griffin have finally—after sixteen weeks—decided they don't want to publish your lovely little novel. Frankly, I don't know what they do want; they don't seem to know themselves; I guess we came pretty close this time, so don't go out and buy yourself that Colt .22. I'm going to try Pauper House next. I'll stay in touch." The disappointment would arrive—although the writer half expected it—as a punch in the stomach, to be followed by a wash of tears and an orgy of overreaction: "Those bastards, those fucking bastards!"

"Aren't all you editors really failed writers?" This strange question was put to Alicia as often as the query, "Wouldn't you like to hear my life story, it would make one helluva book?" Both questions stirred her blood to the boiling point. "If I wanted to write," she would answer, "I would quit my job and write." As for the second, this was not quite so simple: a life story was not the same thing as a book; the magic happened in the process of writing. The folks "out there," as Alicia thought of them, hadn't the foggiest idea of how books traveled from first glimmer to something rectangular and 350 pages long in the window of B. Dalton and Company. Any editor who sat waiting for manuscripts to fly in and land on his desk had better start circulating résumés. At least once a month Alicia stepped into the line at the Eastern terminal at Logan Airport, to board the eight o'clock shuttle to New York, there to court eight agents, sleeping nights at a hotel on Lexington Avenue whose threads were beginning to show, and returned exhausted and with gray fingernails and dirty hair three days and two nights later. Several of these agents were her dear friends, several others spoke a language she could barely decipher, dealing as it did exclusively with first names—"As I told Bob yesterday"; "And I gave the manuscript to Kurt, who loved it"; "Swifty called this morning"—and they looked over her shoulder during lunch at the Four Seasons grill. "Your agent is your key to the garden of profits," Phyllis told her staff from time to time. "You must woo them ardently, you must learn to love them." Manuscripts that came in "over the transom"—an archaism that amused Alicia each time she heard it—were fortunate if they were read within six months. The hope that continued to spring in the breasts of these unpublished writers, should it be turned into something useful such as energy, would keep the planet warm in perpetuity.

Alicia was distracted, although she did not know by what; her agitation floated. She had work to do, a manuscript to read, but her concentration was shot. "Oh, damn," she said, "What's the matter with me?" This was Saturday; by Monday she would have to have finished this manuscript and be prepared to voice opinions about several other matters. It was like school; Phyllis ran her shop like an elementary school. A month earlier Phyllis had set "acquisitions goals," a phrase that had become the source of both joke and torment within a week, and meant that every editor had to bring in so many new books for each list—Fall and Spring. Alicia had been summoned by Phyllis to her office, which she had filled with plants to resemble a subtropical garden. Fronds hung over her desk and tickled the windows, the smell of humus was overpowering. "Alicia, my dear," Phyllis said, "you're taking too long with your books."

"I can't hurry, Phyllis," she said, trying to modulate her anger. "I'm a line-editor, I can't leave a mistake, I just can't skip over a sentence that doesn't sound right."

"You're a dying breed," Phyllis told her. "Nobody cares what it sounds like. Do you suppose your average reader counts the adverbs in a novel by Harold Robbins?"

Phyllis, she figured, wanted her to say she would try to

change. She wasn't going to do that; it would compromise her methods. Instead, she asked, "Have you read that manuscript about volcanoes that I left with you last week?"

"First twenty-five pages," Phyllis said. "It wouldn't sell. It's nicely written, it's perfectly okay, but nobody wants to read about rocks." Alicia doubted that Phyllis had read twenty-five pages of the volcano manuscript; it was rare that Phyllis read anything beyond the agent's name and address and the menu at which she hosted her agents and authors.

With a sigh, Alicia settled herself in the reading chair under the gooseneck standing lamp. Everything twitched and prickled, the skin on her legs and arms, the back of her neck, her scalp. She left the steaming Guatemalan jungle and picked up another manuscript. It weighed about the same as a month-old infant, and was a novel sent her by a New York agency entitled *Habits,* and appeared to be the story of a nun who, following a spiritual crisis, became a West Coast distributor for angel dust. Moving backward and forward in time, and from convent to street, it had a complicated structure and lapsed too often into abstractions like "transcendence" and "authority," but it had something that kept Alicia reading. The convent scenes were crisp and painful. "You should never have left, dear," Alicia told the heroine, a young woman named Franny, identifying with her like mad, in spite of the fact that they had nothing in common.

Having said this, Alicia got out the address book, prompted by an unmistakable tug. Something was wrong with the book, she could feel it. It was unaccountably warm, radiating a steady glow of heat. My God, she thought, what's going on? She skidded the pages past her fingers and stopped at T. What was this name: Roger Tucker. Who was Roger Tucker? Alicia's heart bucked. What was Roger Tucker doing in her address book? She squinted, studying the handwriting. It was exactly like her own, her *g,* the way the *r* collapsed at the end. Why had the man at the pizza parlor copied her handwriting and put this unknown name in her address book?

Alicia perspired. She turned to the F page. Wilma Fearing. Who was Fearing? Were Fearing and Tucker related in some way? On the K page she saw another unfamiliar name: Jared Koenig, followed by M.D. Who was Jared Koenig, M.D., and what was he doing there, among the K's? And there was a Jeannette Ashburton and a Pearl Withers . . . "Who *are* you?" she said to them. This question emerged as a choking sound.

"Did you say something?" Barney asked. He had slipped into the bedroom and was taking off his pants.

Alicia made a sound that wasn't quite a word. "Yes, I did," she managed. "But it wasn't anything." She wondered if her face showed what was going on inside her. "What are you doing?"

"Ernie just called. He wants to play a couple of sets of tennis. He's reserved a court for three-thirty. Okay with you?"

"You don't have to ask my permission," Alicia said. "Don't forget to wear your bulletproof vest. Remember last time he threw his racket and barely missed your skull."

"Ernie's over that childish business," Barney said. "Hey, is something wrong? You look a little pale. Greenish."

"I'm all right," Alicia said. "It's stuffy in here." She made a production of opening the window and taking a deep breath. It was at this moment she decided that she could not tell Barney that her address book had been invaded, entered by five creatures from . . . from where?

"Barney . . ." Alicia began.

"What, honey?"

"Oh, nothing."

"I wish you'd see Tom Brainard on Monday. I don't like the way you look. Are you on one of those crazy diets again?"

"Pizza?"

"Oh," Barney said, "I forgot. But when was the last time you had a checkup?"

"Last September," she said. "I'm fine, really, just over-worked."

"Is it the New York thing?" He surprised her by asking this. "Is it making you sick?"

"Oh, God," she murmured. The door opened, hitting the rubber stopper attached to the wall. Toby stood on the threshold. Her skin looked translucent, like an infant's.

"Haven't you made up your mind yet, Mom?" Toby said.

Barney smiled. It wasn't one of Alicia's favorite smiles. "Adults have to agonize before they can decide things," he explained. He was being careful with his daughter, who seemed not to notice—or not to mind—his patronizing.

"Well," Toby said. "I wish you'd make up your mind. Can I tell Laurie?"

"No!"

"You don't have to shout at her, Allie," Barney said. "We're all in the same room."

"Sorry," Alicia said. She hadn't meant to shout and as she apologized she felt a thin film drape itself like plastic wrap, over her and around her, cutting off some of the sound, some of the light. She wanted to penetrate it to get out but didn't know how. She raised her arm in an odd gesture. It embarrassed her but neither Barney nor Toby had noticed it. The book in her hand was very warm, warmer than her skin. She put it down.

Barney glanced at his watch, then left in a hurry. Toby told Alicia that she was going to meet a friend and buy some running shoes.

"You just bought a pair last month," Alicia said. She wondered how it was possible for her to keep up this normal-sounding conversation when she was about to explode.

"I need another pair," Toby said. "Besides, I have that Christmas money from Granny. I can do whatever I want with it."

"Of course you can," Alicia said. Toby glared and kept her mouth shut tight. Alicia could see her daughter moving away from her again, as she had at seven months, crawling on all fours. Now it would be faster. It was about time, Alicia supposed, but even so, she wasn't prepared.

"Go ahead," Alicia said. "Buy whatever you want, buy out the whole store . . ."

"Mom? Are you having your period?"

As soon as Toby left the house, Alicia stared at her address book, afraid to touch it. The strange new people there called to her, called her by name. "Alicia, it's me, Wilma, it's us, Wilma and Jeannette, we want to talk to you." She picked up the book, it was still too warm. She sat down, dizzy, her heart thrashing, cutting off some of the air coming up into her mouth. Her hands were ice. "My God," Alicia said softly, "I must be crazy." The manuscript of *Habits* lay neglected on her desk. Panic traveled along her calves. They were real, they were her names, what should she do with them? If she drew a line through each name, would they die? "Leave me alone," she said. She took in deep breaths of air, trying to slow down all her systems. Then something occurred to her: what would happen if she called each one of the new names and talked to it? She would discover, then, if the names were in fact connected to real people or to silence. "I can't," she said in a whisper, "I just can't." She let her head flop against the chair's back and closed her eyes, wanting someone to help her. There was no one.

After several minutes Alicia got up and sat down at her desk, taking out a long yellow pad and a felt-tipped pen. "I'm a rational person," she thought, "and I'm going to approach this business in a rational manner." She wrote across the top: *Possibilities.* Then she began:

1. An elaborate practical joke, carefully orchestrated, involving pizza place, Wilma Fearing (if that's her real name), perhaps Barney, and the other invaders. Maybe even Phyllis V. A procedure of complexity, full of risks. Motive: to

drive me crazy? As revenge? To see if it can be done? Likelihood: remote. Too sophisticated.

2. A neurological anomaly. Something in my brain responsible for blackouts, loss of memory, amnesia, etc., but not loss of ordinary functions. Likelihood: plausible but improbable.

3. A form of lunacy, in which periods of activity are later repressed. On and off, without warning. Likelihood: fifty-fifty.

4. The supernatural. Fearing, Koenig, etc. my creatures, only I can hear and see them, they are determined to haunt me. Many stories deal with people who can see "ghosts" no one else can. A curse. Likelihood: unknown.

Alicia tapped the end of her pen against her front teeth. Of the four possibilities the first was absurd. It was too elaborate, the pizza-parlor boy could not have been so convincing. Barney was too busy to engage in anything like the preparations this would entail.

Number two was less absurd, the most logical but the least easy to accept. If she had a lesion, wouldn't she have other symptoms as well? Wouldn't she have splitting headaches, fall down as if drunk, and so on deep into the land of pathology? As for her dizziness, that could stem from anything, psychic or physical. Alicia decided to table number two. And as for three, it was logical and just as awful as two. Although, if put to it, Alicia would no doubt choose lunacy over brain tumor.

Alicia was amazed at her ability to thus analyze the odd situation she found herself trapped in. She recalled a Griffin book in which the author had discussed what he called "selective amnesia." In one such case a man, burdened by a white-collar job, would take off for periods ranging from two weeks to several months, hire out as a rigger and live the tough but rewarding life of the simple laborer. While this was going on, while the sufferer fed himself a varied menu, his wife was at home taking care of his children by herself and trying to figure out whether her husband was alive or dead. The kids did dangerous drugs, the mother was going mad and the father was having the time of his life. The author seemed more interested in the man than in his wife.

For the sake of argument, Alicia gave herself a case of selective amnesia and was unconvinced. Her family, husband and child, would have given her clues to its existence. "Where have you been all week?" "Why didn't you come home?" If Alicia suffered from amnesia she would know about it. Wouldn't she?

As with number two, Alicia tabled number three for future consideration and moved on to the final possibility. This made her most uneasy.

Considering number four, Alicia could not help relating it to her prescience, but was unable to say what the nature of this relationship was, even to guess at it. It all took place somewhere no one else could go with her. It seemed to Alicia that this was what madness might be: the layering of the irrational with the actual until they were chemically bonded, fused, ultimately one and the same.

Alicia held her address book tightly, as if it might fly off. She flipped to the F page and sat down by the telephone. She started to put through Wilma Fearing's number, but her finger slipped against the four button and she had to begin again. This time the call took. The other phone buzzed faintly against her ear. Then a thin voice came on the line.

"Hello?"

"May I speak to Wilma Fearing, please."

"This is me."

"Yes, well, this is Alicia Baer." Her own voice sounded as if she were being shaken by the shoulders.

"Allie," Wilma Fearing said. "Hello again."

"Wilma?"

"Yes, Wilma," the voice said. "Is our lunch still on?"

"Yes," Alicia said.

"That's good, I was afraid you were calling to cancel. Then I'll see you on Monday at the Hedgerow."

"Twelve-thirty?" Alicia asked.

"That's what we agreed on," Wilma told her. "I hope I'm going to recognize you," she added. "My hair isn't red any longer; it turned sort of mushroom a few years ago. But you'll know me. I'll be wearing a purple down coat and carrying a pet raccoon." She laughed. "No, honestly, you won't have any trouble, I still look like I always did."

"I'll recognize you," Alicia said.

Restless and hungry, she went downstairs, found half a cupcake and started in on it, thinking about her conversation with Wilma Fearing. How had she known to say twelve-thirty? Was it only a reasonable guess—what other time did people meet for lunch?—or had she already known what time? The cupcake was too sweet and dry, having sat around too long. She threw the rest of it away.

She could not tell Barney about the invaders, she had already decided this. She might tell Davida, Davida was the only one who would treat it seriously. But with Davida there was the danger that she might run with it, turn it into a wild fiction. Davida's belief in the supernatural might turn out to be less helpful than Barney's skepticism. As for Alicia's mother, this woman would probably say, "Why don't you go down to Bonwit's and buy yourself a nice hat?"

Alicia moved through the rest of Saturday as through a miasma. She prepared dinner for Toby and dressed for a cocktail party down the street, something she would not, under the best of circumstances, be looking forward to.

The Simpsons didn't seem to realize that when she finished work she did not want to meet dentists with manuscripts about how to floss or travel agents with chilling adventures they wanted someone to write for them or therapists with yet another theory about the id. She wanted merely to listen, to take part in some mindless gossip, to sip wine and go limp. She managed to get through the evening by drinking more wine than she should, covering her anxiety.

That night Alicia dreamed she was pregnant and undergoing amniocentesis. When she woke she realized that the doctor who had stuck his needle deep into her abdomen—and it hadn't hurt at all, she couldn't even feel it, though the needle was over a foot long and glinted terribly—looked like Dick Freyburg; he had the same round cheeks and fringy hair and odd glasses, partly frameless. She did not have the inclination to parse this dream, she merely let it register.

Alicia persuaded Barney to take the next afternoon off and go to a movie, where they held hands intermittently—an old habit, begun when they were engaged and never abandoned—and ate yellow popcorn. The movie was a revival of *The China Syndrome.* When they came out into the sun, Barney said, "It's going to happen again. Not just Three Mile Island but a lot of other installations—somebody's going to overlook the crucial valve and the fucking thing will leak all over the countryside."

"The movie's an exaggeration," Alicia said. "It's fiction."

"Nope," Barney said, zipping up his jacket. "It's an understatement. I know the guys who were technical advisers on the movie. They held back, actually, they figured the public could swallow just so much reality. We might all last till the end of the century, but I wouldn't put any money on it." Alicia thought of Toby, doomed, but doomed with all the other children. Barney would come home from his meetings with those other doctors attempting to turn nuclear policy around and tell Alicia he felt as if he were trying to douse a forest fire with a water pistol. "Then why do anything?" she said. "Why don't we just live it up and wait for the blast? Hold orgies and eat all the potato chips we ever wanted?"

"Can't do that," he said. "Have to try to do something for Toby."

The movie upset her, though the invisible wrapping she had been inside since the day before somewhat protected her.

Later, after dinner, while they were still at the table, Barney said, "Have you thought any more about the Tolland and Lutwidge offer?"

"I think about almost nothing but," Alicia said, "But I can't talk about it yet."

"Why not?"

"I just can't, I haven't sorted my feelings from the reality, they're still in too many pieces. It's all in a muddle and if you really want to know, your being so nice about it makes it that much harder. Why don't you just tell me you don't want me to take the job?"

"Because it's not so simple as that for me either," Barney said. "Of course I don't want our family to break apart, I want you here, I like our life together here. But that's not the issue. Even if I don't see any way we can compromise, because the mechanics are so cumbersome, even though I don't know the solution, I know that if I became difficult and said, 'You *may* not go,' that you wouldn't forgive me. I'd feel your resentment and anger every time we ate breakfast together, every time we went to bed and I wanted to fuck."

"I can't talk about it anymore." I can't talk about the address book either, she said silently.

The first thing Alicia thought of when she woke on Monday morning was Wilma Fearing. Barney had left the house at six-thirty, without disturbing her, having surgery to perform. In the silence, Wilma seemed to take up a lot of space. Shaking her head, Alicia dressed and went downstairs to the kitchen, where she found Toby sitting at the table with a plate with half an orange on it in front of her.

"What about some Grape-Nuts?" Alicia asked.

"No, thanks."

"That's what you asked me to buy you. Now you won't eat them. You won't eat anything. What's with you?"

"I'm not hungry."

"You have to eat more than half an orange for breakfast. Ask Daddy."

"I told you, I'm not hungry."

"Have some toast, then."

"*No.*"

"Shit." They tried to stare one another down. Toby caved first. Alicia did not feel as if she had won anything. "I have to go now. I hope your stomach growls in math class," she said. "Loud, so everybody will look at you."

"Thanks a lot," Toby said.

Toby's goodbye was sullen. Alicia was too absorbed in her own nervousness to care much, though it left her with a strange feeling; up until today Toby had made an elaborate ritual of the morning separation.

Far from being dispelled by work, Alicia's anxiety intensified, so that during the editorial meeting Wilma's name punctured her concentration. Five editors, three assistant editors, Mickey Eversharp, who headed up Griffin's Advertising and Promotion departments, a couple of secretaries, one to take minutes and the other to get coffee, and an unpaid intern all had drawn chairs around the enormous polished mahogany table that served the company as a bar at parties as well as for this more serious purpose. Phyllis sat in the center of one side, like the President during a Cabinet meeting. Phyllis brought up Davida's lawsuit, flicking dangerous eyes at Alicia. "Let this be a lesson to the rest of you," she said.

Jane Templer said, "How are we supposed to decide when to get a manuscript read by a lawyer? What criteria do you use?"

"The first criterion is your head, Jane." Jane flushed. "Of course you can't expect every character in a novel to be a total invention, but you *can* go to your author and ask him if he's put anyone whole and entire into his book, like that woman who wrote about her transactional therapist and made a horse's ass of him. Naturally, he sued."

"He was a horse's ass before she got to him," Mickey Eversharp said.

"That's beside the point," Phyllis said. Her eyes lit on one person after another, lingering a split second longer on Alicia's face; Alicia was determined not to drop her own eyes but to return the gaze bravely. "We very rarely ask Doc Gurney to read a novel manuscript, it costs too damn much, for one thing. And for another, what does he see when he reads it? He can't possibly know which character is real and which invented; it's up to the author who has to be completely candid and willing to rewrite and add to a disguise."

Alicia said, "Davida Franklin's suit is a fluke. The plaintiff doesn't have a case; he's crazy."

"Crazy like a fox," Phyllis said, "But we can't waste any more of your time on this. Alicia, can you stay for a moment or two after the meeting? There's something I'd like to discuss with you." Now Alicia flushed; teacher suggested wickedness in front of Alicia's classmates. "Of course," she said. She prayed this would not make her late for her appointment with Wilma Fearing.

"I apologize for the fact that a good deal of what's on the agenda this morning seems to be negative; these are hard times."

"Amen," whispered Mickey to Alicia.

Alicia wanted to open the door to the conference room; the air had grown stale and warm. A headache began, settling over her eyebrows.

"Some of you—and at this point I'm not going to mention names, as that's far too cruel—are not meeting the quotas we mutually agreed on. You know who you are. And I don't want to hear excuses; excuses never alter facts. Some of you"—the eyes whipped back and forth up and down along the length of the table—"are bringing in junk. We can't have that. We can't have books about failed priests, busing or childhood leukemia. Sex, money, the international coke trade, younger men with older women, folks from outer space are fine, are wonderful. Please, all of you, don't forget that your quota doesn't represent mere numbers, it must represent commerce. We're not in the altruism business."

Alicia leaned toward Mickey and said, "I'm at sea here, I don't belong in this room."

"You do, chile, you do. You're too good to let them dump you over the side."

Phyllis did not dress the way articles about working women told one to; she always looked to Alicia as if she were about to take tea at the Ritz. She wore supple challis and heavy silk; most of her dresses had a loose bow below the throat, long sleeves, swinging skirts. Her colors were rust and wine, edging toward pink and orange and blue. Never yellow or green. Alicia and Davida had decided that each one of Phyllis's dresses cost at leat $250. Today her dress was a lovely shade of eggplant; a blouson top hid her enormous breasts. Two tiny buttons winked over each wrist. Phyllis shifted and said, "I'm going to pick on one of you, but please, Harry dear, don't take it personally, I'm using you as an object lesson, I couldn't be more fond of you, nor more sure of a bright promise." Harry gulped and clutched his pad. "It's about the Blessing manuscript," Phyllis said. "I really wanted it for Griffin, I knew we could do a beautiful job with it. But you were cleared to bid up to fifty thousand dollars, Harry, not sixty thousand. That's far too much to bid on a book about Greenwich Village in the Forties. We could have had it for fifty. What possessed you to go so high?"

Harry swallowed again and ran a trembling hand through pale thinning hair. His neck colored. "I must have misunderstood," he said.

"Jesus Christ," Mickey said to Alicia behind his hand, "*nothing* happened in the Village in the Forties."

"I don't quite see how that's possible," Phyllis said. "I wrote you a memo."

"I can't explain . . ." Harry began.

"Dear Harry," Phyllis said, her voice sharpened by indignation. "I realize you've only been out of Harvard four years but, my dear, didn't they teach you to read and follow instructions there?"

"Phyllis," Mickey said, "why don't you leave the kid alone? I think he gets the point."

Harry stared gratefully at Mickey, eyes melting. Several others, not so brave as Mickey, nodded. Phyllis said, "You understand me, all of you. Harry here blew it, Griffin has just spent ten thousand dollars it can't afford."

"She's right," Peter Fairchild said to Alicia.

"And we hate her for it? Does Harry get the hook?" Alicia asked.

"The week before Christmas," Peter said. "That's the way it's done." Peter smelled of sharp cologne. Alicia wondered if the woman in New York had bought it for him.

Alicia glanced at her watch every few minutes; it seemed to be moving faster than usual. Her restlessness made sitting there intolerable, pretending to listen to Phyllis and the others haggling over whether they should delete a passage in a Griffin book about to go into production, a passage that was just a sneering dismissal of Christian Science. "It makes us look tacky," said one. "But to take it out would be censorship," said another, "And I'm against censorship in any form." "It's not censorship, it's a matter of good taste and fairness," said the first. "Baloney," the other replied. Alicia wondered why Phyllis did not step in and settle it, as she generally did. Their voices, muffled by the buzz of impatience in Alicia's bloodstream, came and went. It was her kind of argument, but she could not stay with it. She focused her eyes on each speaker in turn while behind, inside her head, she saw a spindly woman sitting on the Green Line subway, a book on her lap, nervous fingers, and a face closed to scrutiny. So that was what Wilma looked like. She looked like a woman visited often by minor illness.

"What do you think, Alicia?" Phyllis ruptured Alicia's vision of Wilma Fearing.

Alicia said, "I'm sorry, Phyllis, I'm not sure what you're asking me."

"About this passage we've been discussing for the last ten minutes. I want your input." Phyllis didn't want her input, Phyllis had recognized her vacancy and was making the most of it. "I'm against," Alicia said, "even though that particular paragraph makes me cringe."

"Thank you, Madame," Phyllis said.

Next on the agenda was the final decision on whether or not to buy a manuscript about survival after limited nuclear war. When Alicia had told Barney about it he had hit the ceiling, maintaining no nuclear engagement could be limited. It was a work studded with the names and shapes of risks and dangers, descriptions of the drying up of wells, the horrors of radiation. It delivered a biblical portrait of entropy. Alicia had had to force herself to read it; it made her perspire with anxiety. Peter said, "Phyllis, are you sure anyone will want to survive after reading this? It doesn't sound like much fun."

"This is a roots and berries book, darling," Phyllis said. "Survival is a class act. I'm planning to ask someone at Yale to do the introduction if we decide to buy."

"I vote no," Peter said. "It depresses me."

"You're leaving," someone said to him. "That's not fair, Phyllis, Peter shouldn't have a vote on this one. He's leaving."

Alicia knew that votes or no, Phyllis would decide. The votes were meant to co-opt them, to make them feel they were part of the process. How come they all sat there like dummies? Or were they too seething, hiding it so well they looked like children on their first day at parochial school? *Wilma, who are you? What do you want with me?*

The editors and Mickey discussed whether Peter deserved a vote on the survival manuscript, while Alicia's trepidation increased as The Hour grew closer. Nothing in her history had prepared her for this meeting with Wilma Fearing. She felt as if she were about to meet a woman she had dreamed about, an entirely made-up person whom she would recognize but not know.

Phyllis broke up the meeting with a caveat: "You're spending too much time with each other," she said. "I want you out there rubbing elbows with pols and streetwalkers and Harvard professors. And, above all, with agents. You all have your expense accounts: use them, for chrissake, or the competition is going to get the next blockbuster. Hustle up there, these are lean times, and Sales Conference is coming up." She paused, locked gazes with each editor and then said, "That's all for now." She paused. "Alicia?" The group stumbled from the room, all but Harry, who was bent almost double. Alicia watched them go, enviously. "Yes, Phyllis?"

"Doc Gurney's coming in later this week with one of his law partners. I'd like you to be at our meeting, so please leave both Thursday and Friday mornings free. I'll let you know as soon as it's firmed."

"Is Davida going to be there too?"

"Absolutely. It won't be any fun without her."

Alicia swallowed her response to this and said instead, "I've got to meet someone in ten minutes. Is that all you wanted to talk to me about?"

"That's all," Phyllis said, gathering several folders together and making for the door. "I've got a heavy date myself."

Alicia made a quick stop in the ladies' room, washed her face with a stiff paper towel that smelled like glue, combed her hair and put on fresh lipstick. Then she stopped at Jenny's desk in the hall outside her office, and told her she was going out for lunch. Her breaths came shallowly, as if she had been jumping rope for the first time in years. Equal portions of thrill and dread loosened muscles and sent current through her nerves. She was close to a scream.

CHAPTER
Four

ALICIA started walking briskly across Boston Common. She skirted a drunk with one eye pasted shut, a week of whiskers on his face and a loop of green mucus leaking from his nose and pasted to his chin. His coat was held together with a diaper pin, his pants bagged around his knees. He smelled like a subway urinal. Ahead of her lounged a gang of half a dozen teenage boys and a single girl. One had almost no chin, another cheeks scarred by the battle of acne with flesh, a third with hair brushing the middle of his back and jeans that drew tight against his parts, squashing them. All this Alicia took in within seconds. They held bottles of beer stuck into brown paper bags, necks showing. They turned slowly as Alicia drew near and seemed to form a tacit conspiracy, she had become their victim. They leered at her, a look of interest unconnected with anything as simple as sex. At a silent signal, one of them drew an empty bottle from its bag and tossed it with practiced aim on the sidewalk just beyond her feet. It exploded with a popping noise, sending a shower of broken glass briefly upward, just missing her legs. Alicia looked at the kid who had thrown the bottle. His nose ended in a bulb, his cheeks looked as if they had been gnawed by a tiny animal, his hair was bushy, black, filthy. The boy stared back at her, a look she read as "Next time I'll get even closer," although she was certain he had not meant to hit her. Then he said something that sounded like "cunt." Alicia grew light-headed and drifted dangerously a moment, in terror and disgust. Then her legs moved her away from the boys and the splinters.

Alicia recognized Wilma Fearing at once as the woman on the subway before Wilma saw her. Wilma was the one sitting just inside the front door, wearing a purple coat and reading a paperback book held far from her eyes, almost in her lap. Her face struck Alicia as a paradox: she had a young expression, expectant, half smiling, but her skin was old, creased and wrinkled like a sailor's. Her complexion was yellowish, as if she had had hepatitis, but her eyes, what Alicia could see of them, were a deep gemlike green and darted rapidly back and forth across the page. Wilma looked up and, seeing Alicia, rushed at her.

"Alicia Gordon," she cried in a reedy little voice, "I'd know you anywhere." Her mouth was unusually thin and opened and shut between words. She stuck out her right hand; Alicia stuck hers out to meet it, half expecting to find only air, to discover that Wilma had no substance and was a creature wholly dependent on her, Alicia, for existence. But the hand was real enough; its fingers were dry, the grip tight and bony.

Alicia said, "You look exactly the same." The lie emerged with no effort; it was as glib as a truth.

"I know you're flattering me, Allie," Wilma said. "But that's okay, I don't mind, it's the sort of white lie we all want to hear." The woman seemed ill at ease.

Wilma had reserved a table which they were shown to by the head waiter. Wilma had tiny, flat breasts. She wore a cowl-neck top made from a synthetic fabric; Alicia could tell it wasn't wool or cotton because its threads picked up and reflected the light. Her throat was taut and its tendons stood out alarmingly. The hair poking from under the brim of her hat was mushroom-colored and crisp; it looked as if it had been straightened.

"You have no idea how happy I am to be here, Alicia. I don't know why but not very many things have gone right in my life since we were in school together, it's as though each time I made a choice or did something unexpected, it turned out badly, I haven't felt really good, you know, satisfied about anything, even though there weren't any terrible tragedies, any real disasters. Like too much salt in the soup or the milk went a little bit sour. You could still drink it, you understand, the sour was just a trace. But since I moved to Boston, that is, to the Boston area—isn't that what you say?—I don't actually live in the city, it's either too expensive or too dangerous, things have a good feel to them, I have a sort of sense of balance. And your meeting me today, that's a good omen . . ."

Alicia nodded. She didn't have much of an idea what this disjointed person was talking about. "Yes, the Boston area. We don't say suburbs, for some reason."

"I hope we're going to be friends again, like in high school."

Alicia had no memory of Wilma at school; other girls, her best friend, Betty Frank, Ann Davidson, there was a Margo something and Enid Simon . . . Alicia went spinning off into her own past, searching for a Wilma, not finding her. Alicia nodded again, feeling like someone else, disoriented, and tried to grab a conversational foothold. She could not imagine this nervous, creased woman as a girl of seventeen. Was the seventeen-year-old Wilma still there, barely alive, shrunk to moth size, and flapping away feebly inside this middle-aged woman with faded hair?

"Where have you been all these years? What has your life been like?" Alicia heard herself asking these unremarkable questions, astonished at how steady she sounded. Her heart fluttered against her throat, and she kept having to wipe the napkin over her palms. Her mind flew back to the list of possible explanations she had drawn up after finding the invaders, then hidden inside a folder of correspondence in the back of the filing cabinet. This woman was not part of a joke of any sort, there was nothing of the joke about Wilma, who wore her earnestness like a kind of fraternal garment no one else was allowed to wear. The other alternatives—brain dysfunction, lunacy, the supernatural—Alicia could neither credit nor rule them out, since they suggested hallucination; when you're hallucinating you think it's real and so verification is impossible until the seizure is over. Alicia tried, by shaking it, to clear her head. The list she had drawn up seemed irrelevant in any case, a silly exercise designed to keep her from going mad at the time.

She was determined not to let Wilma see how agitated she was. She was a fair enough player of roles and keeper of secrets; covering up was not her immediate problem.

She hoped that Wilma would fill in blanks, shedding light on what was apparently some shared history. If Wilma knew her, then it was reasonable to assume that the other invaders of her address book knew her too. Alicia, hoping for the opposite to be true, realized that there wasn't a shadow of a doubt that she was the person Wilma thought she was; this was no case of a faulty identification: Wilma recognized Alicia.

Without further prodding, Wilma began her autobiography in an inchoate style, but the themes were manifest: "Ted, my husband, was a straightener," she said. "You know the kind of man, I'm sure, who if he sees something not lined up at right angles will move it, so it will be squared off or parallel with everything else on the table or desk or whatever. He didn't like the Kleenex coming out of the box because he couldn't straighten it. He straightened the children's shoes in their closets, it drove me and them crazy. His head was like that, he wanted us to be like him. We couldn't. Well, we didn't want to be either."

Alicia nodded. She was, at least, vivid.

"But his life was a mess," Wilma said, then stopped as the

waiter bent over them to take their order. "I'll have the spinach salad," Wilma said, snapping her menu shut. Alicia ordered an omelet with blue cheese. She wasn't hungry. "Ted made a mess of his life," she repeated. "He slept with his secretary, then after he fired *her,* he started messing around with one of his associates at the lab and after her, he had an affair with someone he met on a goddamn airplane. It never got too messy for him."

"The other side of a straightener is a slob," Alicia said.

"You've got it," Wilma said. She sipped her wine. "I finally took the kids and got away from him. It took me too long to do it, I can see that now." She pursed her mouth together, then went on. "Your letters, Alicia, helped me a lot. Your neat sense or humor. You haven't lost a bit of that, have you? Well, they lifted me out of the blues more than once. Thanks."

"Don't mention it," Alicia said. "I was glad to write." She had no recollection of these antidepressants. She could not remember writing letters to a woman she didn't know. The woman sitting across from her, eating raw spinach with surprising fervor, was as concealed as if she was locked inside a chest. Alicia forced herself to say words to which she felt no connection. She felt funny now, faint. Maybe it was the wine, stronger than she realized, and poured into an empty stomach.

"I put Betsy and Steve in Newton South High School," Wilma said. "They seem to be getting on well enough, Steve made the junior varsity soccer team, Betsy's concentrating on young men." She made a face which said she thought this was an unwise choice. "As for myself, I'm working at John Hancock, I'm what they call an administrative assistant, which is just a fancy name for secretary. I make the coffee. They taught me how to use a word processor, it makes my shoulders ache and kills my eyes. I hate it, it's impossible, I hate the other secretaries, all they think about is clothes and getting laid. I ought to be running an art gallery on the North Shore, or Provincetown, someplace like that."

"Then you're still painting," Alicia said, startling herself by the question.

"Wilma the artist, Alicia the writer. Remember how they called you Edna for Edna Ferber?"

"Couldn't they have done better than Ferber? Millay, at least."

"What happened to us?" Wilma said. "I'm writing letters to actuaries and you're blue-penciling other people's manuscripts."

"I'm perfectly satisfied," Alicia said. In fact, she felt as if Wilma had dropped a piece of ice down her back. Fuck her, she thought. What right has she got to talk about my calling that way? "I enjoy my job," Alicia repeated. "I enjoy it so much I'm thinking of going to New York where there's an even better one. I love being an editor, I'm happy working with my authors. Sometimes, you know, you get a lovely cream pie out of what appeared at first to be sand. You get to help make the thing, the book."

"Well," said Wilma, and her lithe tongue flicked out between her thin little lips and snatched a crumb away, "you may like your job, but mine's the pits." This short speech did nothing to convince Alicia that she had convinced Wilma. Their waiter came by, saw they were not finished, scowled and left them.

"That's too bad," Alicia said lamely.

"Ted's so stingy, trying to get money out of him is like trying to get blood from a stone." She didn't seem to realize that she had scrambled the image.

"Don't you have a lawyer?" Alicia asked.

"Lawyers cost money," she said. "They charge you for calling them on the phone. God, they're certainly not stingy with salad dressing." The spinach remaining lay in a pale green pool.

"You, Alicia Gordon, were one of the first cool people I was aware of," Wilma said. "The funny thing was we all envied you and I don't think you knew that at all. Everybody liked you, you know, except a couple of girls like Marilyn Steinberg and she didn't like anybody but herself and her boyfriend with the zits, Paul Desmond. You know why they voted you Gold Dust Girl? It was because you looked so clean and healthy, even in winter your skin was sort of copper-colored. That sounds silly, doesn't it? You think Gold Dust and it suggests something indoors, at night, but you were outdoorsy and your hair was gorgeous, it just had a bit of curl and it was so nice and thick." Wilma stopped, apparently to think about the youthful Alicia. "Marilyn had a foul mouth," she said. "She was the first girl I ever heard say the word 'cunt' out loud. I couldn't bring myself to say it till two weeks ago. What about you?"

"I can say it," Alicia said. Outdoorsy? When had she ever been outdoorsy? Did she remember this, did she remember any of this? The names Wilma presented meant nothing to Alicia. "Gold Dust Girl" was something straight out of the Twenties; was Wilma in the wrong time warp? Alicia tried to examine each item as it went past, as on a conveyor belt, but nothing felt right in her hands. She did not know what to do with them.

"You also had a terrific figure. *And* legs. *And* eyes. Just your fingernails weren't so great, you bit them."

Instinctively, Alicia tucked her fingers under. "Just what did Marilyn say about me?" Alicia asked.

"I don't know why you care," Wilma said. "She had such a filthy mouth and she was a terrible gossip. She made things up. She told me you were a liar, and implied you were sneaky. I told her it takes one to know one, Marilyn honey. Don't lose any sleep over it, Alicia, she wasn't worth your little toe." Wilma snapped a bread stick in half and crunched a piece into her mouth.

"There's a lot I never told you," Wilma continued. "Things I've kept locked inside me forever."

"Oh, dear," Alicia said. The food tasted like paste and she was having trouble swallowing. She put down her fork and drank some water.

"Not to worry," Wilma said. "It's nothing terrible. In fact it's sort of nice. Nice for you, that is. We were all envious of you. After the senior picnic we got a ride home in someone's father's station wagon and I had to sit on Tommy Salten's lap because there wasn't enough room otherwise and all Tommy could talk about was Alicia this, Alicia that. He told me he loved you so much he couldn't sleep at night, he said you were a golden girl, you could do anything, dance, write poetry, play tennis, cook even. He said you were the most beautiful girl he'd ever known."

"And you were on his lap? I would have told him to shut up," Alicia said.

"I tried and I couldn't. In a horrible, jealous way, I wanted to hear what he was saying. It made me sick with envy but I had to hear."

"What you heard was normal schoolboy romanticism," Alicia said. "I don't know how you could have taken it so seriously. Romanticism aggravated by having a girl on your lap. At that age every boy has a crush on a girl, especially someone who will never love him back. Hopeless love—it's classic. It goes with being eighteen in the spring."

"Maybe," Wilma said.

"Not maybe. Absolutely. We all did." This was partly a lie as Alicia, trying to remember details of her eighteenth year, came up against dark fog. The haze that was her adolescence had all melted together and gone dark. She could not remember Tommy Salten either. But wait, there *had* been a Salten, the name pricked her skin and then connected itself to a young face, looking mournful.

Meanwhile Wilma went on producing events she seemed to think the two of them had shared. "Remember that shack we rented in Eastham, it was just rundown enough to give off sentimental vibrations? It smelled like dead mice, dirty sneakers and rotting cabbage—you couldn't get over it, having come from the kind of house you did, with the amenities in abundance. Anyway, even I thought it pretty neat in spite of how it stank. Artie brought along, wouldn't you know, a copy of *War and Peace*—Artie had to be associated with the best or he had no use for it . . ." Abruptly, Alicia knew it was not *War and Peace* but *Anna Karenina;* she saw it lying on a torn beach blanket in the sun, inside a reddish cover. "Artie read to us from *War and Peace,* out loud, and we all had to listen like school kids. Actually, he read quite expressively, I think he was dying to be an actor. The hand pump in the kitchen sink wouldn't work when we got there but you knew about priming and we found a pitcher of dirty water sitting there on the counter to prime it with. How did you know about priming a pump?"

"Summer camp," Alicia said. Cobwebs were being removed.

"The toilet had a crack in the wooden seat that bit you on the fanny when you sat down," Wilma said.

"The walls were as thin as soda crackers," Alicia said, in a trancelike voice. "I must have heard you two screwing through the walls." She sat up, straightening her shoulders. "This all sounds like a made-up story."

"It's true enough," Wilma said. "I got knocked up and had to get an abortion. My uncle Ben was on the staff of a sleazy hospital upstate; he got it for me. Otherwise I might be dead now."

"There were live mice in the closets."

"And in the eaves," Wilma said. "Artie teased me because I was so scared of them, I thought they were going to run up my legs and start nibbling." Wilma's eyes darted to meet Alicia's. Alicia blinked.

"The toilet wouldn't flush," Alicia said, now thoroughly frightened by knowing these domestic details. And as the scene cleared further, the picture swam into focus and magnified, as on a large movie screen: a boy in jeans and a horizontally striped shirt climbing an abandoned coast guard tower, a shaky ladder up its middle, and once on top reciting "Dover Beach"—what else?—with a fierce moon shining down and the surf so loud it covered most of the words of the poem and she, standing beneath the tower, chin up, listening, in love. She said, "David."

"Your heartthrob, David Lawrence," Wilma said. "I heard he got himself killed."

"He was the first person I ever slept with," Alicia whispered, as he stepped out of the bog of her memory. She felt odd, as if she had been injected with blood thinner. She drew in a large breath.

"Are you okay? You look a little greenish."

"How did David get killed?" Alicia asked.

"I think he was drowned off a boat somewhere. I'm not sure exactly," Wilma said. "He was always playing around with danger."

The news of David's death hit Alicia like a giant fist. The breath was briefly knocked out of her. The waiter stood by their table. "Would you ladies be interested in dessert?" he said.

Wilma said, "I'll have the Jell-O." Alicia knew only one other person who ordered Jell-O in a restaurant and that was her mother.

Alicia said, "Coffee," in a weak voice.

"Aren't you afraid of cancer of the bladder?" Wilma asked.

"I'm afraid of everything," Alicia said. "But what isn't going to get you in the end? We're all going to be vaporized anyway, by some button-happy soldier—whoosh, say goodbye to the human race."

"Gloomy, gloomy," Wilma said. "What about the Russians. You don't trust *them,* do you?"

"The Russians go too. We all go."

"What does your husband think?" Wilma said.

"Barney says we shouldn't stop working, he says we can't stop. Anyway, here's to your health?" Alicia raised her cup in a salute.

Wilma said, "When are we going to see each other again? Now that we've been brought together again, so to speak, I'm going to need you. Though I must say, Alicia, you aren't as funny in person as you are in your letters."

"Maybe the letters aren't the real me," Alicia said.

"If not you, who?" Wilma said. "Or did you get one of your writers to write them for you? Maybe someone who needed a little extra money. I'm not really serious, Alicia, but I *am* serious about wanting us to be friends again. I haven't made very many friends since we got here and the people at Hancock aren't exactly my type, if you know what I mean."

Alicia wasn't exactly Wilma's type either. She wouldn't have to see Wilma ever again if she didn't want to. Wilma was looking at her, the green eyes pleading. "I hope you can meet my family," Alicia said. Wilma grinned, the thin mouth got even thinner as it spread right and left in her face. She seemed much too pleased by this soft invitation. Alicia couldn't say why, but she felt that Wilma had some kind of hold on her and was hanging on for dear life. Alicia looked at her watch and said, "I should be getting back to the office."

"I suppose I should too," Wilma said, sighing. "I keep trying to do things to get myself canned but I can't seem to ruffle my boss's feathers. I take two hours for lunch, he doesn't notice. I use the telephone for long-distance calls, he doesn't mind. I take a day off whenever I feel like it, he says go right ahead. I even fell asleep at my desk once and he had to wake me up. Nothing I do gets his goat. What do you think I should do?"

"Count your blessings," Alicia said, rising. She put on her trench coat.

"I hope you won't be embarrassed, Alicia, if I tell you how much seeing you again means to me, it's almost as if I had been rejuvenated. Look at you, your hair is still glorious, your figure . . . I always wanted to be like you."

"Wilma, that's crazy!" Wilma seemed stuck to her chair. She was just stubbornly sitting there while Alicia hopped from one foot to the other, desperate to leave. "You shouldn't want to be like anyone else. You're fine the way you are . . ." The words came tumbling out, carrying lies. "You *are* embarrassing me. You don't see me the way I am."

"I can't help it, Alicia, I'm taking a leaf from your book. You always say exactly what's on your mind. You always did."

"Wilma, I've got an author coming in at two-thirty; I'm late already. I really have to go."

At last Wilma released herself and got up; they left the restaurant together. Wilma tried to take Alicia's arm but Alicia sidestepped her deftly, avoiding the arm. She wouldn't have touched Wilma except under threat of punishment. They stood poised at Berkeley Street and Alicia forced herself to turn and look directly at Wilma Fearing, whose eyes seemed about to brim over. Where they had been clear and dry before, now they blurred wetly, they seemed the end product of years of disappointment and hurt.

"Before we go our separate ways," Alicia said, "there's something I have to ask you. Why did you call me after all these years? You've been living in Newton for almost a year now, why did you decide to call me?"

"What are you talking about, Alicia? Don't you remember? *You* called *me*. I wrote you a note saying I was here and you called and said let's meet for lunch. I was afraid you wouldn't have time to see me. I was so pleased I almost cried. When you called again on Saturday I was alarmed because I thought you were calling to break our date. This is the best thing that's happened to me since I moved here."

As she slipped back into the Griffin Building, Alicia said, "He didn't drown, his car hit a deer in New Hampshire. He got killed by a deer." Tears slid down her cheeks.

By dinnertime, as Alicia and Toby brought their food to the table and sat down with Barney, she could no longer see Wilma Fearing's outlines; she had smudged. And by ten-thirty, as Alicia got ready for bed, Wilma had gone out of focus entirely.

She was like a person in a dream or the memory of something that happened so long ago it has melted into the pool formed by the union of the true and the merely imagined. Alicia remembered that when she was a tiny child, weighing less than a bag of groceries, her father had dropped a yapping pink puppy into the crib with her, freezing her blood. Had he really done this terrifying thing to her or had she made it up?

As she stood in the shower, letting hot water run over her rounded pale stomach and over her flanks, now large enough to grab by the handful, and wishing for the otterlike body of her daughter (sighing because it would never happen), Alicia tried to restore Wilma but she had slipped away. A pebble, Wilma had fallen into a bottle and was lodged there. Wilma was inside the bottle, obscured by the dark green glass and silenced by its thickness.

Barney looked up from his medical journal as Alicia came out of the bathroom. "You didn't tell me what you did today," he said.

"For one thing, I took Jenny to lunch," she said. "A new Japanese place on Boylston Street." The lie slid off her tongue like soapsuds under a stream of water. The urge to tell the truth—"I had lunch with someone who knows me but I don't remember her"—was so strong she could feel it in her teeth. She clamped her mouth shut.

"I must say, Allie, you're an awfully nice boss. Jenny's lucky."

"Is this something new?" Alicia asked, getting into bed, "Asking me what I did today?"

"I always do," Barney said, and snapped off the light.

CHAPTER
Five

WHATEVER happened at Griffin House—the publishing of a book, acquisition of a new author or property, wrapping up a movie sale, getting a substantial bid from a paperback firm, losing an author, misjudging a book's potential and so on—was viewed as either triumph or disaster, there being almost nothing in the gray area of moderateness. This binary style was due mainly to Phyllis Vance's stress-related view of work. To be good, work must be hard, as Phyllis was fond of repeating while winking at junior members of Griffin's editorial staff. Anything fun, easy or amusing she tended to dismiss. "My father," she said, "educated me in the love of self-discipline. He himself took an ice-cold shower every morning before he went off to his law office. I tried to emulate him in this but have to admit I usually turned on the hot water tap just a tad."

Phyllis's speeches reminded Alicia of pep talks by the coach in the locker room before the homecoming game. But Phyllis had her hand firmly on the helm and kept things swinging along with amazingly few disasters, kept the company somehow out of the red. Alicia said to Barney, "Phyllis is an evil genius. I can't stand her."

Alicia had kept Thursday and Friday mornings free, as Phyllis had asked her to do earlier in the week. This meant breaking a Thursday date with Sarah Dunn, an agent who was in Boston for two days. By the time Alicia found out that the meeting with Griffin's lawyers was scheduled for Friday, it was too late to hook up again with Sarah, who had made other plans. Alicia fumed; Sarah Dunn's client list included six authors whose books were bought simultaneously by publishing house and movie producer, two Pulitzer Prize–winning biographers and three Watergate criminals.

On the phone, Sarah Dunn said, "Not to worry, Alicia, I'll see you when you're in New York next. When will that be?"

"Next month," Alicia said. "I'll let you know well in advance and we'll have lunch."

Still, it was a nuisance, and Alicia blamed Phyllis. Phyllis created nuisance for Alicia without apparently thinking about it. That was the worst part; it seemed to happen with doleful regularity. Alicia made plans, Phyllis shredded them.

On Friday morning Alicia drank an extra cup of coffee—which she fetched herself from the machine in the Production Department—and waited for Davida. She fingered the morning's mail and was reading a letter from Dick Freyburg which repeated something he had already told her about T & L stock options, when Davida blew in, unannounced, wearing a halo of perfume.

"Your person at the front desk told me to go right on up. I guess that means I've finally arrived." She didn't look as if she believed this. She draped her coat on the coatrack and held up a manila envelope.

"See this?" she said. "This is Archie Tanner's pretrial deposition. It's fiction from beginning to end. It's unbelievable. Don't ask me about it now, Allie, I want to react to it freshly later. Do you know both lawyers?"

"Just Doc Gurney. He's the man we consult when we need a legal opinion. The other man is one of the partners in the firm. I've never met him."

Davida paced, walked to the window, looked out, turned and walked back toward the wall of shelves.

"And what have we here?" Davida said, picking up an open box of manuscript and squinting at the title page. "I believe I know the author, we were at school together. She was a year ahead of me. We called her The Nose because she was so stuck-up. That's what we said then, stuck-up. Now we'd say she was on an ego trip. What is this, a novel?" She tightened her face.

"Not exactly. It's an account of the year she spent aboard a schooner with her son, her daughter and a lover."

"Wouldn't you know," Davida said. Her eyes were fierce. "Have you read it?"

"Not yet," Alicia said, telling a partial lie. She had read enough of it to know she wanted to read more.

"I'll bet she made the whole thing up. The Nose I used to play basketball against could not have tolerated a year without a Jacuzzi and a weekly diet of gossip at the trendy spa."

"I don't think she made it up," Alicia said. "The agent says there are photographs."

"Does the lover screw the daughter as well?" Davida, it was clear, was doing her best to light her way through some dark and painful place.

"I told you, I haven't read it yet," Alicia said.

"Griffin had a sailing-around-the-world book last year," Davida said, putting the box back on the shelf and walking across the room. "So you probably won't buy it, right?"

The phone buzzed and Alicia, relieved not to have to answer Davida, picked up the receiver, and said, "We'll be right down. Ready?" she went on, getting up and smiling at Davida to lend her confidence. "It won't be so bad, you didn't *do* anything."

"When was *justice* anything but a word?" Davida said. "Oh, what the hay, maybe I'll get a little notoriety out of this misadventure."

The Hothouse steamed, the windows fogged. Schefflera, ficus, a Boston fern hanging from the end of a chain secured to the ceiling by a large hook swung over Phyllis's desk. The low couch against the opposite wall was occupied by Doc Gurney and another man, who leaped up the moment Alicia and Davida entered. Gurney introduced his law partner, who shook hands so powerfully Alicia nearly cried out. His name was Tom Sheldon and he looked to Alicia as if he never left the vicinity of Harvard except to go to work. Phyllis told Alicia and her author to take the only two chairs in the room.

"Tom Sheldon wants to go over some material I believe you've already covered, Davida," Phyllis said, looking at the pad on her desk. "So I'm sure you'll want to tell him everything he needs to know—"

"Even if it seems redundant," Tom Sheldon said, finishing Phyllis's sentence, leaning briefly forward.

"I'm going to have to leave you folks at some point," Phyllis said. "I'm expecting Stanley Garfield, who's come unglued. He'll be here in a few minutes." She smiled mysteriously. "But you gentlemen don't need me here, I'm superfluous."

Alicia worried lest Davida lapse into flippancy, something she did when threatened. Alicia hoped the men wouldn't browbeat her, but then, why should they, they were Griffin's lawyers, not the plaintiff's. But oh, she saw Tom Sheldon as a formidable number, his suit so gray, his shirt so striped, his tie so yellow, hair silvered as if from a tube, his smile the gesture of one who has never known anything more daunting than a daughter put on the waiting list at Radcliffe.

Alicia watched Davida take out a cigarette and light up, which indicated she was nervous down to her toes; Davida had given up smoking in 1974.

"Well, shall we get started?" Tom Sheldon said, bringing an attaché case up onto his knees and clicking it open. He turned to Alicia and said, "Can you explain to me, Mizz Baer, why you didn't ask to have Mizz Franklin's novel read by Doc Gurney?

I'm aware you've already been over this ground but it won't hurt to have it said once more, will it?"

She thought Sheldon would do extremely well in court. "I guess not," she said. "I didn't ask Doc to read it because there wasn't any intrinsic reason to—or any extrinstic reason either, for that matter. We don't normally ask for legal reading on a novel, not unless the story's based on an actual event or the author thinks one of his or her characters is modeled on someone real. In this case, with *Inside Out,* there was absolutely no indication that Davida—Mizz Franklin—had drawn on anything but her imagination." A neat little speech, she told herself; keep it up.

"I see," Sheldon said, riffling his papers. He cleared his throat that didn't need clearing. Doc Gurney remained silent. Sheldon turned his immaculate face toward Davida, who had crossed her legs; a long black skirt grazed the tops of her boots. A string of fat false pearls glowed against an unadorned rose-colored sweater. Alicia thought she was as beautiful as a game bird. "Perhaps you can tell me, Mizz Franklin, just how much of a case Archie Tanner, that is, the plaintiff, has against you and your novel, *Inside Out?* Please take your time. The idea is not to defend yourself here—we are all on your side—but to get at the truth. Did you, in fact, have Mr. Tanner in mind when you wrote this nov—"

"Absolutely not," Davida said. "He's crazy." Phyllis frowned.

"I'm afraid that's not very helpful," Gurney said. Unlike his partner, he had an informal tone and demeanor. "What we need to know is what there is in your fictional portrait that corresponds to real facts."

"Nothing," Davida said, crushing out the stub of her cigarette and recrossing her knees. "Not a damn thing. Look, I made this character a high school teacher and Archie Tanner worked for an ad agency in New York, he still does, doesn't he?" Sheldon scanned his notes and nodded. "Okay," Davida continued. "My novel takes place in a town in upstate New York and is about a group of moral vigilantes and this character that Archie's suing me over only appears in twice in a minor role and is, for God's sake, a *pre*vert."

"A what?" Sheldon said, staring at Davida's bangs.

"She means a *per*vert," Alicia said, flashing Davida a look of warning.

"I don't see why he wants to be associated with this tacky person in my novel. What has Archie got to prove—I mean, prove *legally?*"

"He has to prove malicious intent and also damages," Sheldon said. "And he's hired the best firm of publishing lawyers in the city. I'm afraid he means business."

"Well, I think it's a lousy, rotten deal," Davida said. Her voice had risen. Like a lot of women, she sounded like a girl when excited.

"Perhaps," Doc Gurney said, "But we have to take this seriously."

"Two hundred and fifty thousand dollars' worth of seriousness," Phyllis said, contributing for the first time; she was exhibiting unusual restraint. Then her phone buzzed, she picked it up and said, "I'll be right there. I'm going to have to leave you now, our anxious author has arrived. Please don't get up, gentlemen," Phyllis added, as she left the room.

Sheldon went immediately to the window and drew it up. "Feels like a Turkish bath in here," he said. "I trust you people won't mind some fresh air." The fog on the windowpanes slowly cleared to reveal a metal sky. Sheldon continued to talk. "You see, Mizz Franklin, the plaintiff thinks you've deliberately set out to ruin his reputation and he has witnesses to prove it. I trust you've read his pretrial deposition by now."

"I have. It's incredible. It's all lies. All those people lied for him." Alicia sighed.

"They were under oath," Sheldon said tightly.

"I don't care what they were under, they lied. Listen to this, Allie: 'Question: How long have you known the defendant?

Answer: On and off for twenty years. Q.: And the plaintiff? A.: For the same amount of time. They lived together on and off until last year, when they split. It was a heavy scene. Q.: Until last year, they lived together until then? A.: That's correct. I was over there for dinner a lot. Davida Franklin made great beef stew, only she had to call it by its French name.'

"I can't believe this," Davida went on, shaking her head back and forth over and over. "I don't even know who this person *is* who's saying this. And I haven't seen Archie Tanner for ten years."

"Can you prove it?" Doc Gurney said. "That's what we need to know."

"How can I prove something negative?" Davida cried. "How can I prove I didn't know *you* ten years ago? What is this, I feel like someone in *The Trial.* Help, Alicia, help me!"

"I wish I could," Alicia said. It was hard not to feel paranoid at this moment, hard not to think that Phyllis had encouraged Gurney and Sheldon to do this to Davida. "How *can* she prove it?" Alicia said to Sheldon. "I would really appreciate it if you would tell us."

"That's extremely difficult," Sheldon said reasonably, while his tone remained hard and unreasonable.

"And what about the so-called damages?" Davida said, springing from her chair and trying to maneuver on her legs, but there wasn't much room and she brushed Tom Sheldon's knees. He drew them in. "What damages does Archie claim?"

"He maintains he lost a board membership at his daughter's school because of your portrayal of him. After all, it isn't a very flattering picture."

"But where is there *anything* for him to go on?" Davida said. She grabbed the deposition notes and shook them.

"Doesn't the character in your book have a beard with a broad streak of white in it?"

"Yes," Davida said.

"And didn't he go to Trinity College, where he was on the wrestling team?"

"The crew."

"And didn't he own a dog that was half Labrador and half, as you call it, mysterious stranger?"

"Yes, yes, yes," Davida said, sitting down once more.

"Those three things are true for Archie Tanner as well."

"Davey—"Alicia began.

"Davey what?" Davida said, snapping her head around. "Those are just superficial characteristics, they don't have anything to do with what the character in the novel is really like, they don't matter."

"They matter to him," Sheldon said. He sat up straight. "It never ceases to amaze me," he said, "how you novelists just write down whatever happens to come into your head without worrying about the possible consequences."

"Oh, is that the way we do it?" Davida said. Alicia saw that Sheldon was going to pretend Davida hadn't said what she had, for he marched right on. "Now tell me, Mizz Franklin, did you and the plaintiff often perform anal intercourse?"

"Now just a minute there," Alicia said. Davida was staring at Sheldon as if she couldn't believe her ears. She began to say something, but Alicia cut her off. "I don't believe that's any of your business," she told Sheldon. "And I resent the way you're treating my author. I thought you said we were all on the same side. Well, I don't think you are, I think you enjoy making people like Davida feel like dirt." She reached out and laid her hand on Davida's arm. Davida gave her a weak smile. "Thanks," she said.

"Do we really have to go into Mizz Franklin's sex life?" Gurney said to Sheldon.

Sheldon cleared his throat and murmured something. Could he have said, "This is War"? Not likely. Alicia read his question to Davida as naked prurience. But he forged on, hacking away.

"The plaintiff's lawyers," he said, "will contend that he was held up to hatred, contempt or ridicule by your portrayal—assuming he can be identified as your fictional character."

"In other words," said Alicia, "first he has to prove the character in Davida's book is enough like him to be recognizable and then he has to prove that even though it *is* him, he doesn't go in for anal intercourse. That's fairly complicated, now, isn't it?"

"Listen to this, listen." Davida, who had been searching in the deposition for the last few minutes, said, "'Now I propose'—that's our man's fancy New York attorney talking in legalese—'I propose to relate this material to the novel in order to ascertain what the purpose, purport, meaning, design of the author was in including this material and whether or not the character depicted in the book was meant by the author to be held up to the public to be hated, ridiculed, to be held in contempt, to be depicted as a drunkard, a coward, a hypocrite, a pervert, dishonorable and in general an oppressive and insulting kind of a man.' Unbelievable! If this wasn't about me I'd think that was the funniest passage since *Decline and Fall* was published. Alicia, how many copies of *Inside Out* did Griffin offload on the public?"

"About ten thousand. But there was a paperback sale, don't forget that."

"The paperback publisher is being sued too," Doc Gurney said.

"And all those readers are immediately going to recognize a minor character in my book as that schmuck Archie Tanner, a two-bit copywriter for an ad agency on Third Avenue. Come on now."

"I keep feeling that all of this is unreal," Alicia said. "I'm shivering, would you mind if I closed the window?" Without waiting for an answer, she got up and did so. "Nobody's going to connect Archie and the fellow in Davida's book—God, I even forgot his name."

"Everett Kane," Doc Gurney said.

"Everett Kane," Alicia repeated. "His mother, maybe, his girlfriends, no one else."

"As I told you, there are people who have sworn under oath Mizz Franklin knew him. He claims he was eased off the board of the Prescott School. But we're starting to go in circles here. I would like your author," Sheldon continued, talking to Alicia's eyes, "to try and reconstruct as best she can just how she came to bestow on Everett Kane some of the characteristics of Archie Tanner and why she made him—ahem—a sodomist." It seemed to Alicia that he said the word caressingly.

Davida's face blotched; she had chewed off a good deal of her lipstick. She looked drained. "You can speak to me directly," she said to Sheldon. "I'm not about to bite you," and she showed her teeth behind a fake smile.

"Of course," Sheldon said. "I'm sorry to put you through all this, Mizz Franklin, but I have to be as hard on you as the plaintiff's attorneys. You're going to have to keep your cool in court—if it goes to that. And if it does go to that I hope you won't wear those jewels."

"They're not real," Davida said, "I don't see—"

"It's the effect, they give the wrong effect," Sheldon said. "Oh, I ought to mention that there's an alternative open to us. We can settle out of court—"

"Settle!" Davida cried. "But why should I settle? He's the one who told the lies. I ought to sue *him!*"

"Nevertheless, in a jury trial they generally find for the plaintiff. You don't have a prayer if it goes to a jury."

"A judge, then," Alicia said.

"A settlement may be more prudent under the circumstances. But it's your decision, that is, yours and your author's. I know what I'd do if I were you." This switch was so improbable that Alicia laughed. Davida was scowling. She held up the deposition. "May I keep this?" she said. Sheldon told her he had another copy and that he wanted her to reread it with care.

"And please be prepared for your own pretrial deposition in the event that we have to go on to trial."

Doc Gurney said, "I think we're through here for the moment."

"So do I," Davida said. At that moment Phyllis opened the door and marched in.

"We're just finishing up," Doc Gurney told her. Sheldon packed away his papers and stood up. His suit was unwrinkled, which was impossible, but there he stood, as smooth as if he had never been taken off the hanger. Alicia wanted to feel he was her friend but couldn't abandon her suspicions. Whatever guided him seemed so alien that she had to chide herself for bigotry.

"I can't get used to people like Tom Sheldon," she said to Davida, back in Alicia's office. "I don't know how his head works."

"He's a stiff and a bully," Davida said. "Why do I have to rely on people like Tom Sheldon? Jesus, it's a cruel world. How much of his fee do I get stuck for?"

"That's something we're working out with your agent and Doc Gurney."

"Shouldn't I bring in my own lawyer?" Davida said. "Who's looking after *my* interests?" She appeared frightened.

"Not yet," Alicia said.

"Okay," Davida said. "Let's try to forget about the lawsuit for the moment. How about you and me going out for lunch? I could use a good stiff drink."

"Davey, I can't, I'm so sorry. I've got to have lunch with Phyllis and tell what happened while she was out of the room."

"In that case, I think I'll give Craig a buzz and see if he's free." Alicia heard the frost on Davida's voice. "I wish I could break it . . ." she began.

"Never mind, Allie, *une autre fois, peut-être.*"

Phyllis insisted they take a cab to the Ritz; Alicia would have preferred to walk but didn't say so. They were given a table right away in the Café—the maître d' called Phyllis by name—and sat down by the brownish glass windows. "I always like this place," Phyllis said. "It makes me think money doesn't have to be a problem." She ordered a double bourbon on the rocks, water on the side. Alicia asked for white wine.

Phyllis's features were at their most dreadful. "Do you know why Stanley Garfield came in to see me? He wanted to inform me he wasn't going to do the Donahue Show. I couldn't believe what I was hearing. Who does he think he is, turning down the Donahue Show?"

"It does seem a little perverse," Alicia said, wishing the waiter would hurry up with her wine.

"Perverse," Phyllis cried. "It's monstrous. That academic prig, he thinks just because he wrote the biography of an alcoholic movie stud which happened, along the way, to have pleased a couple of so-called literary critics, he thinks he's some big deal, and he can turn down an opportunity that comes to one author in ten thousand."

"How did he explain it?" Alicia said. A woman at the next table, eating a chicken sandwich, seemed to be eavesdropping.

"Oh, he said something about how it would interfere with his teaching schedule. But that was clearly a pretext for his real objections. Oh, God, deliver me from infantile authors! What he really meant was that the Donahue Show was infra dig—beneath his contempt. His colleagues no doubt got to him and told him not to go on the show. They're envious, naturally, of his sudden notoriety. I mean, here's this assistant professor of English at Wellesley suddenly coming up with a sure best-seller. They're all snobs, I know them very well. You just see, Alicia, Garfield will be back in six months saying he's changed his mind, he'd like to be interviewed by Donahue and it will be too late by then, they won't want him anymore." Abruptly, Phyllis seemed to realize they hadn't yet got their drinks or given their order. "Where's our waiter? This place is a disgrace!"

Alicia was used to Phyllis's imperial behavior; not so the woman at the next table, who stared disapprovingly as Phyllis raised her arm and began waving it about like a traffic cop.

"What can you do?" Alicia said. Her heart not in this discussion, her heart was with Davida, who *really* had problems, who might have to spend a good deal of money to help defend herself against the miserable Archie Tanner and end up without a publisher for her trouble. "There are compliant authors and balky authors," she added, feeling stupid.

"I don't like it when I'm not calling the shots," Phyllis said in a singular moment of self-portraiture. "It makes me extremely anxious." Their waiter unloaded his tray of drinks. Phyllis didn't sip hers, she gulped. "I'll have the eggs Benedict," she told him as he took out his pad. "And please tell them I don't want my eggs hard. Last time I had to send them back."

"Yes, Madam," he said. His eyes skimmed over to Alicia.

She wanted the crab meat salad but was reluctant to order the most expensive thing on the menu. She ordered the cold roast-beef platter and listened passively as Phyllis let off steam. "I kept reminding him that an author was more or less obligated to do whatever he could to help promote his book. 'Partners, darling,' I said, 'We're in this thing together. You write, we publish, we both promote.' It went over like a lead balloon. He didn't see it my way, he said this was the first time he'd thought of his years of work on this book as a collaboration. He called Griffin House a printing press."

"Just for emphasis, don't you think?" Alicia said, grabbing on to the last part of Phyllis's recital and responding gamely.

"I couldn't budge him, tried every which way. That's the last book of Stanley Garfield's Griffin House is going to publish!"

Their food arrived. Phyllis asked for a glass of Vouvray. Alicia saw an editor from Panther Press come in with something very young and very nervous, a first novelist perhaps.

"That's John Prentiss," Phyllis said, following Alicia's gaze. "They're in trouble over there. He may be the first to go; he's brought in more poetry than any other editor in the history of the firm. I give him six months."

"How do you know all this?" Alicia said.

"Keep my ear to the ground," Phyllis said, jabbing the yoke under its yellow blanket. More yellow oozed out. She smiled. "Just right," she said. "For once."

Alicia looked at her plate. The slice of beef, with its rim of white fat, embroidered with sprigs of parsley, flipped her stomach; she saw it inside a lion's cage.

"Not hungry?" Phyllis said.

"Not very." Alicia bit into a rectangle of melba toast. This was no doubt what Toby felt when she looked at her food: total revulsion. She sliced into the meat and put a tiny piece of it into her mouth, chewing until it was mush, then took a sip of water and washed it down.

"Well, what are you waiting for?" Phyllis said, having polished off one of the eggs and begun on the second. Hollandaise dripped over the edge of her fork. "Are you going to report on this morning's meeting? Or should I have asked for a tape?"

"I was waiting for you to finish with Stanley Garfield," Alicia said, wishing she had asked for a second glass of wine. Phyllis no longer seemed interested in Alicia's appetite once Alicia began her documentary account, leaving out nothing important, saying no more than was necessary.

"Those two chaps are costing Griffin and Davida Franklin many bucks an hour for their time. They better be worth it," Phyllis said.

"I think they are," said Alicia. Smoke stung her eyes. She looked out at Newbury Street and watched a man in his sixties help a leggy young woman—who needed no assistance—out of a limousine. The young woman was wearing a black mink coat. All that was missing was her leash. Alicia smiled. "They were awfully hard on Davida," she added.

"They have to be," Phyllis snapped. "That's what they're there for. Davida has to be responsible for her actions. She's caused us one hell of a headache. I've said it before, Alicia, we've got to cancel her contract and let her keep the first installment on her new book—kiss her goodbye for good. I'd like you to agree with me, of course, but I'm afraid I'm going to have to insist in any case."

Alicia swallowed, though there was nothing in her mouth. "Let's wait until this lawsuit thing is settled," she said, "before hitting Davida with that."

"We can't afford to let friendship come between us and the right decision," Phyllis said. "I know how close you are to Davida Franklin but I'm afraid that's an irrelevant consideration now. Why don't we publish just our friends' books and let it go at that? The House of *Amis,* we could call ourselves. Who cares about numbers anyway?"

"Please, Phyllis, I've had a rough morning . . ."

"You're getting to be an old-fashioned softie," Phyllis said. Alicia thought she heard menace behind the words. "You realize, of course, that this lawsuit may drag on for years?"

"Yes, I know."

"Are you finished, Madam?" Their waiter stared at Alicia's plate. The slice of meat was almost as large as when he had put it in front of her. "Yes, thanks," she said in a steady voice. The waiter whipped her plate away. She wondered what would happen to the beef after it left the table. Would a hungry busboy grab it for a snack? Would the chef feed it to his dog? Would it land in the garbage pail alongside uneaten rolls, puddles of chocolate ice cream, watercress and ends of smoked salmon? Or would it turn up on next day's menu as roast-beef hash?

Phyllis looked at her watch. "I've got to get back," she said, slapping down her American Express card and getting out her lipstick and compact. "I'm willing to leave this Davida thing up to you—*when* you're going to do it, that is, not *if.* I'm sorry, but Franklin's a dead weight. Look, Allie, would you mind very much staying here to pay the bill? I'm late for my next appointment. Just sign my name, they won't bother checking." And with that, Phyllis rose, got into her coat and was out the door before Alicia had said a word.

When Alicia got home, the house was empty—there was a note from Toby on the front hall table telling Alicia when she would be back. Barney was no doubt still at the office palpating lumps and reading vaporous X-rays. She changed into a skirt and a pink velours top and then put the lasagna made by May that morning into the oven. Then she dialed Jeannette Ashburton's number; this time her hand was steadier than when she had called Wilma Fearing. She viewed this as a kind of progress.

The phone rang four times before a low voice answered.

"May I speak to Jeannette Ashburton, please," Alicia said, pretty sure she already was.

"This is Jeannette Ashburton speaking," the voice said. "To whom am I talking?"

"This is Alicia Gordon Baer." Alicia inserted her maiden name into the formula for the first time in a long time.

"Alicia Gordon. I had a student by that name when I taught at Carey College. You wouldn't be that Alicia Gordon, would you?"

"I . . . yes," Alicia said, leaping. Sun lay across the carpet in a pale cool trapezoid. The house was silent except for the hum of machinery in the basement, the hot water heater, the furnace. Far above the house the thin sound of a jet engine proceeding from north to south reached Alicia's ears, then grew softer and finally died.

"Alicia, my dear, this *is* a surprise. I must say I hadn't expected to hear from you after all this time. My goodness. But I must tell you that your call is a remarkable coincidence, don't you know? Your name came up just the other day. You are an editor, I believe, in Boston?" Ashburton's voice was heavy on bass tones.

"Yes, I'm an editor in Boston," Alicia said, her stomach softening.

"My first cousin, Thornton Burns. You are no doubt unaware of his existence but he makes it his business to keep abreast of the financial state of Boston publishing, such as it is. Thornton's in banking, don't you know? He's something of a town gossip but Lord knows he wouldn't hurt a fly. It was Thornton who mentioned your name in connection with I believe it was Griffin House and when he mentioned you I told him I thought you might be my old student Alicia Gordon, who wrote so many lovely stories for my English class at Carey College."

Carey College was the institution in which Alicia had marked time waiting for her life to begin. She remembered neither Jeannette Ashburton nor writing stories. She did remember trying to avoid gym class and learning to play bridge on the floor of her room and testing theories about sex with others as untried as she was. Alicia attempted to squeeze an Ashburton memory from her brain and failed. She sighed. "I do work at Griffin House," she said. And then, these words came out without her having planned them: "I'd like to come and see you."

"Why, that would be very very nice," Ashburton said. "I live alone since my husband Charles Junior died four years ago. The children—well, I imagine you've never thought of my having children—are on the other side of the globe. Margery is in Australia raising sheep and too many children, she married a rancher, poor soul, and just took off for Melbourne with him. Gregory's with the Foreign Service. Imagine, they've posted him to Israel." There was a pause, giving both of them a chance to consider this incongruity. "You were Jewish, weren't you?"

Alicia laughed. "I still am."

"Not to worry—I love company," Jeannette Ashburton said. "Did I tell you that I'm working on a biography of Beatrix Potter, a splendid, remarkable woman, she began as an artist and ended up as a farmer, wore big rubber boots all day long and loved animals to distraction. She sent a letter back unopened addressed to her under her maiden name instead of her married one. I shall probably die before the manuscript is completed."

"Oh, no," Alicia said.

"I'm seventy-five," the woman told her. "I'm no chicken."

"My mother's seventy-eight and going strong," Alicia said.

"How nice for you, my dear, you must have good genes. I hope your mother still has her hearing. That's so important, don't you know? Both these senses are more or less intact. I would rather lose my eyesight than my hearing. The deaf are so cut off . . ."

"When would it be all right for me to pay you a visit?" Alicia said.

"I don't suppose you take tea?"

"I take tea often," Alicia said. "But that time of day is a little awkward for me. I work at Griffin until nearly four and then I like to go home so my daughter won't have to come home to an empty house."

"A perfectly reasonable arrangement," Jeannette said. "Why don't you suggest a time, then?"

"I was thinking maybe of a Saturday or Sunday."

"Come tomorrow," Jeannette said, "and I'll give you a light lunch."

The back door slammed at that moment; Alicia heard Toby climbing the stairs.

"Please, I don't want you to go to any trouble," Alicia said.

"It won't be any trouble. I have a young girl, Pauline, who comes in to help me with my housekeeping, such as it is. She's inexperienced but that's salutary as it turns out because she hasn't had time to pick up a lot of bad habits. Pauline will be glad to prepare lunch for you and me. She tells me I ought to have more company."

Toby appeared in the doorway. She said, "Hi, Mom," and then withdrew.

"Are you sure this Saturday is convenient for you? Tomorrow?"

"Of course I am. Tomorrow will be splendid. Is there anything you don't eat?"

"Unfortunately, no."

Jeannette Ashburton gave Alicia directions for getting to her apartment house on Beacon Street, a large rococo palace Alicia knew already, as one of her authors lived there. They said goodbye and hung up. Alicia was light-headed again, a sort of spinning. She crossed the hall to Toby's room, where her daughter sat on her bed with a book open on her lap. Her stereo was playing.

"Who was that on the phone?" Toby said. "You sounded funny."

"An old teacher of mine from college," Alicia said. "Apparently."

"Oh." Toby looked at her book. "I've got to study, Mom."

"I'll leave," Alicia said. Her daughter wanted her out of the room not for any interesting reason, like dope or masturbation, but just wanting to be alone. Alicia had wanted her own mother out at that age too but there was something else that Alicia saw: a glint of steel in Toby's eyes.

The phone rang, bringing Alicia back to the room she shared with Barney and sparing her an encounter she hadn't the stomach for. It was Davida. The moment Alicia heard Davida's voice she could smell the perfume she wore habitually.

"I want you to know I'm still in one piece," Davida said.

"Glad to hear it," Alicia said. "Did you go to lunch with Craig?"

"He was busy," she said. "I went shopping instead. I bought myself the ideal work costume."

"A muu-muu?" Alicia asked.

"No, dear, a sweat suit. It's fabulous—it's warm, lightweight, loose and so hideous you wouldn't be caught dead with it on anywhere but at your desk." She stopped and shifted gears. "That was some session this morning. I'm just beginning to recover. I'm sorry I barked at you."

"That's okay," Alicia said. "I would have done the same thing myself. I could easily send our Mr. Sheldon a letter bomb."

Davida laughed. Alicia figured the reason Davida had called was to apologize; the apology released her. Across the hall Toby's door clicked shut. The buzzer on the stove went off, indicating that the lasagna was ready to be removed. "Actually," Davida was saying, "I'm almost as worried about me and Craig as I am about the legal mess. I just don't seem to be able to maneuver myself the way I want to. Last night, for instance, we stayed up until almost three talking and drinking ouzo, for chrissake. A writer can't do that, you have to keep monastic hours. And you certainly can't function with a Greek hangover. At least I can't."

"Didn't you tell him you had to get to bed?"

"I tried," Davida said. "Craig isn't so terrific in the listening department."

"But you need him. He enhances your life—or am I wrong?"

"Oh, what the hay, I don't know. Does a man enhance a woman's life?"

"Our mothers believe it—fervently," Alicia said.

"My mother's heavily into marriage. I guess all their generation is," Davida said.

"It seems to mean so much to them," Alicia said. "Marriage is a blessing and singleness a curse. How odd that some women have turned it completely around, and it's now facing in the other direction."

"When in fact," Davida said, "they're both wrong. Why do you suppose mothers put so much store in marriage?"

"It seems so safe," Alicia said, thinking that when she

married Barney it had seemed so safe. "And actually it's just as full of treachery as anything else you do. Oh, the celestial odor of the wedding veil! God, what is it? We all know better."

"*You* shouldn't talk," Davida said seriously. "And I mean that. You've got a good thing going. Even with this New York offer ruffling it, your marriage has been more than okay. You really shouldn't talk like that, Allie."

Alicia felt she was being scolded unfairly. "Davey, I've got a lasagna in the oven that will turn into cardboard if I leave it there any longer. And I'm upstairs. Do you want to hang on or should I call you back or what?"

"No," Davida said. "I've got to run. I'm meeting Kitty Gates for a drink. I'm going to help her publicize some antinuclear benefit she's running. God bless Kitty."

"I wish I thought it would do any good," Alicia said.

"Well it can't hurt, can it? Anyway, I've got to do it so I can sleep at night."

They hung up. Alicia felt herself slipping back in a trough of apprehension. New York, Ashburton, the cloud over Toby, her daylight in shadows and night coming quickly, threatening storm or utter stillness and making an absolute certainty of darkness. She shook her head and went down to the kitchen, twisted the stove knob to kill the buzzer and, protecting her hands with two large padded mitts, drew out the lasagna. The baby emerged somewhat dry but probably edible.

Alicia began pulling apart a head of lettuce for salad. Her mind traveled two hundred and fifty miles to Manhattan. Where would she live if she went there? An apartment, no doubt, with a kitchen window through which she could look at a wall of brick or concrete fifteen feet away. Alicia glanced through the window above the sink and looked at the thin new tree Barney had planted outside, its buds beginning to bulge. Was an eyeful of bud to be preferred over that of brick? And if so, why? Who had the nerve to rank items in this arbitrary manner? Who was to say that anything untouched by human hands was better, more uplifting, morally "cleaner" than something that human hands had created, like a brick? They were all part of nature anyway, the brick as much as the leaf, although the brick was more complicated. "I like the city," she said to her hands. "I like the life of a city." In fact, where there were no people Alicia was half asleep. She would not apologize for that to anyone.

Barney came home. The family drew into its center and sat down for the evening meal, a collaboration between two women who rarely saw each other. Barney was talkative. Toby seemed quieter than usual. Then abruptly she said, "Why do you serve lasagna, Mom, when you know I'm trying to lose weight?"

Barney said, "That's nonsense, Toby, you're absolutely dead center of the normal weight range for your size and age. Dead center."

"That's the trouble, Daddy, I don't want to be in the middle, I want to be below the middle."

"If you go on one of those crazy diets you won't have any energy left. You won't be able to play tennis or soccer."

"Daddy, please, I know what I'm doing!"

"You have to eat, sweetie," Alicia said.

"I hate when you call me sweetie," Toby said. "It's fake."

"Oh, yeah? Then how about, 'You have to eat, dummy.' You like dummy better?"

"Let's not," Barney said. "Let's not get into a pissing contest."

"Oy!" Alicia said, unwittingly echoing her grandmother. "I agree, let us not get into any kind of contest with a fourteen-year-old."

Toby tipped over her glass of apple juice. The amber juice hit the table, spread to form a tiny lake, then spilled over the side, falling onto her knees. "Get a cloth," Alicia said. "Don't just sit there . . ."

"You forgot to say dummy," Toby said, getting up.

Barney was in pain and Alicia was aware that whatever control she had over this three-part organism was breaking down, the organism itself was breaking and she didn't know how to fix it, she didn't even know which instruments to pick up.

Toby took her dishes to the kitchen. Then she went upstairs, leaving her mother and father looking at one another in silence.

"So much for your theory about our goody two-shoes," Barney said. His voice was not unkind.

"My theory has held up until just the last week or so. I swear it, Barney, she's changed, it's as if she's been ticked off for years and was just now getting around to letting us know. You should have seen her eyes, earlier, when I went into her room. They were hateful."

"Do you know what you sound like, Allie?" Barney said. "And by the way, isn't it curious that it was just last week that this job offer came from New York?"

"There's no connection," Alicia said. "And I believe you're saying I sound like a crazy coot. Am I right?"

They both laughed, unwilling to maintain the emotional poise a serious inquiry would have required.

"A coot, maybe, a crazy coot never," Barney told her. "What's a coot?"

"It's an aquatic bird," Alicia said.

"Why crazy, I wonder?"

"The noise it makes, probably. A crazy, scary noise."

Barney said, "Well, coot, I've got to get to work."

"Must you?"

"Oh, Allie honey, don't make it hard for me. You know I've got this paper to finish. They're holding up the issue for it."

"Sure," she said. "I thought maybe we could talk about the job thing."

"I thought you didn't want to talk about it."

"I'm ready now," Alicia said, "but I guess it can wait." Her own patience amazed her.

CHAPTER
Six

ON Saturday Alicia had no trouble freeing herself to visit Jeannette Ashburton; in fact, no one saw her leave the house and, as far as she could tell, no one cared. Barney had office hours—every other Saturday was treated like a weekday—and Toby had gone off to school for an orchestra rehearsal for *The Pirates of Penzance.* Alicia had thought they didn't do Gilbert and Sullivan anymore but she was apparently mistaken. She called Davida, who was too sleepy to talk—another late night with indefatigable Craig—read half a manuscript (deciding against it as "imitation shlock") and then changed into the dress she had worn when Dick Freyburg had taken her to lunch at Lutèce in New York. The dress was gray wool challis with tiny bright flowers scattered over it, a dark garden of bright wild flowers. It was neither seductive nor severe and had cost her just over one hundred dollars at Lord & Taylor.

Looking at herself in the full-length mirror in her bedroom, Alicia tried to make herself feel that what time was doing to her did not matter: a little more flesh here, a little less there, some flecks of gray in the hair (which she was determined to leave as is), the skin on her throat ever so lightly creased and an apprehensive look about the eyes. "You have nothing to feel rotten about," she told the eyes. "You have everything going for you. You can't fail me now!"

Alicia parked, fed the meter, and announced herself to a doorman in a crimson uniform, who spoke into a phone and was told to let her pass. The elevator that took her up to the seventh floor was paneled in polished wood and opened up on oiled gears. The hallway was wide enough to steer a baby grand piano through; there were only five apartments on the floor. Instantly, Alicia knew that Jeannette Ashburton's husband, Chaz, must either have been rich to begin with, especially lucky, or a very concentrated laborer.

Alicia's finger stopped a fraction of an inch from the buzzer's nipple. A tremor of fear went through her, a touch of chill. Again, it struck her that what she was doing made absolutely no sense. Why had she come to see a woman she didn't know, had never heard of, as if she did, as if she had?

"Go ahead," Alicia said. "What are you afraid of?"

A young girl wearing a tight yellow dress and a gold cross resting on her breastbone answered the door, opening it as if she knew who was going to be on the other side of it.

"I'm Alicia Baer," Alicia said. "I've come to see Mizz Ashburton."

"She's in the living room," the girl said. "The first door on your left." She trotted off down a long darkish hallway, her sneakers sounding like the padding of a little dog. The apartment smelled of flowers and spice.

Alicia entered the living room. "Is that you, Alicia?" a voice said. Her name emerged like a song—Al-eece-eeah.

"Yes," Alicia said. She had expected to see a frail body and here was a massive woman who looked as if she consumed three Victorian meals a day and took no exercise. Jeannette Ashburton remained seated in a large, wing-type armchair, letting Alicia come to her.

The room was furnished with things from a much larger house; she had crammed chairs, tables, lamps, a baby grand piano, potted plants of exhibition size, pictures scaled for an immense wall, into this one smallish room. She had come here, evidently dragging her past with her; Alicia guessed she would turn out to be an unabashedly nude bather in nostalgia. There was no sense, in this room, of a woman who viewed the passage of time as a chance to change.

"Sit down, sit down here," Ashburton said, indicating a chair close to her own. "Would you like to see pictures of Gregory and Margery? I'm sure you still can't believe that I have children."

"I'd like to very much," Alicia said. Jeannette Ashburton pointed to two silver frames the size of legal pads. Alicia picked them up, one at a time. The faces inside the frames told her little. Two young people in their early twenties and robust health—how long ago were these photographs taken, at what stage had their subjects been frozen and preserved inside their silver frames? —blond, Waspish, hidden behind bland expressions as if they knew they would end up keeping their old mother silent company toward the end of her life.

"Nice," said Alicia, feeling stupid but not knowing what else to say. They *were* nice, after all. It was not a lie.

This judgment seemed to satisfy Ashburton, for she said, "And how about you, my dear? Are you married? Do you have children?"

"I'm married, yes, to Augustus Baer, we call him Barney. He's a surgeon. We have one daughter, Toby. She's fourteen."

"Toby? Is that short for Tobia?"

Alicia shook her head. "She's just Toby." She could not understand why Jeannette Ashburton wanted to talk about children; it seemed so peripheral. But she wanted to let Ashburton steer this conversation so she did not try to change the subject.

Jeannette called out, "Paulie. Don't you have some sherry for us?" Then she turned to Alicia. "Will you have sherry?"

"Yes, thanks," Alicia said and wondered what Ashburton would have offered her had she said no. Something else? Nothing?

The girl, Pauline, came in, carrying a sturdy oval silver tray with little knobs on its bottom on which rode two crystal glasses filled with sherry. Ashburton had trained Pauline to serve like an old-fashioned servant, for she bent from the waist and held the tray steady and level with Alicia's elbow. Golden, fish-shaped crackers studded with salt swam in a small cut-glass dish. Alicia took several of these. They bit her tongue. "What if she keeps me here?" This odd thought flashed across Alicia's brain and then quickly receded whence it had come.

Having served the two women, Pauline withdrew again. "She's learning nicely," Jeannette Ashburton said. "Though I do wish she wouldn't wear those dreadful sneakers, don't you know."

So far everything either one of them had said could have been said by two people meeting for the first time, like people waiting for a train.

"When did you leave Carey College, Mizz Ashburton?" Alicia said, deciding it was time now to get down to business.

"Oh, my dear, please call me Jeannette, you're not my student anymore, you're my peer, don't you know? Of course, I will always be light-years ahead of you. I was born so long, long ago. Woodrow Wilson was alive. Imagine that. But you're my friend now." And she reached over and gave Alicia's knee a soft little pat that sent waves of shyness through her body. Jeannette's eyes widened and narrowed.

"All right then, Jeannette," Alicia murmured.

"Oh, well, you see, Alicia, I retired almost ten years ago, it was mandatory or I would have stayed on, naturally, until they carried me out in a box. I loved the work, I loved you girls. You may have gathered that my circumstances"—and with this, she made a sweep of the room with her eyes—"were far from straitened. Chaz—Charles Ashburton, Junior—was quite successful in business but I'm not going to discuss that part of it now; it all had so little effect on my inner life but it did permit me these little luxuries, my rugs and my pictures and now my

Paulie. I have plenty to eat, a good firm mattress and a membership in the Musical Heritage Society, which releases the finest recordings available. I indulge myself in a little music at night. It helps put one to sleep."

And how to square this woman with a teacher of stories, as she apparently was? There was no suggestion yet of anything Alicia recognized as a "literary sensibility." Where were the outrage and the nerves and the guilt? Where was the self-pity?

Alicia stole a look at her new friend. The woman's hair was white and unruly; it stuck out all around her head in a halo. Her mouth was wide and expressive and full of teeth, teeth that looked like her own. Her hands, with fat round fingers, opened and closed spasmodically.

Pauline called from somewhere, "Your lunch is ready."

"I've told her not to yell like that," Ashburton said and started to hoist herself out of her chair. Instinctively, Alicia took her arm. "But I find I can't tell her more than one new thing each day, that's all the child can handle. Come!"

Once on her feet, Jeannette took back her arm and led Alicia down the long, dark hallway—pictures hung against the walls, but there was so little light Alicia could not make them out—and on into the dining room. The table was set with lace doilies, crystal stemware, silver salt boats, linen napkins—everything on the table corresponded to the furniture in the living room, all imported from the past. Everything gleamed and shimmered from the work of a strong elbow. Alicia wondered if the elbow belonged to Pauline or to Jeannette herself, who wouldn't be able to tolerate tarnish.

The first course was a cold asparagus soup, served in bowls so shallow they were little more than curved plates.

Jeannette took several spoonfuls of soup, lifting each vertically to her mouth, brought her napkin to her lips and said, "And now, my dear, you must tell me about your work."

"I'm an editor," Alicia began. "You work with the people who write the books. I imagine it's something like teaching, some of the mechanics are very similar. Some writers need a lot of revision, their prose sounds like it was written by a typewriter, not a person. Other authors don't need any revising at all, maybe a punctuation mark here or there. I don't know which I enjoy more; the clean ones or the other kind. The clean ones don't need me as much. How much work I do on any one manuscript varies from book to book. You probably don't realize this—most people don't—but almost all the manuscripts submitted to us come in from agents. I don't know how we'd function without them. So of course, you have to keep in constant touch with them so they won't forget you're alive. Then there are the things you have to go out and look for, you have to be a sort of Indian scout, miner, and egg candler. You read the papers and see who's just murdered his girlfriend and write him a letter saying you'd be interested in his story . . ."

"You don't say," Jeannette said.

"Well, that sort of thing doesn't happen very often." Alicia realized she had been trying to shock the old woman, which she hadn't set out to do at all.

"Or someone tells you about an obscure writer of short stories who's published a couple of things in literary magazines that look beautiful but don't pay anything and have a circulation of ten and a half and so you go out and buy a copy of the magazine and read the story and it removes the top of your head and you write her a letter, knowing that she has as much chance of making money for the house as the woman who checks out your groceries."

"Ah, money," Jeannette said. "I suppose it must enter the picture sometimes. Publishing is, after all a business, don't you know? Cousin Thornton has been educating me. Cousin Thornton thinks it isn't quite a modern business. But you know, Alicia, when I asked you about your work, I was speaking about your own writing."

"My writing? I don't write, I'm an editor." At this, her breathing went shallow; something had her by the throat.

"What a pity, what a waste," Ashburton said, and nodded as Pauline came in and removed their soup plates. "You once wrote extremely well. You handed in story after story. As I recall it, you spent so much time on the work for my little course that the dean had you into her office to talk about what was happening to your other course work. I followed you there and pleaded your cause—did you know that?"

"No, I didn't," Alicia said.

Pauline came with a plate in each hand and set them down in front of Alicia and Jeannette. On the plate lay a triangular slice of quiche and a salad made of blood-red tomatoes sprinkled with herbs. "I taught her to cook," Jeannette explained. "I think she's done quite well considering that she knew only chops and fried chicken." She gazed, round-eyed, at Alicia.

"You must be a good teacher," Alicia said. "It's delicious." She began to feel that this lunch was exactly like her lunch with Wilma Fearing: real and unreal at the same time. The cheese custard coated her teeth, that was real, her tongue knew that, but these assertions by Ashburton—her writing? She could not remember ever having written a story in her life. The sound of Ashburton's voice was reassuring; it hummed, staying low and resonant; it hardly paused.

"Your writing had a certain *je ne sais quoi*—quite unusual, don't you know, for someone so young and unformed. And one of its most striking aspects was its humor. I recall one story you did—my, that was a long time ago—in which you wrote about a young girl's attachment for an older woman and just as it seemed about to fall into the usual postadolescent bathos, it simply took off in another direction when the older woman turned into a crane and flew off to Brazil. I don't quite know how, but you managed to get away with it; it worked. Wouldn't do nowadays, I daresay—all the best stories are written in the present tense and have neither plot nor point of view . . ."

By now Alicia was positive Jeannette was making the whole thing up—but *quel* fantasy, as Davida would have said. The food, good as it was, remained against the back of her mouth; she couldn't swallow. She took a sip of white wine, trying to send it on its way. Her forehead pounded.

"And your poems. Naturally, they were imitative but one could detect that you were trying to find your own voice, which, after all, is the first hurdle any writer worth his salt must clear."

"You have a remarkable memory," Alicia said.

"That's about all I do have, my dear," Jeannette said. "If you live as long as I—and you do have those good genes—you'll understand what I'm talking about. My dead husband, a few outstanding students, don't you know? Are you aware that mine was one of the first creative writing courses on the undergraduate level in this country? Not the very first, you understand. Except that I fought them about the name. I said, all writing is creative, even directions that come with the toaster. Please, I said, let us call my course something else like Learning to Write or some such thing, but they put their feet down, they told me that Creative Writing would draw the students, creative was what students would understand, and that's what they would want. For all its substance, Carey College is hardly what you would call innovative."

As Alicia heard the soft voice go on and on, the lens cleared, the scene came into focus and she saw herself sitting on the grass by the campus pond with a boy whose name was ... *Grant* and she was telling him that the only thing she wanted to be was a writer, no husband, no children, no hearth. "Children keep you separated from your real life."

"That's nuts, Allie," Grant said, touching her arm.

"No," she insisted. "You obviously haven't read Virginia Woolf's diaries."

"Oh, but I have," Grant said, grazing her breast with his fingers. "And you just proved what I said before. Virginia Woolf was mad as a hatter. She was balmy, she had bats in her belfry."

"You're a clod and I wish you'd keep your hands to yourself."

The scene vanished slowly, as if a heavy mist had come between her and it. Alicia returned to the table. She wasn't sure how long they had been sitting there but it seemed a very long time.

The quiche gave way to dessert—sweet oranges peeled and sliced into flat disks. Jeannette explained that this was a favorite of her mother's. A sticky liqueur had been poured over the disks. Pauline brought in a silver dish of Pepperidge Farm cookies. Alicia realized that she ought to have brought a gift for Jeannette, a few flowers or a box of chocolates. She would send something that afternoon.

"If you ask me it's tragic to let a gift like yours fall into desuetude. I realize you haven't asked my advice but since you called and asked to come and see me I can assume a moral stance, don't you know? The prerogatives of age and perhaps a senile loss of inhibition. . . . I assume you don't mind what I'm saying?"

"Not at all," Alicia said.

"At my age," Ashburton went on, "it doesn't much matter what I say. Nobody listens." Incongruously, she smiled.

"That couldn't be true," Alicia said.

"Of course it's true, I'm not sentimental. There's nothing quite so obsolete as a retired teacher, especially one who was always too busy to write her own book. My Beatrix Potter biography occupies me, of course, and I intend to ask you to read it if I ever finish. Now there's a reversal for you, *you* will judge *my* work. And then there are other students who come to visit me from time to time but so many of my favorites live elsewhere. Isn't the Cointreau tasty?" Jeannette Ashburton belched softly.

"The entire lunch was very good," Alicia said.

"If you're finished, why don't we go back to the living room for coffee? Pauline!" The girl appeared immediately, her hands glistening with soapy water.

"Please bring our coffee into the living room and remember the cream and sugar."

"Okay."

"Tomorrow," Jeannette confided softly to Alicia, breathing into her ear, "I'm going to teach her to say 'Yes, ma'am,' don't you know?"

They sat in the same chairs as before. The room was beginning to seem more and more like an attic, airless and claustrophobic, though the furniture was polished and there was no dust anywhere. Jeannette continued to talk to Alicia on the subject of wasted gifts, making Alicia increasingly uneasy. The ring of truth was faint but clear.

And then, without any warning whatsoever, Jeannette made a grab for her upper chest, the color left her face and was replaced by pallor; she made a choking noise. Alicia jumped up and cried, "Pauline! Come in here quickly."

Jeannette's hands beat at her breastbone, she tried to say something, but the only thing that came from her mouth was a long string of saliva which slipped over her chin and dropped onto her dark brown dress. Pauline came in, holding a dishtowel. She said, "Mercy, she's taking one of her attacks."

"What is it? What should we do?" Alicia touched Jeannette's shoulder; she was surprised to find a knobby bone beneath her hand.

"I think it's a kind of hernia or something like that," Pauline said. "It happens sometimes when she talks and eats at the same time or when she gets worked up." By this time, Jeannette Ashburton had slipped down in her chair and was sitting on her spine, her legs splayed like a cellist's. Her head lolled back and to one side. Her eyes rolled upward, showing white.

"Oh, my God," said Alicia, "we have to call an ambulance, I don't know what to do to help her."

"We put her in her bed," Pauline said. "She told me that. Then I'm supposed to call Dr. Bergman, that's the doctor."

It was no easy thing, transporting the floppy woman from the living room to her bed. The noises Jeannette made frightened Alicia so that she grew clumsy; Jeannette kept slipping out of her hands, nearly falling. Her bedroom was, like the other two rooms, a reliquary. The bed was huge and very old, with a high mahogany headboard carved into a flat floral garden, and raised on blocks so that the head was two feet higher than the foot.

"Please call the doctor," Alicia said to Pauline, feeling that she was somehow responsible for what was happening to Jeannette and worried that she was about to die. She eased the woman back against her pillow and removed her shoes. Her stockings underneath were moist and sticky. Alicia pulled the quilt over Jeannette's body until only her head remained outside. Her hair formed a frizzy circle around her face. She saw this face, younger and tighter, the sight went wheeling backward in time. She shuddered and said, "Don't worry, Jeannette, I'll stay here till the doctor comes."

"Not worried," Jeannette whispered. "This happens."

"You're feeling better now?"

"I can breathe," Jeannette said. Her face was the color of ashes. Pauline was looking through Jeannette's black book for the doctor's number. She dialed. "That's the main thing. I'll survive this if I can just get my breath."

"He wants to speak to you," Pauline said, thrusting the phone at Alicia. Alicia could not decide whether Pauline was guileless or clever.

The doctor, young-sounding and impersonal, said, "Are you Mrs. Ashburton's daughter?"

"No," Alicia said, "I'm just a friend, I was having lunch here when she suddenly started strangling or something, I can't tell you what it was, maybe a heart attack. She seems a little better now, but her color is still awful."

"Is she breathing easily?"

"She's breathing."

"It's her hiatal hernia," Dr. Bergman said. "There's nothing really we can do except wait until the contraction passes. Just try to get her comfortable and as calm as possible. Make sure her head is raised. By the way, what did she have for lunch?"

"We had quiche and salad."

"And coffee?"

"Yes, we had coffee too." Pauline went over to the window and looked out of it. Ashburton lay almost motionless on the bed; her breathing sounded phlegmy and her forehead was creased in pain.

"I've told her not to eat fatty things or drink coffee. She knows this, she knows what happens when she indulges her appetite for these things."

"Can't you give her a muscle relaxant or something?"

"I'm afraid not," Dr. Bergman said. "It won't help. See if you can get her to take one of the antacids I prescribed for her. Would you say she's in considerable pain? The symptoms of this condition, as you noticed, are not unlike those of a heart attack."

"Well then, how do you know she isn't having a heart attack?" Alicia said.

"I suggest you check with the patient," Dr. Bergman said. "And by the way, give her my best, she's quite a gal." And he hung up.

Alicia said, "He thinks it's your hernia."

"I don't need any doctor to tell me that," Ashburton said. Pink began to replace the gray on her cheeks. She moved a leg beneath the quilt. Pauline stopped looking out of the window and cocked her head to one side. "She did this last month," Pauline said. "It'll be over in an hour." Alicia was certain that Pauline liked her employer.

It was only when her legs buckled that Alicia realized how

frightened she was. She sat down hard at the foot of Jeannette's bed, just missing her feet. Jeannette took a gasping breath. "I feel I ought to apologize to you," she said.

"Oh, no . . ."

"But that would be silly. I'm glad we had a pleasant time together. I trust my little episode won't spoil your visit in retrospect. Though I'm sure it will . . ."

"But it won't," Alicia protested.

"What are you gaping at, child?" For Pauline was still standing by the side of Jeannette's bed, immobilized by a hidden emotion. "Don't you have dishes to do?" Pauline nodded and left the room. "She's utterly helpless under stress, don't you know? But what can I do?"

Alicia said, "She's very fond of you."

"Naturally, or she wouldn't be here," Jeannette said.

Half an hour later Jeannette Ashburton told Alicia that she was "vastly improved" and thought she would take a little nap.

"Are you sure you're all right now?"

"Absolutely," the woman said. "And Paulie is here, she's a good girl." And Jeannette then presented Alicia with a wide, expanding smile.

Alicia left the apartment house on Beacon Street determined to send a gift to Jeannette Ashburton and to go through the old papers she had saved in cardboard cartons and stored in the basement, in search of the wonderful stories Jeannette had told her about, whose existence she very much doubted. She stopped at a florist's and bought twenty-five dollars' worth of long-stemmed flowers in as many colors as they had and said to deliver them to Ashburton. By the time she reached home, Alicia was aware that Jeannette had joined Wilma inside the bottle and was thinner than a shadow, further away than a first memory, vague as a forgotten dream.

When Barney asked her later what she had done with her day, Alicia told him she had read a couple of manuscripts and done household errands. She knew she was lying; she did not know what the truth was.

On Monday morning Alicia sat down at her desk and cleared her mind of everything except New York. When and if she made the move, she would fly back home on weekends. Friday afternoons up to Boston, Monday mornings down to New York on the first shuttle. That would mean three nights out of seven she could sleep in her own bed. Toby would go to a school like Concord Academy or the Cambridge School, where she could board on weekdays—just as her mother did. Barney worked almost every night; he would hardly notice their two absences.

Who was she kidding? The phone rang, bursting Alicia's fantasy. Davida was on the other end. She said, "*Diaskeuast.* And you're not allowed to look it up in the dictionary."

Alicia had never heard this word, nor had she seen it in print. "Someone who *does* something. Splits rails, makes billiard cues."

"Take your time, *chérie,*" Davida said. Her voice was happy.

"I don't have much time this morning, Davey," Alicia said. "I had to make an unscheduled appearance in Phyllis's office."

"Tell Davey," Davida said.

"We lost an author. Apparently Phyllis thought it was my fault. I suppose, in a way, it *was* my fault. This author thought our advertising department was neglecting her."

Davida laughed. "My God," she said, "I know exactly what she means. Who is she?"

"Come on now, Davey, you know I can't tell you that." The sun slapped the window of the building across the street, indicating to Alicia, who told time by primitive bouncing and sundial techniques, that it was late. Davida babbled: "Craig and I are going to take a vacation together he never bothered to tell me about. Yesterday he just said, 'Let's go to my place in Londonderry.' He wants to teach me how to fish. Imagine. I don't know that I have the patience. All my patience goes into sitting in front of the typewriter and staying there when I'd rather be reading a book or at the movies."

A cloud obliterated the sun. A cool shadow fell across Alicia's papers, graying them. Something urged her to say, "Don't, don't go." Instead she said, "When are you leaving?"

"*Demain matin,*" Davida said. "I'll be back Saturday. Most people go away weekends. Craig hates to do what other people do, he prefers to go away during the week and to stay home Saturdays and Sundays. It's okay with me, my time is my own. And in case you were dying to know, I think I've finally got my book under control. I've broken its poor back. It's mine now, not some monster's."

"Terrific news," Alicia said. "Aren't you scared your holiday will break the rhythm?"

"Just the opposite," Davida said. "I can go because I want so much to get back and work. Oh, it's too complicated. I want you to come shopping with me; I need some warm things for his cabin. It's not insulated."

"I can't go shopping with you, Davey, I've got too much to do here. You wouldn't believe it, they fired our only reader because she disrecommended two books that sold immediately to television and they're too stingy to hire anyone to replace her. Phyllis says, 'Oh, you don't mind taking home a few of these manuscripts to read, do you, sweetie?' and I say 'Yes, I do mind, my family needs me,' and she lays them on me anyway."

"Strike," Davida said.

"Management doesn't strike," Alicia said.

"Listen," Davida said, "Come with me to Eddie Bauer's. It's just over on Boylston Street, you can buy a sandwich and take it back with you so you're only using a lunch hour. I need your advice or I'll spend my entire advance. Allie?"

"God, you're worse than a child," Alicia said. "Okay, I'll meet you. But just one hour, I can't afford a minute more. By the way, what about the word?"

"Ha!" Davida cried. "I knew I'd stump you one of these days.

It's you, you're a diaskeuast. It's just a fancy word for editor. You like it?"

"I love it," Alicia said. "But I doubt I'll ever get the chance to use it."

"Knowing you, you'll find a place for it sooner or later. So how about it? In half an hour, inside the front door of Bauer's?"

"Sure," said Alicia. "What the hay?"

Every time Alicia got out on to the street and walked in the city she felt good; no matter what was happening in the office, the motion of her legs, the quick glance off other people's faces, the streak of her reflection in store windows, the liberating sense of being completely alone. No one on earth knew exactly where she was—she was lost and found at the same time. Each time she left her office she left with guilt, a feeling as tangible as her gloves. Sometimes it seemed as if the more she did, the more there was to do. A mountain of work stood there for her to conquer—that was the word used with mountains; one did not simply climb them, one *conquered* them, and Alicia doubted if she would ever, so long as she was employed by Griffin House, conquer the mountain of work she had deliberately set out to do.

"Hey," Davida said, coming up and attaching herself to Alicia's arm. "We got here at the same time."

"We were supposed to, weren't we?" Alicia said. "Don't go blaming that on E.S.P."

"I wasn't about to," Davida said.

They went in. It was, Alicia discovered, the Church of the Holy Goose. Racks of down vests, down parkas, shirts, knickers, pants, shelves of sweaters as thick as sirloin steaks, socks, gloves, hats to wear over the head and others over the face, turtlenecks, undershirts punctuated by holes—these stretched down both sides of the softly lighted interior, leaving an aisle in the middle. "The altar's in the wrong place," Alicia said to Davida, pointing to the blond wood checkout desk by the front door. "That's the holy font," Davida said. A young woman with yellow hair and a smooth forehead tailed them.

"May I help you ladies with something?" She had on a crimson corduroy wrap-around skirt, turtleneck and a mustard-colored flannel shirt over that, tucked into the skirt. "We're just looking," Davida told her.

"Do we look like shoplifters?" Alicia asked.

"No one looks like a shoplifter," Davida said.

"Every last one of them is wearing the Bauer vestments," Alicia said. "I wonder if they get to keep them after they leave."

Customers moved about, larghetto, over the grayish carpet, as if meditating. A man strolled toward the dressing room, carrying two pairs of bright green pants to try on.

"What exactly do you need?" Alicia said. "What are we looking for?"

"I could use a heavy flannel shirt and some very warm pants. Wool maybe, except wool itches."

"Here's something that says you all over it," Alicia said, taking up the sleeve of an orange jacket, puffy with goose down.

"How much?" Davida said.

Alicia looked at the tag. "A bit steep," she said. "Two hundred and forty-nine bucks. What's two hundred and forty-nine dollars about it?"

"The way it's made, stupid," Davida said, smiling. "Maybe we should have gone to Filene's Basement."

"I'm sure they have some less expensive items." Alicia was fairly sure Davida could not afford the jacket. Nearly all her authors were quixotic with money. They would take their advance on a book and blow most of it immediately, forgetting that they might have five years of work still to do on the book before another cent came in. "Look, that rack over there says 'Sale,' let's try that."

"Seconds," Davida said. "Something wrong with them."

"Let's find out," Alicia said, feeling like Davida's mother. They discovered a heavy flannel shirt that had nothing visibly wrong with it, and a pair of woolen pants lined with soft cotton. Davida, thought Alicia, had something on her mind and then she saw what it was: no larger than a walnut, it was a doubt inside Davida's head, a suspicion, hard and programmed to grow. Davida, Alicia realized, suspected Phyllis's plan to cut bait, to dump her. She almost knows, thought Alicia, and I haven't the guts to tell her she's right. "Why don't you get these mittens?" she said, picking up a pair of down mittens.

"Don't need them," Davida said, abruptly switching from exuberant to glum.

"What's the matter?" Alicia said. Her secret lay heavier than a backpack filled with rocks.

"Nothing. I guess I'm just worried about the lawsuit, and money . . ."

"And about Craig?"

"No, why should I be worried about Craig? Craig could have written the book."

"What book?" Alicia looked at Davida and realized what she was talking about. "Oh, sorry, I understand. Well, dear, I'm very happy for you if he's as great as all that." They left the store together. Alicia said, "I forgot to ask you about the deposition. When is it?"

"Two weeks from today," Davida said. "I'm boning up on the fine art of perjury."

"Are you putting me on?"

"Never more serious in my life. Archie got people to lie for him under oath and if he wants to play by those rules then, by gum, I'm going to play by them too."

"You can't do that, Davey."

"I can't? Just watch me."

They walked in silence for half a block, then Davida began to talk about her new book and to swing her package at the same time. Her shifts of mood were dizzying. The heat Alicia abruptly felt over her heart was nothing more than a spurt of love for Davida, a child who has no idea how glorious her voice is.

CHAPTER
Seven

THAT afternoon, while still at work, Alicia called the next name: Roger Tucker.

After a single ring, a man said hello. His voice was hollow as if he were talking through a wide tube. She said, "This is Alicia Baer."

"Alicia," the voice echoed. "Where are you? Why didn't you meet me Friday like you promised? You said you'd be here at one and you never came. I waited over an hour for you and you didn't come, you didn't call." The man seemed about to break down and cry. "I should never have promised you not to call. If you really want to know, I almost broke my promise and phoned you at home; this is excruciating, I don't know if I can bear it. I never stop thinking about you, not for a day, not for a moment. Sometimes, when you don't show up I get the feeling I'll never see you again. Never, it's as if when you're not here with me, you don't exist at all. Jesus, do you hear the way I'm talking to you? I sound like I'm ready for the rubber room. Darling, Alicia, that's what love does to you. Does to me. Does to us. Alicia, are you there? Say something."

The man was either crazy or putting her on. She considered hanging up: there was something in it of the obscene. An obscene phone call without dirty words.

"Roger?"

"What do you have to say to me, my sweetest Alicia. I love your name. Have I told you that?" He waited, she was silent, he went on. "Do you have any idea what you've done to me? I used to be a rational man, I hid my feelings just like everyone else. I went daily about my business, my shirts were pressed, my hair was kempt."

"I don't know what to say," Alicia said. Her hand moved toward the phone's cradle, but still she did not hang up. His urgency had the same effect as an insult: it kept her at arm's length.

"Well, I must say, that's a change." His voice grew more mellow. "I do love you, whatever you say, and even when you say nothing. I love your sweet eyes. And your breasts."

"Roger, please."

"You've managed to invade my entire existence," he continued, as if not feeling the brakes she had applied. "Everything is Alicia. And if it's not Alicia, it has no meaning for me. It's quite meaningless."

Alicia began to feel uneasy. The man's language scared her. If he had been talking to someone else she might have found him funny. She made a humming noise.

"What's wrong?" Roger said, obviously alarmed. "Something's wrong, I can tell, you sound different, cool. Please tell me, Alicia, I can't tolerate not knowing what you're thinking. I've got to know if something's happened. Is it your husband?"

"Barney doesn't know anything," she said.

"I have to see you," Roger said. "I'll go crazy if I don't see you right away. I'm starving, dying of thirst. I'm tied to four stakes in the Sahara and the ants are crawling all over my poor parched body, they're eating my balls . . ."

"Roger!" The man was unhinged. She had got herself entangled with a maniac. Jenny opened the door and walked into her office, holding a sheet of paper expectantly. Alicia waved her out of the room, her heart racing. "Roger, I can't talk to you now."

"You mustn't feel guilty about us," Roger said. "We have a powerful love, it's right and good. Dearest girl, trust me."

"I'll meet you tomorrow," she said, wondering where these words had come from. "I can meet you for lunch."

"I can't make it through another twenty-four hours without you," Roger said with tears in his voice.

"You'll just have to, Roger."

"You won't stand me up again?"

"I promise I'll be there."

"Anthony's at one then," Roger told her. "Alicia, say it, let me hear you say it."

"I can't now, Roger, I shouldn't even be talking to you on this telephone."

"Jesus," he said.

"Roger, you've got to let me hang up. I'll see you tomorrow at one. I promise."

Alicia hung up the phone; her palm was shiny with perspiration. In agreeing to meet Roger she was risking more than an hour or two, she was risking her own history. She pulled away from this situation and tried to view it as someone who didn't know her would: there she glimpsed a woman swimming equidistant between two shores and beginning to panic.

That night Alicia slept badly, as if she were in pain. Between bouts of wakefulness there were dreams whose contents were perfectly obvious even to the dreamer: a glinting knife poised above her pelvis, a smoldering kiss bestowed by a man she did not recognize; he had a thick black mustache and somewhat feminine, sloping shoulders covered with silky hairs. When she woke at four-thirty her cunt ached. She glanced at Barney, an old cat, snoring, and felt guilty. Then she drifted again and when she woke for good at six she reached out to touch her husband, who was no longer there. She heard him in the kitchen, then heard the back door close softly and the car crunch out of the driveway. Off for a morning of cutting and excising. What Barney did, she realized, was not so different from what she spent her working hours doing. He removed the rotten parts of bodies, she of manuscripts. The fact that he made more than ten times what she did for a similar service was only in keeping with the American Way; things like this disparity had long ceased to seem unfair (though she had longed for fairness most of her life). She wished she could tell Barney what she had just thought of—it was such a good analogy—but he had left the house.

She argued with Toby about breakfast, urging her daughter to eat her eggs. Toby was about to breathe fire, but held back. They parted without a kiss or touch; when Alicia reached to touch her daughter, Toby jumped back as if on the end of Alicia's arm there was an electric prod.

The morning was relatively free of interruptions. Alicia dictated several letters to Jennifer, spoke to an agent about a manuscript that had disappeared somewhere between New York and Boston. Alicia had the distinct feeling that the agent didn't believe her, but thought it was floating around the Griffin Building, lost. "I've never had this happen before," the agent said. "We're very scrupulous about return addresses. Are you sure your secretary checked out the mail room?"

"Yes, I'm sure, Brenda, it just never arrived. We have a log book at the reception desk. Every manuscript that comes into the building is immediately entered into the book." At that moment, Alicia saw the manuscript, half out of its wrapping, its pages coming through the brown paper like bone in a compound fracture. It was on the floor somewhere, partly hidden by a low shelf. She saw black shoes. She said again, "It simply isn't here, Brenda. Can you send us another copy?"

Brenda said, "I'll have to think about it." The woman was maddening. Then an author called and wanted to know how many copies of his book B. Dalton had reordered. "It's going into a third printing, Don," Alicia said. "Don't worry about Dalton. They're on their toes."

And all the while she was thinking, *Roger Tucker, what do you want from me, what do you need, how can you assault me this way? I didn't ask for you. I don't want you, I can't deal with your ardor.* But the memory of his voice drew her, she had to see the face that went with the voice; she could almost feel his hands against her skin. She shuddered in the wind of this recollection. I am obscene, she decided, I am meeting an obscene lover. The idea of being wanton after all these virtuous years made her light-headed. She looked in the mirror above the sink in the ladies' room, leaned over the soap dispenser with its liquid soap a pink puddle on the porcelain and stared into her own two wicked eyes. You must not go to meet him, she told the eyes, and the eyes winked back. She opened her purse in order to find the lipstick buried there and discovered, to her horror, her blue plastic diaphragm case, and a small tube of jelly. She did not remember putting them there. "I can't believe this," she said aloud and then shut up, as Jennifer had come in the bathroom and was staring at her.

"I talk to myself from time to time," she told her secretary. Jennifer laughed uneasily. "It's all right, dear," Alicia said. "You will, too, when you're my age."

Jennifer said, "Well, have a nice lunch."

"I'll try," Alicia said.

She followed the periphery of the Common—ever since the boys had exploded the beer bottle in front of her she had not been able to cross the Common itself—and headed for Anthony's.

Roger Tucker was waiting for her in the dusk of the restaurant. She could feel his presence before she saw him and when she did see him it was as a shape rushing toward her. He grabbed her above the elbows, squeezing, his eyes swam, looking for hers. His own seemed about to brim over.

"Oh, God, I thought I'd die waiting for you," he said, steering her to a table back in the murk. "Sit down, sit down." Dumbly, she sat. "I'm like an adolescent," he said. "You're my obsession, I can't think of anything but you. What should I do, Alicia, I think I'm going crazy."

"Maybe you should see an exorcist," she said, attempting to smile.

"It's not funny. I'm in agony when you're not with me."

"You don't look so happy now either," she said. He swallowed some beer. Foam flecked his mustache. He pulled the back of his hand across the wet.

"You're right, I'm not. My anxiety that I may never see you again has lifted temporarily, but no, I'm not happy. I may lose you tomorrow."

"I'd like a glass of wine," Alicia said.

"Oh, my God, I completely forgot, I'm neglecting you," Roger said. "What's the matter with me, I'm so neglectful . . ." He waved his arm, trying to catch the waiter's attention.

"For heaven's sake," she said, "don't carry on, it's no big deal."

"A glass of red wine for the lady," he told the waiter. "For Alicia." He blushed. She looked down.

Alicia studied Roger covertly; he was younger than she, by six or seven years. She could not tell, from the way he was dressed—a darkish pair of pants, cotton shirt with tab collar, no tie, sports jacket—what he did for a living (she could hear him say "if you call this living"), where he weighed in on society's scales. In fact, his clothes were neutral enough to put him anywhere. He appeared to have social polish, but he wasn't using any of it on her; he was distraught, a child terrified.

"Poor Roger," she said.

"You say that so often," he said. "But then I must deserve it." He seemed not to know what to do with his hands. First they huddled together on the table in front of him, then they took off in opposite directions, the left one landing above his ear and the right one crawling, on the table, toward Alicia's arm. She watched it as she would have a snake whose venomous potential was as yet undisclosed. She withdrew her arm; he looked up, hurt.

"What's wrong?" he said.

"Nothing," Alicia said. "This isn't the sort of thing I had in mind when I was twenty. Or even forty."

"Nor I," Roger said, sniffing. "Nor I." He cleared his throat. "Are you hungry or can we leave now?"

"I'm always hungry," Alicia said. "Aren't you?"

"You know what I'm hungry for," Roger told her. "Not much else. Since we started seeing each other again I've lost six pounds. Don't you think there's been some divine intervention, having us meet again this way after so long? I wonder you take it so lightly." He stopped talking as their waiter came back to take their order, his pad ready. "I'll have a bowl of clam chowder," Roger said. "And another one of these." He pointed to his empty beer glass. Alicia ordered antipasto.

"You're irretrievably lovely," he said.

"I haven't gone anywhere," she said, smiling.

"Did I say irretrievably?" Roger asked. "I meant irreducibly."

"That's pretty funny too."

He seemed not to notice her efforts at jollying up the conversation. He kept backing again into a thick sea of emotion. "You're even lovelier than when I first knew you. Some women get dry and crisp when they get older. You're like a flower that keeps bringing forth more and more beautiful blossoms." He paused and seeing her pained expression, said, "Do you mind so much my talking this way?"

"I do," she said. "It embarrasses me. But on the other hand, I don't entirely believe you."

"I wouldn't lie to you, Alicia," he said. "You have to see that!"

"You don't mean to, I'm sure," she said. "You're smitten. You're seeing stars the way people do in the funnies when they're hit over the head. You don't seem to know how old I am."

This fired him. "Of course I know how old you are. What difference does that make? For chrissake, Alicia, what a terrible thing to say." He began to scoop up spoonfuls of chowder and swallow them as if he hadn't eaten for days.

"I'm long in the tooth," she said. "Over the hill."

"You're not," he said, eyeing her above a spoonful of chowder. "Eighty is old, ninety is old. Forty-three is young. I can't bear to hear you talk like that."

"I'm sorry," she said, realizing that she did not want to hurt him. She was somehow firmly attached to this incredible man.

"Eat up," he said, nodding to her plate. "We don't have much time."

She did not ask "time for what?"

The soup seemed to have a tranquilizing effect on Roger Tucker. He was calmer now, almost jovial. She could see he was a nice person. Behind the man in genuine distress there lay a perfectly reasonable human being, someone she might, under less peculiar circumstance, take as a friend.

"I have an hour and a half," she said, wondering where these words came from. She had meant to say *no* but had come out with *yes.*

He beamed and made a grab for her hand. "Oh, joy of my dreams, my living dream," he breathed. He paid the bill by leaving some money on the table, no doubt too much, but for him time was clearly more precious than money, and led her out of the restaurant. She walked the three blocks to his apartment dumb and blind, passively entered the elevator, watched, as if drugged, as he pushed the button for the fourth floor and followed him like a compliant pet as he unlocked the door and shoved it open. His apartment was white and bare; nonstructural elements had been wrenched off and carted away, leaving a flowing whitish space, with windows at all levels and a brick wall of soft dusty pink that looked like felt. Instead of chairs and couches there were platforms buried under huge pillows covered with soft, drifty colors; strip and recessed lighting in the ceiling; bamboo shades and a kitchen with its bones showing. The place told her Roger was an architect and had no doubt done this himself.

Roger removed his jacket. "We don't have much time," he said, repeating himself.

"Very businesslike, aren't you?" she said.

"It sounds that way, doesn't it?" he said. The mouth under the drooping mustache turned briefly upward. "Oh, come on, Allie, take off your things and come to bed. I'm burning, I'm on fire. Love me. Let me love you." He took her hand; fire shot up her arm, cauterizing her brain. Her reason went to sleep. She followed him into a small room off the big one, equally bare. A double platform bed floated above the floor, a rectangular ship on a hardwood sea. She felt as if she had stepped into someone else's body, someone younger and lighter than Alicia, someone on fire herself. Roger's sexual energy radiated in an aura, reached the lower part of her torso, then dove between her legs. She felt a spurt leave the delta of her vagina and moisten her crotch. The joints of her knees dissolved. "My God," she said.

"Come come come, Alicia, don't stand there, remove thy clothes."

This archaic imperative worked. She unbuttoned her blouse and unzipped her skirt. She sat down and pulled off her panty hose, piling it all on the only chair in the room. Naked, she slipped between sheets which were as smooth as water, and chill. Her brain slept on, she could have been in a coma for all its activity, while at the same time her body was charged with life, electrified. He was whispering in a raspy voice, incredible things: "Glorious, lovely Alicia, you have the body of an odalisque, you are my treasure, I can't believe you're really here. You've been inside my head for so many years and here you are inside my bed. I dream about your loveliness every night."

He put his mouth over her nipples, sucking like a baby, he sucked so hard she thought her milk would start up again. Her body was limp and taut at the same time, she felt as if she were going to shatter. It seemed impossible but she was both liquid and rock. Impossible. His hands kneaded her softly, each finger charged with high voltage; she felt like screaming. His hands were all over her, here and there, in crevices and down broad planes and dunes. She could not help comparing him to Barney, the only body she had known for so many years. The signs of youth—comparatively speaking—were here in Roger; they had disappeared into Barney's past. Roger's arms were iron, the tendons over his armpits stood out, hard and round. His neck had hardly a crease in it and was tight and hard, thin and tight and hard. The hairs on his mustache scraped against her flesh but didn't hurt. She said "Ah," swimming in pleasure. She reached for his penis, it filled her hand, she felt his blood moving in spongy veins beneath the skin. His cock was like Barney's but different, the veins were smaller and differently placed, the skin smoother. As Roger's shoulders inched southward, she gasped with a noise that surprised her by its strangeness. Then she felt his ears smack against each of her thighs, two soft sea shells, and his liquid tongue lapping against her clitoris. She cried, "Please!" pleading with him to save her from drowning. He emerged for air, smiled in an inward way that gave her assurance, and entered her. She welcomed him by winding her legs around his hips and squeezing. It seemed as if his prick could have found its way home blindfolded. This was not strange, this was repetition. They moved together, two swimmers making for an island.

He came first. "My God," she said again as he lay heavily over her. She felt wet on her shoulders, his shoulders were shiny, the tiny silk hairs glistening. Alicia looked into Roger's face and saw there the dumb look of bliss. She knew that if she tried to get up now she wouldn't be able to; she had no strength.

Presently he shifted his weight and rolled away, and put his hand on her flank, holding it firmly. He said, "We came together."

She did not argue. "It's not supposed to matter," she said. She touched his face. His skin was sticky, his mustache fierce. "Who are you?" she murmured, counting on his misunderstanding.

"It's funny you should ask," he said. "Ever since we started seeing each other again, I haven't been all that sure myself." He moved down and grabbed her thigh, squeezing so hard it hurt.

"They're solid flab," she said.

"No," he said. "You don't appreciate yourself enough. They're lovely. You're not fourteen anymore, Allie darling, you're a grown woman. Your flesh is gold. Treasure it."

As his overripe talk drifted over them, her brain began to wake up.

"I really have to get back," she said. "Don't you?"

"My hours, as you know, are my own," Roger said, hoisting himself on one elbow and staring at her body. The sheet lay tangled at the foot of the bed. Her skin began to prickle with cold. "It's my work that counts, not how many hours I spend doing it. This line"—and he ran his hand from just under her arm clear down past her knees, raising gooseflesh—"is perfect, it makes my throat ache. Turn over on your stomach a minute." She did. "Your vertebrae are tiny round knobs, your ribs embrace you—"

"Roger," she said, interrupting him, "you're not seeing the real Alicia. You're seeing some fantasy woman. I look like everyone else who isn't deformed. Even my heart is pedestrian."

He scowled. She turned over onto her side and closed her

eyes so she wouldn't have to see his disapproval. "Tell me you love me. Tell me," he demanded.

"Roger, don't . . ."

"What's the matter, Alicia, you didn't have any trouble the last time. I knew when I heard your voice yesterday there was something wrong." He seemed about to burst into tears.

"I love you, then," she said. The words had a life of their own. They may have been her creatures but they were wild and untamed; uncivilized. *Barney,* she thought, *I love you too.* The idea that she might love two men at the same time was very dangerous; Alicia pushed it away.

"I suppose you're going to tell me you can't live without me," she said.

"I wouldn't commit suicide," he said. "But my life would be dead without you." Noise sifted through the walls of the apartment building, muffled and shy. He saw she was listening. "That's a composer who lives upstairs," Roger said. "He also plays the oboe. Nice fellow; he composes all day and sometimes all night. When he's not at the piano he's playing his oboe."

"Don't you have a legal right to ask him to stop after eleven at night?"

"I suppose I do," Roger said. "But that sounds so bloody-minded. Besides, the walls in this place are so thick it doesn't really bother me. I rather like the oboe. The only thing that really disturbs my sleep is you. Sometimes I lie here awake and conjure the most fantastic orgiastic things for us to do. You have ten mouths, and a dozen cunts. I have the pricks to match. We are like hydras. We love each other for hours, then fall blissfully asleep, exhausted."

"How piquant," she said. She wondered why she kept lying there instead of getting the hell out. It was his sexual radiance that had trapped her in his bed. Davida would understand, though she might be surprised by Alicia's uncertainty. Phyllis would say, "You're as weak as the rest of us. You're no better than Marabel Morgan." But she wouldn't tell either Davida or Phyllis—God, certainly not Phyllis!—about Roger. Roger was as securely sealed off as if she had only imagined him and he lived in a small rented room in the back of her skull.

Alicia's thoughts begat action. She reached again for his balls and held them, hard. He moaned slightly and his eyes closed. "Jesus Christ," he said. His penis inflated rapidly and began to throb. With a sort of whoop, she flung herself on top of him, their skins pasted together. "What am I doing?" she asked. "Keep it up," he said from underneath. "*Whatever* it is. I didn't know you were such a tiger. Imagine that." He grinned at her, rubbing her buttocks with both hands and parting them. He explored between with his little finger. In the meantime he continued to talk nonstop, to tell her about herself, to describe her flesh, her spirit, to flatter her in ways so convincing she almost believed him. "You're perfect in every way," Roger said. "Your pubic hair is a sky full of stars."

"Now that really *is* too much," she whispered. "You make me want to laugh."

"Go ahead and laugh. I love your laugh." He rose up into her and she sat straight, looking down at him. He wiggled inside her. For a moment, he was her victim. He looked at her as an infant at its loving mother about to pop a breast in its mouth. "Oh, God, Alicia, this is too much."

"No," she said, "and shut up. Can't you shut up for a minute and just do it?"

This time there was more activity; they thrashed about, then rolled over so that he was on top, ending with both of them, beached, side by side. As he separated himself from her, groaning that he wanted to remain inside her forever, she sighed deeply, ending with a little shudder of punctuation. "I'm a wicked woman," she said. "I like this too much."

"That's an oxymoron," he said, kissing her face. "It's impossible to like love too much."

"I was talking about sex," Alicia said.

"This isn't just sex," Roger told her. "This is love."

She went into his bathroom and said, "Where am I?" But she knew exactly how far to reach for the light, how far to bring the tap around to keep it from scalding her. She stepped into the glass stall and showered quickly, then wrapped herself in an enormous towel. She would not look at her reflection in the mirror. I must get out of this place, she thought. I have no business here. But she knew that leaving, or the onset of amnesia, would not alter the fact that she had betrayed her husband. She blamed herself wholly, then began making a list of excuses: she was forced; she had fallen under an evil spell; she didn't know what she was doing. The inanity of these excuses was so obvious that Alicia began to giggle, then to tremble with laughter, then was seized by crying. She came out of the bathroom red-eyed and covered by the towel. Roger said, "Why do you cover yourself that way?" He asked, "What are you ashamed of?"

"Roger?"

"If you lived with me I would make it a rule that you would have to spend at least three hours a day without any clothes on. Remove thy towel."

"You're balmy," she said. "I don't think I've ever met anyone like you. You're a space cadet, Roger, you really are."

A moment expanded during which Roger seemed to be deciding whether to laugh or allow himself to be stung. He ended by smiling. "If that's so," he said, "it's because you've driven me mad. I don't think you have any idea how much your life is part of mine; its almost as if you had taken possession of me."

"Like I said before, maybe you should get an exorcist," Alicia said. She was touched by his distress. Still holding the towel against her side, she went over and sat with him, on the edge of the bed. Roger hunched over his torso; his cock lay curled down, resting. She put a palm on his shoulder. He looked at her and tried to smile.

"You continue to joke about something that to me is as difficult to manage as cancer. There's nothing funny about this."

"I'm sorry, Roger."

"What am I going to do?" he asked, fingering her knee. His prick woke and stretched. She saw that she would have to get away now or they would end up fucking again.

"We'll talk about it," she said. "But right now I've got to get back to the office. Someone's coming in to see me at three. It's almost that now."

"Who? Who's coming to see you?"

"An author."

"When can I see you again?" Roger's eyes pleaded.

"I'll call you," she said softly. "I always do, don't I?"

"No, you don't. It's pure hell, waiting for your calls. Sometimes I don't leave the house so I won't miss you when you do call."

"Roger, that's crazy, you can't do that!"

"I wish you'd stop telling me I'm crazy." The phone rang. Roger reached across her lap and picked up the receiver. He spoke into it in a voice so crisp that Alicia couldn't believe her own ears: this was the voice of another man. He told whoever it was that he could see them in his office at four. Then he hung up. "A client," he explained. "He tracked me down. I hate nervous people," he added.

Alicia had begun to put her clothes on. "One last kiss," Roger said, back in his old treacle voice. How could she deny him? He came toward her where she stood with her skirt on, and her bra, shoeless. His penis stuck straight out, pointing at her. The incongruity of this and his sad and serious expression reminded Alicia that while love was the ringleader, sex was only a clown. What, she thought, was more clownish than a penis erect? Roger locked his arms around her so that they met across her back. He pasted his face against hers. The mustache tickled her cheek. His parts made a tight fist against her skirt, and his kiss, when he located her mouth, melted her joints once more and her knees buckled. She thrust her pelvis so hard against him that she hurt the bone there. After a minute or so, during which they studied each other's mouth and tongue, they both drew back.

"I think you're a warlock," Alicia said, gasping. "This isn't real."

"Your husband must be a terrible clod," Roger said.

"He's not," Alicia said. "But I don't want to talk about him."

"That's your prerogative," Roger told her. "I don't especially want to talk about him either."

CHAPTER
Eight

BY midday Monday, six days after Alicia and Roger Tucker made love, the memory of it was as indistinct as a Life Saver that has just melted away on the tongue. Roger had slid into the bottle, which was now getting crowded. Fearing, Ashburton, now Tucker. But while the memory had dulled and dimmed, the sense, in Alicia, that something critical had happened to her remained and she did not want to look Barney in the eye.

She was not certain if her husband noticed this evasiveness; it was hard to tell with Barney, who always had an edge of preoccupation about him anyway. The wicked Alicia laughed, the upright and honest shed tears.

Davida had not called over the weekend. Alicia put this down to the springlike weather; Craig and Davida had decided to stay after all, how could they leave with the season turning so bright? But when by Monday noon Alicia had still not heard from Davida, she began to worry. Davida checked in with Alicia—or vice versa—several times a week; for Alicia talking to her friend was as refreshing as a dip in the old swimming hole on a blistering August day.

Several other things crowded Alicia's apprehensions about Davida. One was her appointment with Pearl Withers, the fourth invader of the Book. And the other, of course, was the ever-present pull of Dick Freyburg, Tolland and Lutwidge, and the soaring future she saw for herself in their offices high above Fifth Avenue.

And so, on Monday, Alicia had just settled down at her desk to compose yet another rejection letter. "This is the most loathsome drivel I've read since *The Two Million Dollar Honeymoon*. Please take my name off your mailing list"—this is what she wanted to write. Instead she wrote: "Thank you for sending me this manuscript on what to do about your aching feet. I'm afraid it's just not right for our list"—when Jenny came into Alicia's office.

"Here," she said, holding a piece of paper covered with mimeographed writing. Jenny held it out, waiting for Alicia to remove it from her hand.

"What's this?" Alicia asked.

"It's a statement. We want you to join us. We're initiating a job action." Jenny's straight back was okay; her slightly trembling mouth signaled that she was nervous.

"Just leave it with me, Jenny, I'm in the middle of something. I'll read it when I'm finished. *Whose* statement?"

Alicia looked at her secretary for information and found instead that she was admiring the young woman's appearance—her stylishness, her youth, the unmistakable bloom on her creamy cheeks. She wore a soft gray tweed skirt and a rosy cowl-neck, none of it man-made, and no doubt bought with Daddy's dollars. Jenny's pay was one hundred and seventy-five dollars a week—after taxes.

"Ours," Jenny said. "I mean the secretaries here plus Nine to Five, that's an organization of office workers. I guess you could call it a union. Jane Fonda made this movie . . ."

"I saw that clinker," Alicia said. "I think it set back The Movement about forty-five years. I may be wrong, of course. Why don't you tell me what this is about?"

"We—the secretaries and some of the women in Advertising and Production, not secretaries, real people, are joining us. We want you to, too."

She's nervous as a rabbit, Alicia thought. "I'll read this in a few minutes," she told Jenny. "Then we'll have a little chat about it. Okay?"

Jenny left the room. There was a new little lift in her step.

Curious, Alicia put the rejection letter aside and took up Jenny's statement. "Women of Griffin," it began, "We have been exploited for too long. We take home 59 cents for every dollar made by a man doing the same job. We have no security, few benifits, long hours and no over-time. Our working conditions are appalling—the bathrooms are only cleaned once a week and the couch in the women's lounge is as old as the Griffin Building. The tampax machine has been out of order for three months. Our bosses make us bring them coffee and danish and then we are not thanked for this service. We will no longer be treated like cattle or taken for granted. Management would rather see us in jail than allow us to join a Union. Declare yourself side of justice. Join Nine to Five. Help cement the women of Griffin Inc., into an invincible army. Come to the pre-demonstration meeting, Tuesday, nine-thirty in the women's lounge for instructions."

God knows we don't need any cement armies, she said, going out to Jenny's desk. It was cute, though, it made her think of children. "Jenny," she said, "what do you want me to do about this statement?"

"Join us." Jenny stood up. She was taller than Alicia. "We're having this meeting tomorrow morning—you wouldn't have to come to that. Then, if management doesn't meet our demands, we're going to demonstrate on Wednesday morning. The people at Nine to Five called the media."

"You want me to carry a sign and march in a circle in front of the building?"

"That's what I'm supposed to ask you," Jenny said, squinting at her feet.

Alicia realized how hard this must be for her secretary. Was this girl—it was hard to think of Jenny as a woman; there was nothing womanly about her—was she afraid of Alicia? This was an interesting, new, and not altogether disagreeable notion. "How do you spell 'benefit,' Jenny?" she said.

Jenny blushed. "I didn't write it," she said.

"Well, someone, whoever wrote it, should have consulted a dictionary. Also, there's a sentence in your statement with a couple of words missing."

"Does it really matter so much if we can make a statement that's meaningful to a lot of people?" Jenny asked.

"Oh, boy," Alicia said. "Look, I'll tell you what. I don't promise to join the demonstration but I promise not to go into the building till it's over. How's that?"

Jenny's eyes filled with disappointment. She could feel the body shrink. "Oh," Jenny said, and her mouth twisted down.

"Don't go soft on me now," Alicia said. "Oh, what the hell, what have I got to lose? I'll carry a sign. Okay? Only, Jenny, I won't carry it if it's not spelled correctly, that's where I draw the line."

"Oh, will you really? Oh, that's cool, that's really great." And Jenny threw her arms around Alicia's neck and kissed her on the cheek. She smelled so fresh, a light, floral perfume behind the ears.

Alicia, moved by the gesture, flushed. "Hey," she said, "I didn't say I'd go blow up any bridges, I just agreed to carry a sign for you."

"They told me you wouldn't," Jenny said. "They said there wasn't even any point in asking you and I said you would, so they said go ahead but don't expect anything."

"Oh, yeah?" Alicia said. "Exactly who do they think I am? Do they think I'm another Margaret Thatcher or what?"

"I think they think you're not very political," Jenny said. Her confidence had returned, her eyes had cleared.

"Well, then they—whoever *they* are—don't know me very well."

"Anyway, it doesn't really matter as long as you join us.

We've got an editor from Houghton Mifflin and somebody from Little, Brown and Margaret Bannister from Panther Press. Plus a whole bunch of secretaries from all over. We're beasts of burden," she finished, surprising Alicia by this metaphor. Jennifer was pleased by the image and smiled in a knowing way. Alicia figured this demonstration business had done as much for her secretary's self-esteem as a year and a half of therapy. It would, however, do nothing for her spelling.

"You remember, Jenny, when I told you not so long ago that you shouldn't read manuscripts unless you got paid for it?"

"I'm not going to do that anymore," Jennifer said. "They said we were scabs."

"That's what *I* told you," Alicia said.

"I know," Jenny said, and looked at her feet again. "I guess I had to hear it from them."

"Does Phyllis Vance know about what they're up to? The meeting and the demonstration?"

"They don't know for sure. But somebody's making an effigy of Mrs. Vance. We're going to burn it Wednesday morning, hopefully when the television's there."

"Phyllis may be Management, Jenny, but it's the head office in Chicago you should really be making effigies out of," Alicia said. "Hey, wait a minute. Suppose they agree to your demands? Then what happens to the effigies?"

"Oh, goodness, they better not," Jenny said.

At three-thirty, Alicia was talking on the telephone to an author when she saw her second button blinking. "Ira," she said, "I've got another call. Want to hold?" He had turned into a pain in the ass. Nervous author, out of self-control, in the middle of a mini-psychosis.

"No, thanks, Alicia, I guess you've told me what I needed to know. I just don't understand why it's ninth this week. Christ, it's been stuck there for three fucking weeks."

"Ira honey, please. Don't be greedy. Ninth is pretty damn good."

"Okay, okay," he said, sighing. "I'll call you tomorrow." He was gone. Rolling her eyes, Alicia pushed the other button and took the call. Phyllis's secretary came on the line. "Mizz Baer, one moment please, Mizz Vance wants to speak with you."

"Alicia?" The voice of the dragon came on the line.

"Hello, Phyllis."

"I want to ask you something," Phyllis said. "I've heard that you're thinking of joining the ranks of our secretaries with their petty little complaints. News has reached me that you're going to participate in some sort of demonstration. Please assure me, Alicia dear, that this is rumor and not the truth."

"My, doesn't news travel fast," Alicia said. She felt prickles cross her skin. "Almost faster than the speed of sound, though that's not possible, is it?"

"Of course not," Phyllis said. "So it isn't merely a rumor."

"I'm thinking about it. I may very well join the demonstration for a few minutes. It would mean a lot to them, apparently."

"No doubt," Phyllis said. "They have co-opted you, Alicia."

"No," said Alicia. "I'm very sympathetic. Their grievances are justified."

"I don't believe my ears," Phyllis said. Alicia could feel her body tensing up. This often happened when she and Phyllis took opposite sides; she suspected this was a throwback to a feral existence. She showed her teeth. "You're Management," Phyllis went on. "You're not some little simp in the secretarial pool who can't even spell the name of the town she was born in."

"Well, I guess I *am* Management, strictly speaking, but I feel like one of them. All they want is a fair shake and equal pay. For chrissake, Phyllis, even Schlafly is for equal pay."

"The folks in Chicago aren't exactly going to send you a

telegram congratulating you if you join these silly girls," Phyllis said.

"Do they have to know?"

"I don't very well see how it can be avoided," Phyllis said.

"It can be avoided if no one tells them," Alicia said, testing. There was no point in trying to persuade Phyllis to abandon her attitude, no more than there would have been a point in Phyllis's trying to dissuade Alicia from joining the demonstration. And they both knew it. Meanwhile, Alicia congratulated herself on taking a visible stand; she was a woman of the people. How many times did such an opportunity arise? The Civil Rights movement, the anti–Vietnam War, the burgeoning antinuclear movement and now this. Hardly in the same league but all the same—worth it.

Phyllis said the strikers were "dummies," sleep-easies (a characterization Alicia found touchingly irrelevant), disloyal troops (there was that army image again) and finally, "greedy bitches," which was not fair, not fair at all.

"Phyllis," Alicia interrupted, "All they want is a little more money, a few benefits. Don't you think they deserve that?"

"Certainly not," Phyllis shot back. "If I did I would have done everything I could to make sure they got it. Not that I have that much say in these matters. It's what the boys in Chicago want. And Dave Gill. *He's* the financial boss, not me. I'm an editor, I have nothing to do with that end of things."

"Not your table?" Alicia said, softly.

"What? Look, Allie, you know as well as I do that half the girls can't type, the other half can't spell and the third half have their minds on clothes. What's left are after our jobs, yours and mine, Alicia dear."

"That's an awful lot of halves," Alicia said. "Maybe we ought to applaud their ambition. At least the ones who are after our jobs."

"You're impossible, Alicia. Still, go ahead, do what you feel you have to do. But without my blessing. And keep in mind, will you, that the boys in Chicago take a very dim view of unions and demonstrations."

"I certainly will," Alicia said. They hung up. The conversation left her drained. But at least Phyllis's malevolence was consistent. She was like a bad cook who turns out one tasteless meal after another. Who would choose to live on such a diet for life?

Alicia began to fill her Lucy's Canvas tote with homework. (She would not buy a proper leather briefcase, lest she be confused with the woman in the Hanes panty-hose ad.) Today the homework consisted of two manuscripts to read and judge, only one of which she would have time for, and a letter to compose to the agent whose client's manuscript was still missing. Toby would be getting home just about now, alone. The phone rang.

"Damn," Alicia said, answering. It was Dick Freyburg.

"Well, hello there, Alicia," he said. "I'm tracking down a rumor. Someone told me you'd disappeared."

"What do you mean disappeared?"

"Well, not literally, of course. I was just looking for an excuse to call you."

"And to lean a little?"

"No way," he said. "Just checking in. I wondered if there were any questions you'd like to ask me."

"No questions," Alicia said. "And as you can see I'm still here. As a matter of fact, I think I'm molded to my chair."

"How picturesque," Dick said.

"How's business where you are? Here, it's terrible. They've invoked a hiring freeze."

"Good God," Dick Freyburg said. "Actually, considering the state of the economy, you might say we're flourishing. We have on our Spring List two sure blockbusters, one about a disaster on an oil rig off Georges Bank, two first novels about incest, a diet book featuring enemas, the confessions of a CIA malcontent—this one will blow your socks off—one movie script turned into a long piece of crap—excuse me, I mean fiction—and a how-to book about what to do with peels—grapefruit, orange, and potato. Also yet another biography of Frank Sinatra and a keen book about teeth."

Alicia wasn't sure whether he was kidding or not. It sounded like a plausible list.

"You really want to know if I've made up my mind?"

"There's no special hurry," Freyburg said. "I just thought that if you'd decided one way or the other . . ." He trailed off a moment, returning with fervor. "Look," he said, "I might as well level with you, Alicia. Lena Adamson, I believe you met her, she's the one with those gorgeous buck teeth, she went and got herself pregnant and is using it as an excuse to quit. I thought that sort of thing had gone out with the twist but there it is. She's thirty-four years old, for chrissake, she's been at T and L thirteen years. I can't see why she'd rather have a baby but she seems set on it. I told her she could bring it in and nurse it here, we'd even find a little room for it, but she says she wants to stay home and free-lance. Free-lance—now there's a dead end for a top-flight editor."

Alicia heard all this from far away. She glanced at her watch and the mist in front of the screen cleared, revealing Toby moving about in the Baer kitchen toward the refrigerator. It was dusk and she had not turned on the lights. Her face, trapped in shadow, looked not like a young girl's but like a ghost's. Alicia drew in a breath and held it as her daughter opened the door, bent slightly to explore, moved her head slowly back and forth and then shut the door. She ran each hand down her sides and as she came to her hips made a terrible face, an expression of hard unhappiness. Alicia wanted to cry out, "Stop! You're beautiful. I love you. Eat." Six miles away the child moved out of her mother's vision. The mist closed over again. Alicia shuddered.

"Dick," she said, "I'm trying to decide but I'm going to have to do it slowly. That's the only way I can be sure. But if I do come to T and L, I'd like to take Davida Franklin with me, assuming we can work out the contractual problems. She's never going to write a blockbuster and she isn't really into teeth, but she's a class novelist. We work together like Simon and Garfunkel."

"I've been a quiet fan of hers for years," Freyburg said in a voice that sounded to Alicia more neutral than enthusiastic.

Quiet fans were Davida's cross; she bore them like an old-fashioned good sport, the kid who doesn't bitch when the umpire makes an unfair call. Fans she had, but they did not make noise. They passed her books around, from one friend to the next, they put themselves on lists at the public library, didn't mind waiting a year and a half for the list to shorten to them. Some wrote her letters but movie studios and producers ignored her; her novels depended for their appeal on the kind of prose that was not primarily visual. Davida, the good sport, rarely complained except in self-mocking tones, but Alicia knew, from the shape of her expression while she was doing it, that she would not have minded if her fans had not been quite so subdued. "I told Davida it was as if my decision were locked inside a safe and I didn't have the combination worked out yet. But it's coming along."

"I suppose I'll have to go with that," Freyburg said. "By the way, did you hear the joke about the Wasps and the light bulb?"

"Yes," she said. "Two. One to mix the martinis and the other to call the electrician. We're not a complete backwater up here. We do hear some jokes." She considered her next statement carefully, then made it: "Dick, you make me nervous."

"Not to worry, Alicia," he said, unfazed. "I'm a man of my word. You just take all the time you need. I don't want you to feel that I've pressured you into making a decision you might regret. There'd be nothing but trouble in it for me if you did. I want you to be absolutely sure about what you decide when you finally hear that lock click."

"Do you ever have the idea the world is mad?" she asked, surprising herself.

"All the time," he said. "Never stop."

"How do you manage to work?" she asked. She realized how raw her apprehensions must be if she was displaying them to this man, who, after all, was almost her boss.

"I don't see that there's much else one can do. Unless you want to turn into one of those survivalist freaks." Freyburg's fatal simplicity touched her. Then he said, "If I'd had any idea we were determined to challenge the Russians to a race to Doomsday, Kate and I would never have had our two point eight kids."

"Good God, how bleak."

"Isn't it?" The ensuing pause gave them both a chance to lift their chins. "Look, Alicia," he said. "I've got to go now. But keep in touch, will you? Give me a call when you've made that decision."

Wasn't Freyburg fortunate that he could so easily dismiss his despair, as easily, it seemed, as he could fire the mailroom boy caught with his fingers in petty cash. For Alicia it was far more difficult, partly because Barney was so busy organizing other medical people and partly because, well, it was simply in her nature to contemplate the worst, the unspeakable, the ultimate horror. After she hung up, Alicia froze, watching a pigeon on the ledge of the building across the street peck at the granular cement. A horn blared in the street below; the pigeon took off as if nicked in the tail by buckshot. Alicia jumped.

CHAPTER
Nine

PEARL Withers had a voice like faraway thunder. With it, she intimidated Alicia, who sat in the living room of Pearl's apartment drinking a cup of roseate punch and listening to her with a mixture of curiosity and fear.

"You're probably wondering why I live in Somerville," Pearl Withers said. "It's cheap and it's working class, but did you know the original McLean Hospital was located down the road from where you're sitting right now? Whenever Aunt Julia felt peckish in the springtime they would pack her off to McLean Hospital for a rest cure. Everyone had a crazy Aunt Julia in those days. Did you?"

"Not that I know of," Alicia said. She felt uncomfortable. For one thing, the chair she was sitting in had an uncoiled spring somewhere deep in its interior and it poked her. For another, the air was close and moist; she began to perspire.

"I think you should know what happened to me after you and I lost touch some years back," Pearl said. Workmen were hammering on the roof of the house next door to Pearl's. The noise was interesting: sometimes the hammers were in sync, instruments playing together, then they would go out of sync and sound haphazard. Alicia's ears kept wanting to put them back together.

"Long after I married," Pearl said, and the thunder rumbled

on, "I became convinced that my only child, William, was going to suffer some terrible calamity, not excluding death itself. When this obsession began he had just finished up at college—he went to Reed, in Oregon—and embarked on a trip which he said would take him around the world. His grand tour was essentially camping and scrounging for a place to bed down in. He called it crashing. William had done well, extremely well in school, much better, in fact, than either his father or I would have predicted from his previous academic performance. He had been a dreamy sort of boy and quite an accomplished artist. He drew beautifully, one of those children everyone always asked to do their portraits. His line was sure and clear; he almost never used an eraser, he was so often right the first time. Once in college, however, William put away his charcoal sticks, or perhaps he threw them out, and he gave a fellow student his drawing pads. Then he concentrated on history. He had decided—overnight, it seemed—to become an historian. He especially liked the earliest period in American history. He told us—his father and me—that the Puritan period was centripetal, explaining that while it was a passionate time, it was also simple. That is, there existed only the narrowest range of choices in life. It was a far less complex society than most others before or since, at least in the so-called civilized world. Ambiguity was almost unknown, William said."

Someone, a man, began to shout, on top of the roof next door. Alicia could not see the man and could not make out what he was saying; Pearl's windows were shut in spite of the warm air. "One of William's teachers had fired him and once alight, he shone like a bright meteor. It was wonderful to see him like this after so many years of watching him threaten to fail most of his subjects. It was even more gratifying to see *his* pleasure at the results of some serious application.

"A lot of young girls seemed to think William was a knockout. I can say without false modesty that he was extremely handsome. Not that he had regular features or anything as unexceptional as that. His nose was large and veered slightly to the right. His eyes were not the bluest—they were blue-green—and his brows were thin, as if they had been singed. It was chiefly a kind of mournful intelligence and sense of humor illuminating his features that drew the females to him as bees to pollen. They did not turn to watch him, as they would a movie actor or politician, but reacted toward him as they would a favorite professor who only has to open his mouth in order to have his students fall in love with him. I'm sure you understand what I'm talking about."

Alicia nodded. She could almost see the William his mother was describing. She wondered if the real William was as appealing as she made him out to be. She looked around for pictures but didn't see any. Withers was not Ashburton.

"William was graduated—he'd been awarded a Phi Beta Kappa key that year, one of six in his class, and, in the company of his current girlfriend, a superficially pretty, acerb young person named Jackie, set off for Europe. It was quite clear to me from the moment he brought this creature home during their winter break that Jackie felt the world would be a better place were I not in it." Alicia began to find Pearl's slightly archaic speech extremely soothing. It was like being transported backward in time or into a historical novel whose characters spoke with a formal cadence. It was nice.

"Jackie never said this to me directly, of course," Pearl said. She stopped to sip some punch, then wiped her mouth with a handkerchief she had up the sleeve of her dress. Alicia judged her age to be above fifty but not yet sixty. There was a blurred quality to her face; some of it looked old but her eyes, clear and pointed, seemed young. "However, I read it in Jackie's expression and from the fact that she would not look at me directly. She had what used to be known as shifty eyes. And I can tell from looking at you, Alicia, that you believe me to be projecting or employing another such psychological maneuver."

Alicia shook her head. Pearl continued: "There's no sense in my denying it, however, because you have no basis for which to believe a denial any more than you have my initial statement about Jackie and her feelings. Allow me to state—for this record if for no other—that never once did Jackie initiate a conversation with me, look me straight in the eye or praise anything I had done, from the preparation of a meal to a gift I made to the two of them just before they departed. It was an illustrated guidebook to the French provinces. William would say, 'This pie is delicious, Mother,' and I'd glance at Jackie and she would be deep in conversation with my husband John or, if we had a guest for dinner, with that person. She did help me with the cleaning up and she made herself generally useful in the house when he brought her home, but having her there with us was a little like having a dog that is known to bite without provocation. But I am spending too much time on the girl."

Alicia shifted in her chair. Her bottom hurt dully but something kept her there. It was as if moving would break the spell which Pearl had settled around her.

"William always was a good boy. He worked every summer from the time he was fifteen, principally at jobs like frying hamburgers and stocking shelves in the local A and P. One summer he worked in the fish store on the pier selling striped bass and lobsters to summer people at outrageously marked-up prices. He would come home, reeking of fish, and tell us about his employer who bought a load of bluefish for twenty-nine cents a pound and sold it for one dollar and forty-nine cents. He reported this with a visible mixture of triumph and disgust. I knew he was thinking simultaneously of both the man he worked for, whose material existence depended upon how much commerce he could manage during a three- or four-month period, and what William called the 'poor saps' who ought to have known better than to pay these inflated prices. What I am trying to communicate to you is that William was blessed—as most of us are not—with the ability to detect virtue in more than one side of an issue or of a person. As you know, we are most of us half blind. Even as a small boy William was surprisingly free of the sort of dogged opinions that have made our planet such a savage place.

"I am rambling, am I not," Pearl said rather than asked. She put her hand against a cheek, then ran it over her temple and hair. Her fingers were wrinkled and she wore an oval diamond girdled with either garnets or rubies, an old ring. Then she cocked her head, listening to the racket next door.

Alicia felt more and more as if she were being drawn into Pearl's story, that the point of *her* entry into it was not far off and that once inside it, she would not be glad to be there.

"What are you staring at?" Pearl asked.

This unnerved Alicia, who realized that she must have a rude look on her face. She was staring at Pearl, whose features seemed to have spread as if they had begun to melt. "I'm terribly sorry," Alicia said. "I didn't mean to stare."

"It doesn't matter," Pearl said. "I'm ugly as sin."

"Oh, no," Alicia said. She felt like a child facing, close up, a mean teacher. The older woman did nothing to mitigate this.

"My appearance is not worth discussing," Pearl said. "God made me this way and I am resigned to it. I don't like it, but I am resigned."

Alicia did not know what sort of response to make so she applied herself to the punch. It was too sweet. For a panicky moment, she thought that the sweetness might mask a poison.

"To get back to my story," Pearl said, smoothing her skirt over her knees. "So William and his Jackie went off to Europe on one of those charter flights, carrying sleeping bags and backpacks and looking for all the world like two homeless waifs. They had an itinerary of sorts but nothing definite. They knew that they would be in Berne mid-July and Brussels the first week in August. I must say, they did go to the most unusual places. Had it been I, we would have gone to Italy, Egypt, anywhere with a rich and lustrous past. Switzerland has always seemed to me impossibly arid. I suspect it was Jackie who, perversely, chose these petrified and stoutly middle-class cities rather than cherished centers of art. Simply to irk me, something she accomplished: I told her I thought they would be wasting their time in Berne. Now this misty itinerary of theirs was all very well if you want to be footloose. It is not so happy for the people at home who want to keep in touch. John and I were told we could write to the young people in care of American Express in several key cities and they could write to us whenever they chose to, but, in the event of some emergency, they were out of reach, quite out of reach. They would be floating over the map of Europe and God knows where else, two specks adrift . . ." Pearl's eyes closed as if trying to hold these specks in her head, behind the eyes. Opening them, she said, "Oh my, I've forgotten the cookies." And she got up out of her chair, disappeared into the kitchen and came back with a plate of pale round cookies with a dab of jelly, a red eye, in the middle of each one. "Take one," she ordered. Alicia rarely ate cookies, but did as she was told. The cookie was buttery, not so sweet as she would have guessed. Alicia smiled.

"Made them for you," Pearl said, sitting down once more. "You always did like pastry," she said.

Alicia stood pat, said nothing, swallowed.

"I'm aware," Pearl said, taking up the thread again, "that I have not been generous to my husband John in this account. At this time John and I were not getting along as well as we might have. Our difficulties began when I discovered, quite by chance, that he had been behaving in his law practice in ways I could not approve of. I suppose you might say that, unlike my son, I held strong and unshakable opinions about certain things which occasionally made for more trouble in my life than seems entirely fair. We are all looking for justice, are we not? We *do* exult when good triumphs. In this way, Alicia, you and I are very similar. I had been brought up by a stern Episcopalian father to believe that a lie, even a partial lie, was as grave a sin as murder. It topped the list, so to speak, of the crimes it was possible for one to commit."

Where is she going, Alicia thought. Her drift was so wide it covered a lifetime. The hammering next door stopped, several men with saws began to move down through wood.

"Noisy, aren't they?" Pearl said. "The people next door cannot seem to have done with their house. They are always either adding on or subtracting. I have complained to the local police but they tell me that if work is being done on any day but Sunday they cannot do anything about the noise. Sundays, it seems, are different. You can stop anybody from doing almost anything on a Sunday"

"I didn't know that," Alicia said. It didn't sound right to her.

"I am not implying that John lied outright, mind you, not at all. It was more as if the truth had become something flexible and personal; he had begun to bend it here and there to save one or another of his immensely rich clients money. I told him I thought he was in league with the devil. I was my father speaking with my voice. John simply dismissed me as he would a child demanding the impossible. He told me I knew nothing about tax law—which was true—nor about how financial affairs are standardly handled—which was also true. What he refused to admit was that he was cheating and that cheating is a form of lying. And I could not tolerate lying in a member of my family. We started by quarreling and soon discovered that our fighting drove us further apart. Gradually our marriage cooled to a point where we spoke to each other with excessive politeness, and I couldn't be sure, one day when he came home wearing a new coat, that I had never seen it before. I suspected that he turned to other women, one of them a close friend of my own. I remained faithful to him. That is, faithful to our marriage vows; my infidelity of spirit was the lie and there was nothing I could do to assuage my guilt about that. You're wondering why I am telling you all this?"

Alicia nodded. She had lost track of time. Only the fact that it was still light outside, that the workmen were busy with their tools, told her it was not yet five o'clock.

"And you are looking at me as if you cannot wait to get away. You can leave anytime you wish. The door is locked, but only from the inside." The walls of Pearl's apartment seemed, then, to lean inward from the top.

Alicia took a deep breath. "I'd like to hear to the end," she said softly.

"Then try to maintain some semblance of interest," Pearl said. "The end? The end occurs only when I die." She continued; "You have turned transparent in your middle years, Alicia. You never used to be.

"John urged me to seek medical help at about this time, claiming I had undergone a personality change. Isn't it odd the way we tend to blame our own faults on others? You can imagine how his suggestion inflamed me. I actually accused him of trying to make me think I had lost my mind. No one else agreed with him, which was the only thing that saved me. None of my friends agreed with him, none of the women with whom I worked as a volunteer at the museum, not my brother Paul, no one to whom I appealed. It was only John who insisted I needed 'help.' Naturally, given the nature of our relationship, I responded in kind and urged him to go into therapy in order to search for his lost sense of virtue—as if a character defect could be remedied by something as superficial as therapy. In the end neither one of us went to see anyone.

"One week after William and Jackie had begun their trip to God knows where, I did, in fact, begin to change. I felt isolated. My women friends, the people I relied on to provide warmth, amusement, sympathy, what is generally thought of as the female fabric of life, seemed silly and arrogant and selfish, their concerns too trivial to take seriously. Martha Rose, to give you one instance, a woman whom I had always believed to possess a stealthy intelligence and wonderful judgment, went on at incredible length about the redecoration of her dining room; it was all I could do to keep from hanging up the phone as she talked about wallpaper. But worst of all, I could not stand listening to their chattering about their children. They seemed, all of them, to live entirely through and for their children; their sons and daughters had assumed a central place in their lives and would not move off. I listened, with growing impatience, as they talked to me about whether this daughter ought to go on to graduate school or that son take a job in his father's law firm. And all of this, of course, was based on the assumption that what they wanted their children to do their children would do automatically. There was no awareness that they and their offspring might want different things. I knew better."

Under Pearl's words lay a message for Alicia that she could not quite decipher. Or did it? Was she reading into this woman's rather pathetic story something that wasn't really there?

"It was all a wicked waste of time," Pearl was saying. "The conversations with my friends, my making the appropriate remarks to their trifling concerns and wondering, as they talked, where William's feet were touching down. For a week or so I awoke every morning with a headache so fierce it sent me scrambling to the window to draw the blinds. The pain lodged in my right temple, behind my right eye and filled my ear on the same side. It lodged in my jaw. I could hardly bear to open my eyes to see or my mouth to eat. For ten days I swallowed two codeine tablets as soon as I woke up; I kept the pill bottle and a glass of water by my bedside so that I wouldn't have to get up. The pills took the edge off the terrible pain but did nothing to alleviate my conviction that there was something wrong with my body. A visit to my doctor, however, told me that these headaches were, as he put it, not abnormal, part of the hormonal changes I was undergoing as a result of an early menopause.

"I looked forward to cards and letters from William as if they were food and I was starving. When, during one two-week period, not a single word arrived from him, I persuaded myself that he had been swallowed by earth, wind, fire or water, had disintegrated, was gone forever. To compound these matters Jackie was extremely cavalier with her family and wrote them even less often than William did his father and me. One night near midnight our phone rang. It was Jackie's father calling from Chicago to ask if we had heard from the 'young people,' as he called them. I myself had not received mail from William for ten days. I tried to read in the man's voice evidence of the kind of bone-melting anxiety I was experiencing and could not be certain what I heard—my heart was making too much noise.

"When I revealed to John a tiny part of what I was suffering, he was no help. He called me crazy and said that there was no ostensible reason to worry about William. He said we would have heard if anything had happened to them, that the worry was coming from inside me and that I ought, at my stage in life, to be able to control these fly-away panics. Several times he left the house and twice did not come home all night. If I suspected that he was sleeping with my friend I could not have cared less; at that time it was as important to me as the fact that our cellar needed scrubbing. Nothing mattered but William. Where was he? Left alone, my fears intensified. I was certain I would never see him again. I had to force myself to eat. I remember exactly how this felt: I had to will my throat to open in order to sweep the food along. Even swallowing soup took an enormous effort. You're nodding."

"I understand what you're talking about," Alicia said.

"The panic took my life captive. I lay on my bed for hours, unable to read, to watch television, to think straight. The radio by the bed provided background noise, music to accompany dread. I lost more than ten pounds. Under ordinary circumstances I would have cheered; now I barely noticed. My cleaning woman would come in, look at me as if I were a bag lady—she had no sympathy for my suffering because it was obvious I had allowed it to overwhelm me—and left without cleaning the stove. Whenever I heard from William—yes, I did get a card from time to time—I would examine the postmark, reckon the time span between his sending it and my receiving it—and realize that a week or more had passed. Within which some calamity had surely occurred. Things went on like this for nearly three months. I retreated into a world that only the most experienced of mental sufferers have explored. I think it must have been like the world that causes lunatics in asylums to continuously scream." Pearl stopped and her body seemed to relax; there was a slight motion backward; her spine curved and her chin dropped.

Then she went on. "The only reason I did not scream was that, deeply buried but still active, was a sense that if I displayed my wretchedness in this way, I would have been dispatched to such a place posthaste. John, I believed, was waiting for me to succumb so he could pack me off to the lunatic asylum." Pearl stopped again, considering the noise next door, which was now being augmented by a motor-driven drill, a high whining sound that hurt the ears. Pearl's litany filled Alicia with horror and disgust; she could not call up the pity she knew was there, somewhere in hiding. Pearl stared at her, challenging. Alicia stood firm. "I could not say the word 'William' without nausea rising within me. I was certain he was dead. I believe I underwent what is vulgarly and inaccurately known as a nervous breakdown, inaccurate because far from breaking down, the nerves are energized, revitalized, waiting to do their worst. No, the nerves do not break down; quite the contrary. I was determined, however, to prevail over my symptoms. It was strength of will and nothing else that kept me out of the hospital. I cannot escape giving myself this credit."

"And what happened to William?" Alicia asked.

"He returned on schedule." Pearl's voice shifted to match the matter-of-factness of this statement. "He walked in through the front door and I fainted dead away. The scene was as in a nineteenth-century novel when women fainted at the slightest provocation and babies died in alternate chapters. In a diabolically clever story by Saki which you may have read, called 'The Open Window,' a man we have been led to believe is dead turns up at the end of the afternoon and casually asks for his tea. It was like that. My head went black, a strange loud noise filled my ears, and I slipped to the floor, giving my shoulder a nasty bump on the way down. I was not unconscious for long. This sleep was, in fact, only the briefest respite from the emotions that were slowly strangling me. There stood my William, silken, tan, healthy, half-smiling. He had grown a beard during his travels and he looked even more beautiful with part of his face hidden."

Alicia thought this story to have taken a curious turn; she had expected Pearl's fantasy to have been borne out. She had expected something far more dramatic than a beard.

"You are wondering," Pearl said, "why I'm telling you this. I've only just begun. All this has been a prelude."

My God, thought Alicia, I'll be here all night. She looked at her hands. The diamond in her engagement ring looked up at her dully, trying to wink. This and its partner, her wedding band, slipped as she tilted her hand upward; the fingers were getting stringy while her body thickened. Where was the girl Alicia hidden? The girl had bitten her nails; the woman had tamed the impulse to bite. "As a matter of fact—" Alicia began.

"And I'm not finished," Pearl interrupted. Alicia felt a touch of fright as she wondered whether the door might be locked from the outside as well. Was Pearl holding her captive? And if so, why? If she called for help, who would hear?

Pearl reached over and picked up a small purse lying on the table beside her chair. From it she took a tapestried glasses case, withdrew a pair of tortoiseshell glasses and stuck them on her face. They enlarged her eyes so that they looked like translucent grapes. "Jackie," she said, staring at Alicia, "was not with William when he came home that day. Immediately I decided what I wanted to believe, namely, that they were no longer together. But I was the victim of wishful thinking: they were very much together; she was merely paying a visit to her family before joining William. He was changed. It was Jackie who had changed him."

"Changed how?" Alicia asked. She was aware that some of the commotion from next door had ceased. Steps sounded, going past Pearl's door and climbing the stairs. Pearl saw her listening. "Those are the upstairs tenants. You didn't think I occupied this entire house all by myself, did you?"

"I didn't know," Alicia said.

"Well, I don't." Pearl took some punch. "William was changed, as I said before. Where he had been sweet, loving and attentive, he was now cold, superficial and arrogant. He was a different person, as different as the pieces of broken vase are from the whole. I hardly recognized him and it wasn't just the beard. It was as if she had removed one spirit from his body and inserted another, one I didn't like."

"She? You mean Jackie?"

"Yes, Jackie."

"I don't understand."

"Of course you don't. I don't myself."

"Were there drugs?"

"How tactfully you put things, Alicia. What you mean is did they *consume* drugs? Did she *feed* him drugs?"

Just then a line of rain flew down the coast and fell in drops on Boston and Somerville. The windows of Pearl's rooms streaked and glistened. Pearl turned to look at the sudden rain; her eyes seemed to take it in without registering what it was. Then she said, "The rain hurts my bones." She stopped and drifted a moment, then returned with a twitch of her body. "Who is to say about drugs? Can taking drugs so alter a personality that it is no longer recognizable?"

"I don't think so," Alicia said. "At least I've never heard of it.

No, that's not quite true. There was a boy of seventeen or so, the son of someone my husband works with, who dropped acid for a long time and it made him psychotic. They had to put him away. He tried, I think, to fly out of the attic window. He looked straight into the sun and damaged his retina. *He* changed."

"That boy you are talking about went mad. William did not turn into a lunatic; he simply became another person. There's no comparison. I hardly knew my son when that woman got through with him."

"I don't mean to be nosy but how can you be so sure that *she* changed him? Are you trying to say that Jackie had some magic power over him?"

"She was an alchemist of the soul. She set out to alter his personality to suit her perverse taste and she succeeded. Jackie and William live near Denver now; he teaches history in a private school. She makes quilts at home and sells them to expensive boutiques. I imagine that William is an exacting and not very popular member of the faculty."

"How sad," Alicia said. "What a sad story."

"You don't believe a word of it," Pearl said. Her glasses, with the magnified eyes behind them, looked cloudy. Alicia blinked.

"Of course I do," she cried. "Why shouldn't I?"

"Because it simply is not an easy story to believe. How do you know I haven't made it all up in order to gain your sympathy?"

Alicia sensed that she and Pearl were twisted together in some kind of struggle and that it was crucial she not show any sign of weakness or confusion. She smelled a moral, too, hidden behind Pearl's words, to take home with her. Pearl's obsession with William, her own with Toby—there were parallels enough to feed her speculations for quite a while. The woman scared Alicia, her intensity was like a fire in the house next door with the wind beginning to act up.

And so far Pearl had alluded in only the most marginal way

to the fact that she had known Alicia in a former time. "You know James Joel? Dr. Joel?" Pearl said.

"Dr. James Joel? I don't think so." This name fell flat on its face.

"And why should you?" Pearl tossed her head as if to remove impediments to a memory and then continued. The light grew softer, darker. All was quiet next door and footfalls sounded in a muffled way above their heads. Alicia began to smell something cooking, something with meat in it, or fowl. "Before the days when one could simply enter a clinic and request an abortion, the way one requests a shot against Asian flu," Pearl said, "Dr. James Joel made a lucrative living practicing the art of abortion. This was illegal, of course; he was aware of the risks and so were his patients. But, as far as such things go, he was better than the rest. He employed a nurse and he sterilized his instruments. You might say he did this because he didn't want a death on his hands; you might also look at it from the other side and say he was humane. In any case, his reputation among our peers—and now I *am* beginning to be surprised you haven't heard of Dr. Joel—was excellent."

"Dr. Joel," Alicia repeated, twirling the name around, hoping it would catch on to something.

"Compared to what I am about to tell you, Alicia, the other parts were a snap. It is a story I know so well it emerges in my dreams the way it does while I am conscious. I have lost William; he might just as well be the man who reads the gas meter. In point of fact, I see the meter man more often than I see William. This is a dismal fact of my daily life but in a way I think I have resigned myself to it as I have to my plainness; not accepted it, just resigned to the daily pain of it. Now I must talk about you and me." At this, Pearl rose from her chair, crossed the room and stood looking out at the rain-splashed street, the wet trees, the heavy sky, in which huge blue and black clouds were rolling around, as if in labor. Her skirt, in which a muted geometrical pattern was woven into the threads, made her hips seem wide enough for two women.

"You probably don't remember the Garret, either, do you?" she said to the window.

"The Garret? No, I'm sorry," Alicia said, realizing as she spoke that this was probably a tactical error.

"Your apology is meaningless. Why should you be sorry? Your stubborn memory is obviously something you have no control over."

"Oh, God," Alicia breathed, signaling the weakness she had been determined not to betray. A look of triumph spread across Pearl's face, as she turned around to stare at Alicia.

"Selective memory is a most effective weapon of denial," she said.

"Tell me what the Garret is," Alicia said. Underneath her question a tremor started.

"The Garret is the café where we promised to love one another for the rest of our lives. I believe it has long since ceased to exist, but I won't forget it as easily as you apparently have. Not the taste of the coffee or the blood-red color of the strawberries in the cake we shared or the groaning sound the front door made whenever it opened."

This speech so stunned Alicia that she felt the blood leave her head. Whatever you do, don't protest! she told herself. Her face went slack with wonder and horror.

"Ha, ha!" Pearl cried. "You looked astonished. Either you are a most capable actress or a part of your head is missing. I think you are a very good actress . . ."

"Pearl," Alicia began, "I think I must have something terribly wrong with me. I can't remember . . ." Alicia pleaded with her eyes for Pearl to believe her. Pearl's face remained stony. "I can't remember things," she repeated. "But I also *have* to tell you that what you're saying doesn't sound right. I've never had a homosexual relationship in my life, I swear—"

"Oh but you *have,* my dear. We—you and I—shared far more than a taste in art and in food, in clothes. We shared a cottage. We shared a bed."

"No!"

"Yes, indeedy. Yes, we did. More than once. Would you like me to try to refresh your recollection? No, I don't want you to answer that because I will do so whether you would like me to or not."

Alicia jumped up, throwing off all pretense at fortitude. She felt toward the woman facing her, with her back to the fading light, as if she were a mortal enemy, about to cut her in half. She felt as if she were already bleeding.

"We were young. We swore eternal love to one another in the Garret Café. I kissed you on the lips, you squeezed my hand, you held my hand beneath the table. Your nails, I remember your nails, bitten to the quick. I see you have managed to let them grow."

Alicia stared at Pearl's mouth. She could see the teeth inside when Pearl opened her mouth. They gleamed. "I went off to one large city, you to another. Don't look so vacant, Alicia. We wrote regular passionate letters. I still have yours if you would like to see them."

"I don't think so," Alicia said. A sudden weakness bent her legs at the knee and she sat down again.

Pearl sat too. Their both being on the same level evened them off physically, but Pearl still had a mighty edge; the force of her personality swept Alicia from everything outside this room. The rain was still coming down but not so hard as before. Pearl reached over and turned on a table lamp. The light, thrown down by a large cone-shaped shade, was warm. It made Alicia's hands seem tannish. "And then, and then came another turning point in my life," Pearl said. "I heard that you had taken up with a man. You had betrayed our love and formed an alliance with a male. I went into a terrible depression. I felt as if my life was over. I slept for days—does this sound familiar? I lost my job. In anger and hurt I too formed a liaison with a man. His name was Anselm Webb and he taught music in a high school near where I lived. He was a composer manqué, a man who filled his life with sad dreams and he was what some women would describe as a superb lover. He roused the female in me, the woman whom I had covered with dead leaves for your sake, Alicia. He was also married. Alas. I saw Anselm at odd hours, early in the morning when the sun cast smoky shadows or late at night when the moon peered in through the window like an intruder with a powerful torch. When we made love your face burned behind my tightly closed eyes. It was all I could do, at the moment of climax, not to call out your name, Alicia!"

Alicia drew back into herself. Of all the things she had been asked to believe thus far this was the most threatening. She closed her eyes and prayed for Pearl to get quickly to the end of her story.

"And of course, because it was the thing I least desired, I found myself pregnant with Anselm's child. I went to him and told him. He was decent enough about my predicament, as he called it, and he gave me money to go to Dr. Joel, who did what he was paid to do with a minimum of blood and pain."

"Oh, God," Alicia said.

"And so I killed my first child," Pearl said.

"But it's not a child, it's not murder. A fetus isn't a person."

"Have you had an abortion, Alicia?"

Alicia shook her head. "No."

"Well, then you simply have no idea about the guilty residue left after you go through this experience, after the fetus is sucked from your body with a terrifying noise and unbearable pain. You cannot possibly understand if you have not been through it yourself, the hours you lie awake accusing yourself of murder, wondering what he would have been like, having him come to you in your dreams and saying, 'Why did you kill me, Mother?'"

An awful thought wormed its way into Alicia's skull at this moment and was simultaneously mouthed by Pearl: "If it had not been for you, Alicia, if you had not betrayed our love, I would not have fallen into the arms of Anselm Webb, I would not have murdered my first child. I lost him, I lost William. I am that most miserable of women: a mother with no children. Have you any idea of the depth of my misery?"

"You can't blame me," Alicia cried, springing from her chair again. "That's crazy. I'm not responsible for what happened to you. You did it yourself!"

"You must not allow this to destroy you," Pearl said, speaking now in a monotone which Alicia found sinister. "I'm aware that effects have more than one cause. Nevertheless, I blame you for what happened to me. Our lives had been as one. We were closer than most men and women in a marriage—certainly closer than John and I ever were. I cannot talk for you; I don't know anything about your marriage."

"It's a good marriage," Alicia said. "We're very close."

"You're lying, it's obvious, but that's neither here nor there. What I want to impress on you is your cowardice; it was not you who came and told me about breaking your vow to me; it was someone else who told me, a girl who did not know about our relationship, who mentioned your love affair in passing, as a piece of idle gossip. Your lack of courage was a weapon you used against me. I hated and loved you at the same time . . ." Pearl's voice went fuzzy and her eyes glittered wetly.

The air around Alicia was oppressive, as if all the oxygen had been sucked out by a giant vacuum. She couldn't breathe. But she managed to say, "Pearl, if I say I'm sorry it would only represent how bad I feel because of your pain. But it wouldn't have anything to do with what happened to you—how many years ago was this?"

"Twenty-four," Pearl said. Pearl had briefly removed her armor and stood naked and shivering in front of Alicia. Oh, the awful power of love, Alicia thought. But she was uneasy still and convinced that Pearl would get suited up again as soon as she could muster the strength. "I think you're lying to me," Pearl said at last. "I have never called anyone a liar in my life with the exception of you and John. Odd, isn't it, the two people I have had the closest bonds with have both lied to me. And I know you are lying, Alicia, by the way your eyes have narrowed, by the way your mouth curves, by the way you keep putting your hand to your mouth. You are not telling me the truth . . ." Then Pearl's voice changed again, this time sounding like a funereal wail. "But why, why after all these years have passed and both of us having lived respectable married lives, why you still choose to deny what may have been for you—as it certainly was for me—the one extended moment of pure, illuminating love, I cannot imagine. Your denial is inconceivable."

Alicia called upon God, whatever that was, a gray wisp, not an actual presence, who came and went casually and could not be relied on for assistance. Nevertheless, she gave it a try. "Dear God," she said, "please!"

Pearl rolled her eyes. "There's little point in that," she said. "This is something for you to come to terms with yourself. He's not going to help you. I know him. God doesn't give a damn."

"It was only a figure of speech," Alicia said.

"But one that betrays your sense of helplessness," Pearl said. Some of the fight was coming back into the old dog.

"What do you want me to do?" Alicia asked. Her throat was impossibly dry, but her glass was empty. She was surprised by her own question; it was not something she had meant to ask.

"You must make it up to me," Pearl said, hugging herself. Her upper arms, strained under her sweater, seemed muscular, as if she exercised daily. "My two children are gone. Nothing matters anymore. My husband is dead, my so-called employers no longer seem to want me, I live in almost total isolation. I do not even know the people upstairs, the two who daily pass my door and seem to have such a happy life above my head. My memories choke me, strangle me. I go out seldom, most of my friends have fallen by the way or have died. My view here is frightful; look at that alley: garbage, detritus, ashcans, never collected. A woman across the street sits in her wheelchair all day long, crying, crying, I see her weeping hour after hour. I think it is me."

As Pearl spoke, the odor of cooking grew stronger. The smell was nauseating. Alicia felt strings of saliva gather in her mouth and spread over her tongue.

"I cannot forgive you," Pearl said. "Until you called me I had placed you in the distance, you were so far back in my picture's perspective you were small enough to ignore. When you called, you moved forward, grew larger. You are here. Why *did* you call, Alicia?"

"I can't explain it." Alicia began and then, as if she had been punched in the nose, the tears lined up quickly behind her eyes and fell steadily over the brink, advancing across her cheeks. They fell on her hands. She bent her head, covering her face and sobbed and sobbed. The sobs filled her mouth and burst through her lips. She heard her own noise, a noise like muffled coughing. She didn't question why she was crying; the course of this grief was far beneath the surface, too far for her to distinguish. The crying was like the pure and terrible certainty that the world has gone mad.

"It's good to see you weep," Pearl said. "It shows you have some feelings after all."

"I do have feelings," Alicia said into her hands.

But Pearl didn't hear this. She said, "I will be with you for the remainder of my life—or your life. Whichever ends first."

"How?" Reinforcements for Alicia's tears began to slack off.

"I will write you, call you, visit your house when my health permits. I will disturb you at work, at home, wherever you are, I will remind you of what you did to me."

"You can't do that," Alicia said, sitting up straight and looking at Pearl.

"Who will stop me? Will you have me arrested? A harmless, aging eccentric who sleeps alone, reads Jane Austen and listens to Mozart? A former volunteer at the Museum of Fine Arts, the widow of a distinguished lawyer? A woman as articulate as any you will find walking around today? They won't believe you. They will think you are crazy."

"I think we should talk about this," Alicia said.

"You want to give me money to leave you alone," Pearl said.

Alicia flushed; she could feel the heat rise off her face. The smell seeping into Pearl's apartment made her gag.

"They must be gourmet cooks up there," Pearl said. "They have never asked me to share a meal. But that's the way of the world, isn't it?"

"I have to go!" Alicia said firmly, standing and looking around for her jacket. "I'd like to talk some more about this, perhaps agree on something that would make you feel better about things."

"You *are* offering me money to leave you alone."

"Yes, I guess I am."

"And if I accept, what's to assure you that I will keep my word?"

"I suppose nothing," Alicia said. The crying had left her washed out. She felt considerably weaker than when she had walked into Pearl's apartment—how many hours earlier?

"I'll think about it and let you know, but I don't think I will take *any*thing from you," Pearl told her. "Now I must lie down. This has been an ordeal for me."

Alicia found her jacket on a chair and walked to the door to let herself out. She looked back and saw Pearl, revolving smoothly as if she were on a turntable, with no motion in her legs. Alicia blinked.

"Goodbye for now, Alicia Gordon," Pearl said and left the room by a door Alicia had not noticed.

Once on the sidewalk, Alicia breathed the air with the same sense of freshness and relief she would if she had landed on a beach by a warm clean sea.

On the drive home, looking through the windshield of her car, Alicia saw, in a flash of white light, the inside of the Garret Café. The front door groaned.

CHAPTER Ten

AFTER her visit to Pearl Withers, after Pearl had faded like the others, leaving Alicia with a residue of uneasiness, she realized that maneuvering in what she had begun to think of as reality one—as opposed to that one populated by the invaders of the address book, reality two—required more and more concentration. She had to force herself to move her eyes across a line of typescript, to listen when someone spoke to her, to put out her hand to collect change. Without knowing why, she was certain that if she let herself slip away from this concentration she would end up adrift in mingled voices and blurred sensations. There were moments when she was quite sure she was losing her mind.

Alicia felt like a picture out of register, her outlines overlapping.

Fearing, Ashburton, Tucker, now Withers—although they were inside the bottle, their faces materialized from time to time in unexpected places, up out of the pages of a book, the eyes staring; in the upright coffin they call an elevator in the Griffin Building; on the bathroom floor.

Several times she tried to talk to Barney about her strange feelings, her uneasiness, about the invaders of the book whose faces came and went, whose conversations were a babble, but she could not begin. Davida was still not back from the country.

It was only a week, of course, but this silence was so unlike Davida that Alicia was certain something had happened. She thought of calling her mother in one of Florida's mossy suburbs but had drawn back. Her mother, on hearing something so distressing, would make Alicia reverse roles and become her mother's mother, obliged to comfort.

Toby? How could Alicia bring herself to tell her daughter, this person fourteen years old, that she had been entertained—so to speak—by four people, one of whom she had fucked? This was hardly something you could lay on a delicate child. Do you tell her that you have cysts in your breasts? Do you report that Daddy was impotent last night?

The demonstration started outside the Griffin Building at nine-thirty sharp, Wednesday morning. Channel 5 and Channel 38, alerted by Nine to Five's publicity staff—and sensing that here was an event which, if it turned out to be not exactly thrilling, would at least offer a view of young female flesh—sent camera crews, youths with cameras mounted like saddles across the shoulders and two overeager reporters whom they followed around. Alicia was one of the few demonstrators not a secretary; she and the others were distinguishable not by age so much as by what they were wearing. The secretaries were smartly turned out in clothes featured in *The New York Times*'s and the *Boston Globe*'s Lord & Taylor and Bloomingdale's advertisements, with eccentricities muted and prices scaled down for the working woman: suede flight jackets, high- and low-heeled boots, bright hose, skirts longish and swinging, pants somewhat baggy at the knee and tighter over the ankle. As always, Alicia was struck by the poignancy of so much salary swallowed by articles of clothing (though she had spent her money this way at their age); she guessed many of them went without the right food or dental checkups in order to be chic. Alicia did not think of herself as dowdy but when she assembled with the others to get their marching orders and picket signs, she said to Margaret Bannister from Panther House, "These kids make me feel like a bag lady." Margaret, nodding, said, "Will you look at those boots. At least one hundred and fifty dollars exchanged hands when those things were bought." Alicia had on her ten-year-old trench coat with the removable lining: it was short and her skirt hung down beneath its hem. She had brought in her girl scout shoes for the occasion.

Bonnie Farber, secretary to the Griffin treasurer, was in charge. Bonnie had a faceful of freckles and wrists like a wrestler. She picked up a cardboard sign stapled to a stick and said to Alicia, "Have you got gloves? These things splinter in your hand, look." She held out her palm in which were embedded tiny shreds of wood.

Alicia said, "No. I'll have to risk it. What does it say?" Bonnie showed her. "GRIFFIN SLAVES UNITED! Support Nine to Five. Boycott Griffin Books."

"What an economical message," she said, picking up the sign.

"It took us a long time. Some of us wanted to say 'Cut the Griffin's Throat." But we were outvoted. Didn't we luck out? They promised not to fire us if we went back to work after lunch."

Alicia lined up with the others and began to walk in the oval formed by the demonstration. A few of the women were chanting: "What do we want? Justice! When do we want it? Now!" over and over again, back and forth. A microphone with a sock over its head appeared under Alicia's nose. "Are you an employee of Griffin?" the reporter holding the microphone asked.

"Yes, I am," Alicia said.

"Oh, are you a secretary?"

"No, I'm an editor. I believe passionately in their cause and that's why I'm out here."

The reporter took this in without the slightest change of expression. "Are your feet getting tired?"

"Not yet," Alicia said. "I expect they will soon."

"How much salary do you make?"

"I don't think that's any of your business," Alicia said, regretting it as soon as it came out of her mouth. The reporter smirked and went off to interview someone else. "Damn," Alicia said, "Why did I say that? I should have said seventeen thousand—before taxes. It ain't too far from the truth anyway." She cursed herself two times around the oval, then looked up to a window so crammed with leaves they seemed about to burst out through the glass and come raining down on the sidewalk. The face of Phyllis Vance stared down at Alicia; she could almost feel the Vance eyes burning into her cheek. It occurred to her that Phyllis no doubt read this act of hers as a personal gesture of defiance, an insult, a thumbing of the nose, a flip of the bird. Alicia felt Phyllis watching only her as she made her way around the oval, up around, back, up around, back, her knees beginning to protest. Now, if Phyllis took it into her head to retaliate by firing her, then it would solve neatly the problem of whether or not to quit Griffin. For a moment, Alicia half hoped that she would be permitted the coward's way out of making a decision. The moment passed.

Alicia tried to recapture Pearl Withers, but Pearl was a wisp of a dream, an echo, a slim memory. She felt sure Pearl had threatened her, but not why. Alicia thought of Toby; her stomach lurched. Something had happened to Toby, she was sure of it. The blood tingled in her legs; she wanted to rush upstairs to her office to see if there were any messages for her. Calming, she realized that she was not out of touch; she would be told if anything had happened to Toby. What are you doing now, Toby, are you thinking about love, are you dreaming yourself into trouble? If I go to New York, what will become of you?

Shortly after noon the picket line began to thin out; Alicia figured some of the strikers were hungry and had gone out to forage for a burger and a shake. Margaret Bannister came up even with Alicia and said, "Why don't we go and get a bite to eat? I'm starving. Besides, my knees feel like they were on fire."

"Isn't that funny, so do mine. I guess we're a little over the hill for this sort of thing."

"Maybe," Margaret Bannister said. "Maybe we're just not in such good shape. How about it?" Margaret was almost six feet tall. She had kinky brown hair, not frizzed by hand but curled by nature. She wore steel-rimmed glasses and had powerful-looking hands. She bore a reputation for being what men called an "aggressive" editor, and her directness was seen, by some, as lack of tact. Alicia thought this unfair; a man like Margaret would be "candid," "forthcoming."

The two women stashed their picket signs and set off toward Quincy Market. "I can't help thinking of myself as twenty-three years old," Alicia said. "My legs say different."

"That isn't what I heard. I heard you were plenty grown up," Margaret said. She had a fearful stride; Alicia had to hop to keep up with her.

"What do you mean?"

"Only that you inspire—how shall I say—respect. Yes, that's the word. You don't let anyone hand you any shit, that's your rep, Alicia."

"You mean they're afraid of me."

"I didn't say that," Margaret told her. "Will you look at that mean bunch of kids. Does one of them have a pin through his nose or am I seeing things?"

"It *is* through his nose," Alicia said. Dressed in black, five or six boys stood near the corner, flicking their gaze on and off, their hair short, like wet feathers, and scars like mosquito bites on their innocent faces. Alicia thought she recognized the bottle thrower but it didn't matter one way or the other; they were all alike. She guessed they were scared and terribly angry.

Margaret took up the previous topic. "And anyway," she said, "what do you care if they're a little afraid of you? It keeps them on their toes, it reduces the amount of chitchat and fraternizing. I for one don't especially want to be the confidante of the kid who brings me my mail in the morning. God, how they love to go on about their meaningful relationships. It *is* a pin through his nose. How revolting."

Davida, where are you? Alicia suddenly thought. She felt ill. They stopped for a red light that seemed to take forever to change.

"You like Chinese food?" Margaret said. "I don't really want to go to the market, it's too effing crowded. There's a reasonable Chinese place a couple of blocks from here."

Alicia nodded. Her guilt at escaping from the picket line was compounded by the fact that she was violating one of the unwritten rules of Boston publishing: don't fraternize—or sororize—with editors from another house; they may slip you some truth serum and pry off your secrets. On the surface, rivalry between Griffin and Panther was a ho-ho-ho affair, lighthearted, enhanced by an annual banquet held in a Boston hotel, a ritual of camaraderie and publishing jokes. But beneath the surface the rivalry between the two firms was about as benign as that between the Red Sox and the Yankees; people had been known to have their skulls cracked at a Yankees-Sox game. Because both publishing firms were never on the steadiest ground, the loss of one big author, or the payment of one miscalculated advance—too large, no hope of getting even half of it back—might lead to near disaster. Or so went the message, circulated by two anxious managements. Critics of the way publishing was conducted claimed that its business methods languished in the nineteenth century, its techniques similar to those of the dipped candle and whale-oil–rendering industries. Where other businesses made use of electronic data-processing and sophisticated instrumentation, conducted market surveys and samplings of taste, using them to point their advertising and promotion at the vulnerable targets, book publishing stumbled along, a clerk on a high stool scratching numbers into a ledger. Every so often Griffin, in the clutches of a terrible enthusiasm, bid one point five million dollars, most of it underwritten by a reprint house, on a book for which blockbuster status was predicted. More often than not this status was a chimera that failed to materialize while in the meantime the house's less showy, less "successful" authors suffered from skinny advances on the chimera's account. "It just isn't fair," Davida had complained, "that that shlockmeister"—referring to a Griffin author whose huge advance was noted in *Publishers Weekly*—"makes so much money. He has a tin ear."

"People don't read books for their prose," Alicia said. "You ought to know that by now."

"Fuck," said Davida. "I wish I could write like that."

"No, you don't." Alicia smiled ruefully at Davida. "Phyllis and David Gill think the shlockmeister's book will be the biggest thing since Christ made Corporal."

As Alicia saw it, however, the muddling and guesswork, the primitive strategies, the ledger books, the colossal errors of judgment, were part of publishing's piquant charm; they made it seem more like an art than a business. "You never know what's going to happen or when it's going to hit the fan," she was saying to Margaret Bannister as they sat down together in Kwa-Sum's, whose decor was typically resourceful: Popsicle sticks, bits of basket and rice paper, kites and string were incorporated to form screens, room dividers, aeries and backdrops in what must have been one large, drab space.

"The Asians are so clever," Margaret said.

Alicia felt like telling Margaret the joke about why Jews went so often to Chinese restaurants ("because they're treated there like any other white person") but didn't know her well enough. Perhaps by the end of the meal, while they split their fortune cookies. She opened the menu.

Margaret was telling Alicia what she should order, while Alicia studied Margaret's face; like her own, it had settled into a kind of early middle-aged charm, relying more on the suggestion of sensibilities behind the features than in their placement on the skull.

"Why don't you order for me," Alicia said, "while I use the facilities."

The ladies' room was small, one toilet and a sink. The kitchen was evidently on the other side of the wall; Alicia heard good-natured laughter. Someone dropped an echoing pan; some shouting; then a burst of silence. Alicia sat and peed. Graffiti weeds sprouted in a lush, untended garden. "Pete and Gerri," paired inside a lipsticked heart. "LESBIAN POWER" in capital letters. "Sex is like bridge; if a woman has a good hand she doesn't need a partner." This one made Alicia smile. "Reagan did for America what panty hose did for finger-fucking." Alicia thought this sentiment belonged more properly in the men's room.

Alicia gathered herself together, and went back to the table, where she found a glass of wine at her place. "I didn't think you'd mind," Margaret said. "Now it's my turn."

When Margaret returned from the bathroom, she said, "Did you see that sweet message above the tampon drop: 'Radcliffe Diplomas—Take one'?"

"I guess I missed that one," Alicia said. "Who makes up those things?"

"Someone who ought to apply her gift to a book," Margaret said. "Speaking of which," she went on, "I hear you're taking off for the Big Apple."

"Where did you hear that?" Alicia asked.

"Boston's mouth is large and loose," Margaret said calmly. "You're not really surprised that I know, are you?"

"As a matter of fact, I am. I haven't told a soul—except my closest friend, and she wouldn't say a word. And, oh yes, my husband. He's hardly a blabbermouth and besides he doesn't know anyone who would be remotely interested." She tasted her wine. It was slightly bitter. "I haven't decided whether or not to go," she added, looking into Margaret's glasses. Kwa-Sum's was filling up. At a large round table in the corner, seven Chinese men in dark business suits were resolutely eating, holding cups of rice to their chins as if they were afraid of dribbling. Their eyes, over the rims of the cups, looked happy. The sight of them cheered Alicia. "No one at Griffin knows about this," she said. She heard her voice as smug.

"You think so?" Margaret released a tiny smile. "Because I heard it from someone at Griffin."

"Oh, hell," said Alicia.

"Not to fret," Margaret assured her. "You're not the first to leave this town and you're certainly not going to be the last. It's news when the traffic goes in the other direction." Margaret seemed to make complete sentences so easily; it was as if the script had been prepared for her and she was merely reading it.

The waiter came to take their order. "I'll have number thirty-seven," said Margaret. "And one number fifty-six." She slapped her menu shut. At the same time both women became shy, and each looked elsewhere, like two adolescents whose mothers have forced them together and who realize they like each other, despite the parental nudge. Alicia, disarmed by the fact that her secret was no longer private property, felt reckless.

"You know Phyllis Vance?"

"With bells on," Margaret said, nodding.

"Phyllis isn't at all happy about the demonstration," Alicia said.

"And as for my boss, Martin Chambers, well, he like to threaten me this A.M. as I was getting ready to join you people. Imagine the chutzpah! I'm the one who brought in Syd Carpenter and that other money-maker, Glenn Barton. Both of them kept us from going into the red last year. And Marty has the nerve to threaten me. In the politest possible terms I told him to shove it. It eludes me what he's so afraid of. Is he afraid those poor girls are going to occupy his office and spill cigar ash in his Out box? Pee in his private bathroom?" Margaret glared, as if Martin Chambers were right there with them. "Those poor girls, all they want is a container of yogurt for lunch and, in the end, a pliable husband with an M.B.A. from Harvard."

The food arrived, along with a fat pot of tea. Margaret asked for chopsticks. Alicia felt her mind wander off. What would happen, she wondered, if you didn't have to eat. Would all work stop? All work, play, all activity. We would just lie around thinking and screwing. In the distance she heard Margaret vilify her boss, Martin Chambers. She wondered if Margaret really liked anyone; she sounded so bitter. Alicia started eating. The food was so hot it left a ring of fire around her lips.

"That man is staring at us," Margaret said. "But don't look around yet."

Alicia disobeyed and met the eyes of a man who looked familiar but whose name she couldn't bring out of the muck of memory.

"He's good-looking enough," Margaret said. "But his hair wants combing." The man passed their table, switching his eyes as if to catch Alicia's. Her memory spun frantically.

"And how about New York?" Margaret said.

"I'm having a hard time making up my mind. It would mean reorganizing my life. I have a husband, you see, who can't leave Boston. And a fourteen-year-old daughter. It's difficult."

"Yes, I see," Margaret said. She poured herself some tea and held the pot above the table. "You?" she said.

"Thanks," Alicia said. It occurred to her that Margaret was leaving something out of her conversation. "Why do you want to know? I mean it can't be all that interesting. People get offered jobs all the time."

Margaret used her chopsticks as dextrously as she would have a fork. She held each morsel of food between the sticks without having to squeeze it. She transferred a cube of bean curd from her plate to her mouth and said, "Boston sends its best to New York to line up for the fast track. We pretend it isn't like that, we like to think of ourselves as the hub, not only the hub of New England but the world, the universe." She smiled at Alicia. "Ain't that so?"

"I suppose." Talk like this made Alicia uneasy.

"If you go," Margaret said, "you'll have to live in a place with five dead locks on the front door and you'll have to take your earrings and gold chain off before going down into the subway. You'll spend six dollars on a hamburger. But it's the Big Apple and that will make the inconvenience and the cost worthwhile. Am I right?"

"No doubt," Alicia said. There was nothing new here. "New York's an old woman who's had her face lifted once too often."

"Yes, but you forget, she's royalty."

"Why do we spend so much time talking about New York?" Alicia said.

"It's irresistible," Margaret said. "Like sin."

"You're right," Alicia said. "You know, I'm not at all sure why Tolland and Lutwidge is so eager to hire me. No, don't smirk, I mean it. There are plenty of decent editors in New York. I'm not being falsely modest, I just don't altogether understand it."

Music started up and spread around Kwa-Sum's via holes in the ceiling. It was a Mozart concerto, a piece so inappropriate that Alicia wondered if someone were playing a joke on the patrons. She absorbed the notes into her brain, where they expanded. She *was* being falsely modest; she knew herself as an editor who rated an A. She was steady and reliable, she had marvelous taste, her marketing instincts, while not unerringly correct, were right enough of the time to make her valuable to the other editors and, she liked to think, to Phyllis as well.

"As a matter of fact," Alicia went on, "I haven't anything like the record you've got. I should think they would have asked you."

"They did," Margaret said.

"What?" Alicia fell through the ice.

"I said, Dick Freyburg offered me the job he's offering you last fall. In point of fact, when I turned him down he asked me about you. I gave you a triple A rating. Easy, Alicia, don't look so shocked. I told you I've been bringing in the Panther bacon recently. I've had five really big books in the last three years. I'm something of a sport for Boston publishing. I'm also very lucky. For chrissake, say something or you'll make me sorry I told you."

"I'm sure luck doesn't have anything to do with it," Alicia said. She felt as if her insides had been scooped out but was determined not to show how terrible she felt. She thought she tasted blood in her mouth.

"That man who was staring at us before is coming over here," Margaret told her.

So she was second in Freyburg's list. Perhaps not even second. How could she be sure there were no others to whom he had made earlier offers? Well, the truth was she couldn't and neither could she ask him. The sick draining of confidence left her as it had when *The New York Times* ran, some years back, a feature on rising female stars in book publishing and had left her out, not a picture, not a mention, nothing, although, as far as she could make out, everyone else was accounted for. She had burst into tears of disappointment and humiliation. Barney said to her, "Forget it, by next week, no one will remember."

"I will."

Thus wounded by Margaret Bannister's disclosure, Alicia did not see the man come to their table. He now hovered, a presence in chinos and a dark blue sweater. The presence bent from the hips in a mocking bow. "How do you do," he said. "It is Alicia Baer, isn't it?"

Alicia looked up sharply. "Yes," she said. "Do I know you?"

Margaret flicked her gaze from one to the other.

"Roger Tucker," the man said.

"Hello, Roger," she said cautiously. "This is Margaret Bannister." With realities one and two colliding like this, Alicia was in the eye of a storm; everything seemed to whirl around her.

"Howdy," he said to Margaret without taking his eyes off Alicia. "Any friend of Alicia's," he said, sticking out his hand. His eyes wobbled, as if loose in the sockets.

"It's nice to see you," Alicia said, praying for him to leave. She didn't know which she minded more: the fact of his appearing at all or the fact that she couldn't remember anything about him. *Please go away,* she begged him silently.

"We've been demonstrating," Margaret said to Roger Tucker. She explained to him about Nine to Five.

"Workers of the world," Roger began. "Do you ladies need some help? It just so happens I have a free afternoon . . ."

"No, thanks," Alicia said quickly. "But thank you. As a matter of fact, I think it's probably all over."

"Well then, in that case, I'll just mosey along," Roger said. "It was a pleasure meeting you, Mizz Bannister, perhaps we will meet again." He whipped two fingers of his right hand along his right temple in a salute and started back to his table.

"Do you think he's drunk?" Alicia said, hoping to divert Margaret from deeper questioning.

"I don't know about that but he certainly is the cliché expert. One solid wall of clichés. Do you know him or don't you?"

"I think I met him somewhere at a book party. Well I must have, he seemed to know me, didn't he?"

"I'd say he had a thing about you, if you want to know. Did you notice the way his eyes never left your face?"

"You must be imagining things, I barely know him!" Alicia said.

"That's when it's the worst," Margaret said, laughing.

"Oh, well," Alicia said desperately. She had no idea how to get away from the subject of Roger Tucker, which hung about thickly after he had gone. She backed up several spaces.

"Would you mind telling me something, Margaret, would you mind telling me why you didn't accept T and L's offer? What made you turn Dick Freyburg down?"

"I know I sometimes sound flip, I know it, but I had a terrible time deciding. I asked too many people what they thought and in the end, of course, the advice just balanced: some told me take the job; an equal number said I shouldn't. It's amazing how strongly people feel about things that have nothing directly to do with them. Mary Pratt—do you know Mary?—she said I'd be making the biggest mistake of my life if I didn't go to New York. The biggest mistake? How could she be so sure I hadn't made a much bigger one ten years earlier? Anyway, the next person I asked for advice used practically the identical words telling me not to go. What finally tipped the scales was when I went to Marty Chambers and told him flat out that I was thinking of leaving. Ostensibly, I went to ask him what to do—men like to believe we women need their advice the way a drunk needs his booze—but actually I went to see if I could scare him into giving me a better deal at Panther. Which is exactly what he did. He not only made me a senior editor, he elevated me to vice-president, gave me some stock options and promised me my own imprint—under certain conditions which I can't go into here, but it looks very promising. Bannister Books—how does that sound? Of course it doesn't mean much in terms of advertising budgets or promotion; they'll get the same old Panther treatment. But they *will* have my name on them. Lord, how we all love to see our names set in type. And I won't have to go through that awful Editorial Board rigamarole each time I want to take on a new book. It will be my private book."

"They must love you there,"Alicia said.

"You might say I used T and L's offer shamelessly," Margaret went on. "On the other hand, that's the way things are done in a man's world, isn't it?" She picked up the handleless teacup and drank. "Cold," she said. "Besides, Walt didn't want me to leave."

"Who's Walt?"

"Walt Steele, the guy I live with. We bought this little house together in Watertown. He was my divorce lawyer and, well, you might say one thing led to another. He's a sweetie pie." Margaret paused. "Your friend seems to be leaving."

"I have to get back too," Alicia said. Their waiter had disappeared in the time-honored style of waiters. "Do you mean, Margaret, that you turned down Dick's offer for the sake of a man?"

"Of course not," Margaret said. "I wouldn't do anything as self-defeating as that. It was a case of all other things being equal. Although, as I said before, Marty Chambers coming through with that nice promotion and Bannister Books—that helped tip the scales."

"Yes, but Walt . . ."

"Walt was fed into the equation, too. It doesn't help to analyze things too deeply, I think." Margaret frowned.

"I suppose you're right," Alicia said. She decided not to tell Margaret the joke about Jews and Chinese food. They split the bill and left Kwa-Sum's. Contrary to folklore, Alicia felt uncomfortably full.

They walked back toward the Griffin Building, Alicia trying to think of a way to reopen Margaret's door a crack. "You were risking more than I was by joining the demonstration, weren't you?"

"I wouldn't say that exactly," Margaret said, taking her giant steps. "I'm married to Panther, Marty knows he can't mess around with Margaret Bannister. She's too valuable."

Above them lay a layer of gray clouds, obstructing the sun, smudging the sky. The temperature had dropped and it felt more like early winter than early spring. "I hope it's all over," Alicia said. "Do you suppose the demonstration did any good?"

"Probably not," Margaret said, "except maybe make those kids feel better about themselves."

"That's something," Alicia said.

Without warning, the mist behind Alicia's eyes lifted to reveal Roger Tucker sitting with a glass of something orange on the low table next to his knee and his head dropped back in an attitude of despair, his eyes shut. For one moment Alicia thought he was dead, having drunk from a poisoned cocktail he had prepared for himself, and this so scared her that she grabbed for Margaret's arm. But then she saw the chin drop, his eyes open and his hand reach out for the glass. Tears glittered on his cheeks. You're a perfect mess, she thought. Look at you, mooning like an adolescent over a middle-aged woman. She wanted to instruct him to pull himself together and get back to work. Then the mist closed over and her eyes refocused.

They stopped in front of the Griffin Building. All evidence of the strike had vanished: the sidewalk had been swept clean of mimeographed propaganda, the signs had disappeared. Spectators had been reabsorbed into the ebb and flow of street life. "Well," said Margaret, "I guess I better get back to work. I've enjoyed this. Maybe we can do it again soon."

Alicia wanted to do it again. "I'd like that," she said.

"Will you let me know one way or the other, what you decide?" And before Alicia had a chance to say yes, Margaret said, "And look, don't lose any sleep over what I told you about T and L. I only told you because I like you, Alicia, and you would have heard from someone else eventually. These things have a way of surfacing—like dead fish."

"I won't," Alicia said, knowing this assurance was untrue. The hurt was general, it filled her with dull pain.

"Would you like me to give you a bit of advice?"

"I don't think so," Alicia said. "I don't know whether I can handle it right now."

Margaret turned to go. "I'll call you," she said. "Be of good cheer."

"Thanks," said Alicia. She got into the elevator and for a moment, the very briefest moment, saw Roger's face in a close-up, a tear at the lip of either eye. "Be of good cheer," she said to herself as she sat down at her desk.

CHAPTER Eleven

ALICIA discovered that she was exhausted. Her knees burned, her chest felt cold and flat, her head ached. At her desk in the hall, Jenny sat typing letters, fielding calls that Alicia had, for once, asked not to have put through. Alicia used the next several hours in going over a manuscript that needed everything from punctuation to translation into English; the writing seemed to be in code. "The conceptions of dramatic and directive dominance, as contrasting types of power in a performance, can be applied, mutatis mutandis, to an interaction as a whole, where it will be possible to point out which of the two teams has more of which of the two types of power and which performers, taking the participants of both teams all together, lead in these two regards." Mutatis mutandis? Alicia reached for her American Heritage. M-M meant "the necessary changes having been made." Very apt. She would have to make these necessary changes, that was what she had been hired for. She hated this manuscript as much as any she could remember; it made her think of decay. "How do I get into these things?" Alicia said, sighing heavily. She had bought the manuscript—having lined up the entire Griffin editorial staff, sent Phyllis four urgent memos and procured two outside witnesses to attest to its author's importance—on the basis of an outline; unwritten, a chrysalis. How could she possibly have foretold that the author could not write?

When her phone buzzed Alicia was surprised; she had said, "Dire emergencies only, please, Jenny, I've *got* to get some work done." It was Barney on the other end, his voice in splinters.

"You sound awful," Alicia said. "What's the matter?" Oh, my God, she thought, something's happened to Toby. The blood left her head in a rush.

"Listen, Alicia, I've got some rotten news for you. Are you sitting down?"

"Yes," she said. "What's happened to Toby?"

"Nothing happened to Toby," Barney said. Then everything went briefly black. "It's Davida, honey, she's been hurt. I'm terribly sorry, I don't know how to tell you . . ."

Alicia jumped. "Davida!" she cried. "How hurt? I mean, how badly is she hurt? Is she okay?"

"I'm afraid she's not okay." His voice had taken on a professional inflection; this was the way, Alicia guessed, that her husband talked to the families of his patients who were not going to pull through.

The second button on Alicia's phone blinked and kept blinking. Alicia tried to ignore it. Below, on the street, a car screeched on its tires. An angry shout followed; some horns. "Tell me," she said.

"She's gone, Alicia, Davida's dead."

Gone. Gone where? The space inside Alicia's room glittered as if handfuls of Christmas tree sparkles had been released from the ceiling. Her breath seemed to be sucked from her lungs. She tried to say something. Nothing came out. Then she managed to whisper: "What happened?"

"They don't know for sure." The "they" was no doubt meant as a comforter. *They* are looking after you, *they* will make everything all right. "They tried to reach you earlier, but it seems you weren't there," Barney said. "So they tracked me down at the hospital. They wanted *me* to tell you. Considerate of them, wasn't it?"

"Who's they?"

"The New Hampshire State Police. I always thought those fellows were storm troopers but it turns out they're human after all. This fellow, his name is Dick Kelleher, called, and said he'd been trying to reach you. He found papers in the cabin with your name and work number on them. I suppose he could have left you a message."

"Don't go on like that," Alicia said sharply. "Just tell me what you're talking about." What papers, she wondered.

"Apparently there was some kind of violence but Kelleher wasn't all that specific about it. Look, Alicia, don't leave the office. I'll come by and pick you up. Okay? You promise you won't leave the office? I'll be there in ten minutes. Will you be all right?"

"Of course I'll be all right. What could possibly happen now?"

"Just wait there, don't leave," Barney said. Did he think she would do something weird? Then he didn't know her very well. After they hung up Alicia tried to absorb what had happened. From this moment life would be different, as it had been after John Kennedy was killed. She had been in the shower and when she came out her boyfriend, Bill, told her, looking up from his book: "The President's been zapped." That was why they had split; Bill had no feelings. Since then Alicia had two times: B. K. and A. K. Now it would shift to *before Davida* and *after*. She did not cry: there was no water in this stone. She touched her calendar; the symbols that together made up the word *April* looked entirely new, she had never seen them before. She ran her finger over the letters, hoping her touch would restore them to their original size and color. The manuscript she had been editing when the phone rang had altered too. Her hand holding the pencil, her stout, low-heeled shoes, the pain in her joints all had assumed a different shape. Everything hurt, everything shimmered.

The phone rang again. This time it was Toby. "When are you coming home, Mom? I have to ask you something."

"Daddy's coming by to pick me up in a few minutes," Alicia said, striving to sound normal. "Did May leave something in the oven?"

"I don't know," Toby answered. "I'm upstairs."

A phone rang and rang somewhere in the building beneath her and went unanswered. She realized then how late it was. The heat had been turned off. The building had emptied without her knowing it. Strange. Alicia's body began to shake. She vibrated, her jaws clacking against each other. She had to force the words out: "I'll be home soon, Toby. Be a good girl and go down and see what May left for us. Turn on the oven."

"Mom, you really sound weird. No offense."

"No offense taken," Alicia said.

In the Volvo Alicia glanced at Barney's profile. He looked as if he were concentrating very hard. It occurred to her that perhaps her husband thought he liked her more than he actually did. Or perhaps he was trying to contain his own distress.

"Bearer of bad news," she murmured. "Doesn't get off so easily."

"What did you say?" Barney asked. His voice seemed kind.

The traffic, as usual at this hour, was gummed into a solid mass. Lights came twinkling on in buildings flanking the avenue.

"Nothing," she said. "I want you to tell me more." She twisted her fingers together in her lap until she thought they would snap.

"The New Hampshire State cops got a call from one of Craig's neighbors who went over there for some reason, probably just snooping around, and found Davida on the floor." Barney stopped talking. Alicia waited.

"More," she said. "Where was Craig?"

"No Craig."

"What do you mean, no Craig? How did he escape?" It amazed Alicia that she could form a sentence in her head and then have the words emerge from her mouth in the right order.

"They think—they only think, now, they haven't come to any conclusions—that maybe Craig had something to do with it." The car in front of them inched forward. Barney put the Volvo into first.

"Oh, my God, you're not suggesting that Craig killed Davida, are you?"

"It isn't clear, nothing's clear yet. They only think he might be implicated, as they put it, because there was no trace of him. That is, his clothes were there and he'd been eating but he was gone. They're looking for him right now. They'll catch him."

"Wonderful," Alicia said. "They'll catch him. Don't let me see him. I'll kill him, I really will. I'll slice him in half. I'll dismember him." It was anger that brought on tears rather than sadness. Sadness dry, anger a flood.

"Alicia, please," her husband said. She did not understand what it was he was pleading with her about. Did he want her to shut up altogether or did her fury frighten him?

"They must have some idea how Davida was killed. This man Kelleher must have said *some*thing to you?"

"What difference does it make?" Generally a placid driver, Barney now stamped on the gas pedal and missed hitting the car in front of them by inches. "Shit," he said.

"Stop trying to protect me!" Alicia shrieked. "Watch out, you're going to kill us!" Alicia was almost glad that her husband was driving so badly; it gave her something to fix on, however briefly. "How come you know so much! How come they told you and not me! My God, this is crazy—listen to me . . ."

"I am," Barney said. "You shouldn't be fighting me, Alicia. I'm damned if I know why they called me, why they didn't wait for you, but that's the way it happened. I can't change that." He put his hand out and placed it on her thigh. Alicia felt the pressure of his fingers through the layers of cloth. But the gesture penetrated further, through her skirt and coat—it brushed her heart and she began to weep in earnest. A quiet, steady supply of tears washed over her cheeks. "Davida," she said, "how *could* you?"

"Allie, I'm so sorry," Barney told her. "Craig was bad news from the word go. He had rotten eyes and a Hapsburg nose, but did you ever notice his hands? They're like a stevedore's—huge hams. His parts didn't fit together right."

"Why do you say *did?* Do you think Craig's dead too?"

"Did I say did? I don't really know why I said that."

"She fucked a murderer, she ate lunch with him. She cooked meals for the man who was going to kill her. What did he do to her? *You* know, Barney, you're just not telling me!"

Barney's head swiveled sharply, his eyes taking her in, then they went away. "I don't see why it's so important," he said.

"Then you *do* know," Alicia said. "Why do you men always feel women are incapable of absorbing shock or sadness. We're better at it than you are. We're more used to it."

"Any other time I'd be eager to have a contest with you on that little point," Barney said. His voice was neutral. Silence filled the automobile. The car ahead moved clear and then began to move steadily. "They think she was strangled," Barney said simply.

"With that goddamn chain!" Alicia finished. "With that gold chain he gave her. Davida said it was ostentatious, she hated it. But she wore it. I guess she never took it off, not even in a cabin in the woods. She didn't like it, she said, but she wore it anyway. Gold is terrible."

"I don't know how it was done," Barney said.

"I'm sure of it," Alicia said. There was something salutary in discussing the operational mode like this, removing the blood and gore. "I thought it was Toby," Alicia said after a pause. But she hadn't meant to say this.

"Thought *what* was Toby?" Barney asked. "What does Toby have to do with it?"

"I thought something happened to Toby, the way you started out on the phone. But never mind, it's too stupid, really." She began to cry again. This time Barney said nothing. Finally he said, "Darling Allie, you've still got me and Toby. Davida was doomed."

"What are you talking about?" Alicia said.

"I'm angry at that fucking son of a bitch, so I'm sticking it on Davida. Writer she may have been, judge of men she certainly wasn't," Barney said.

"Oh, Barney, it's so awful. I've never known anyone who was murdered. Suicides, lots of suicides, but nobody murdered. I can't believe it, I don't want to believe it. How can you say Davida was doomed? She took the risky side of things, but she loved what she did. How can you *say* that?"

"Reading backwards I can," Barney said.

"And reading forwards we're all doomed!" Barney did not respond. He continued to drive, looking straight ahead. Alicia noticed that his hair had more gray in it than the last time she had looked. It was creeping up on all of them.

When they reached their house, Toby rushed at Alicia. "Mom," she cried, "can I get my ears pierced? There's a new place in the mall that'll do it for two-fifty. *Please,* Mom?"

Alicia tried to hug her daughter, but the child squirmed free and seemed interested only in getting Alicia's permission. "Of course," Alicia said, holding the tears back with a fearful effort.

Somewhat surprisingly, the law began immediately to hunt down the missing Craig. Alicia had assumed that police departments were manned by rejects. It was that old joke—"A defective on the Police Force. Oops, sorry, I meant to say a detective on the police farce"—that joke which made the police seem so inept. But this time, as in a television playlet, their people trailed the suspect to a loft in SoHo, where an old friend of his, a woman who covered cork surfaces with bright acrylic paint, had taken him in, not asking—or caring—why he had turned up on her doorstep at three-thirty in the morning looking as if he had spent the winter with a pack of wolves. The woman gave him a place to crash and fed him some eggs and then went back to sleep. When the detective rang her doorbell later that day she was at work. The woman answered his question and pointed to Craig, sleeping on a mattress in a corner. "You mean him? He's been here for the last six weeks." The detective, fingering his gun under his jacket, informed her that if she were lying she would be considered an accessory and asked her if she knew what that meant. She nodded and said, "He came here last night." Craig, awake now, sprang at his hostess and tried to take her by the throat. The detective and his partner who lingered in the hall, quieted their catch, two trained soldiers against one frightened civilian, no match at all, and hustled him out to their car, calling to the woman that she'd be hearing from them by and by. Once inside the automobile Craig tried smiling but it came out a snarl.

As soon as Alicia was certain that legal wheels had begun to turn, she lost interest in the details. They mattered about as much as the fact that too soon after Davida was murdered, someone rented her apartment and agreed to help pack up her stuff. The picture of Craig which appeared in the Metro/Region section of the *Boston Globe* showed an animal baring its teeth out of the side window of an automobile. His face was the face of a lunatic. Alicia had a hard time putting it together with the sleek person she had known as Davida's boyfriend. When she saw the picture in the paper, she flung it across the room, where it opened out like a fan, its pages scattering on the rug. Toby was full of questions about what happened to Davida Franklin;

Alicia bucked each one to her husband, who answered them with sad patience.

Sleep was a problem. Alicia woke at two-thirty and thought about what it would be like to be living in the same house with someone who was going to murder you but you didn't know it, you weren't even sufficiently aware to be frightened. You were, in fact, so disarmed by this person that fear had never entered the house, had come nowhere near it, was hundreds of miles away in the next county where beatings took place and people went to the hospital with cracked skulls. At what precise moment had Davida recognized in the man who gave her so much enjoyment in bed the man who would kill her? Or had it happened not all at once, but, like an outage, by a flicker here, a dimming, then a brightening, then the lights go off for good?

Would it happen over a meal, and Davida looks over and says, "Where are you, Craig? I mean, you're sitting here with me, eating your tuna fish sandwich, but you're a million miles in outer space. Where *are* you?"

And Craig glances at her as if he hadn't the faintest idea who she was, his eyes disheveled.

And when the truth sinks in—he wants to kill you—*then* what? Do you try to escape? Do you try to defend yourself? The movies say you pick up a pair of shears and just as he's about to do you in, you stab him in the back with it, turning the tables. Or, if there's no weapon around, do you run and lock yourself in the bathroom—stupid, because all he has to do is wait you out. Maybe he's impatient and, crazed with murderous lust, takes up the wood-splitting ax and hacks the bathroom door with it, drags you out by the hair, throws you down and begins to hack *you* up. Alicia found she was breathing hard and shallowly, the excitement ran through her body as fast blood. And what about the chain, does he twist it as you would a wet washcloth and what happens then? Does your flesh break and bleed or do you simply choke? What are your eyes doing?

Open? Shut? And your legs, do they scramble and kick or do they go limp? How long does it take? As long as five minutes? What are you thinking during that time? A *No* so loud and strong it bursts the blood vessels inside your skull, a betrayal beyond belief, a regret for your own frailty. "Oh, God," Alicia moaned.

Two days after Davida's death her mother, Hulda Kracow, called Alicia from New York. "You'll speak at her memorial service?" Hulda said.

"Of course."

"You were her best friend," the older woman said. She had a faint trace of Europe in her voice. Alicia did not know what Hulda's apartment looked like but she saw it now: a stale apartment, in deep shadow. The furniture in the room was lined up at right angles to each other and through the window she could see a thin stripe of Manhattan's sky and an apartment building across the street. The predominant color was brown—brown rug, brown couch flecked with metallic threads, tan walls, brown picture of a woman in a floor-length dress. She also saw part of another room she imagined to be a bedroom. It all fit Davida's description of her mother's general circumstances. Mrs. Kracow was a vast woman with butcher's arms and a bosom that seemed too enormous for one woman to carry around without substantial assistance. She sat in a mustard-colored wing chair. She wore a loose housedress but her hair was done up, she had been able to fix her hair. She seemed to be alone.

"I'm glad she told you that we were friends," Alicia said.

"Her editor," Hulda said this proudly. My daughter the writer.

"She was a marvelous writer, Mrs. Kracow, a joy to work with." Don't go on, Alicia told herself, or you'll start to cry again.

"Davida was a stubborn child. And please call me Hulda. She was very stubborn. Her father wouldn't let her cut her hair when all the other girls did. She was terribly angry with him but it didn't do no good, her father had the last word. Everything else Davida won. She stood her ground like a boy and she won." My daughter the man.

"She won about the disposal of her remains, too." At this, Davida's mother began to cry. She drew a handkerchief from a pocket over her hip and put it to her face. Alicia felt as if she were going to be sick. "How could she have herself cremated?" Hulda cried. "It's against nature."

"Please, Hulda, she did what she thought she had to. It was her choice to make, what to do with." The word "body" stuck to Alicia's tongue and wouldn't be freed. "Please, Hulda, we'll do a memorial service that'll make it up to you, I promise." How could she promise such an unbelievable thing? "Would you like me to come down to New York and stay with you for a while?"

"No. No, thanks, my sister Annie is here with me." At that moment Alicia saw a tiny woman, wearing a housedress six sizes smaller but just like Hulda's, walk into the room and put her arm across Hulda's shoulder, a gesture which produced more weeping. The two women's faces, fat and thin, were identically pinched with grief.

Then Hulda shook herself and blew her nose. Alicia waited. The smell of the cologne with which Hulda had moistened the handkerchief traveled over the telephone wire. It was lemony. Then the scene blurred, started to fade, and finally misted over. Only Hulda's voice remained. Hulda said, "I know you'll think of something nice to say about Davida. Not too long or fancy, just something my daughter would have liked."

Alicia, sickened, said she might read a passage from one of Davida's books. "I'll try to find something appropriate," she added.

"Appropriate?" Hulda said. "She didn't write about . . ." Hulda couldn't finish her sentence. The topic took away her powers of speech. Alicia, having already mapped a talk about

Davida's new book for the sales conference scheduled for the following week, realized that her next public appearance on Davida's behalf would be as eulogist. She had never done a eulogy: how does one get from one end of it to the other without breaking down?

Barney tried to help Alicia but his brand of aid—"Talking it out"—worked against her, and Alicia found herself hiding from her husband, leaving the room on a pretext when he entered it, falling asleep immediately after dinner, having to wash the dishes or make a telephone call, avoiding the conversations he seemed determined on holding.

Everything in Alicia's life during the week after Davida's death floated and bobbed as she struggled to accept the fact that she would never see her friend again. There were sharp moments when she would have liked to slip under and join the dead.

On Sunday morning at two-thirty Alicia woke up and saw the following:

Davida moved sleepily around in a kitchen with a large black stove in it, a window, a rough oak floor, a closet with a Franz Kline poster thumbtacked to it, a galvanized bucket by the sink and an old-fashioned toaster whose sides opened out to receive the bread. She was wearing her new woolen pants, which stretched over her thighs, and a blue bandanna on her head, tied on the nape of her neck. She had on a turtleneck sweater under her burnt orange flannel shirt, which she hadn't buttoned. Davida's face was shiny. It looked very warm in the kitchen. Sunlight slanted across a wooden counter and hit the corner of the stove. Davida removed a carton of eggs from the refrigerator and set it on the counter next to a bright yellow mixing bowl. The scene was tranquil, awash in domesticity. Davida made a contented, humming sort of noise and her eyes seemed unfocused. She neither smiled nor frowned; her body was detached from her thoughts. Alicia knew that she was rewriting a passage, in her head, a passage about, of all things, keeping a large house in order. She tossed out several words and added some new ones. Then she smiled, showing her fine teeth. She whispered something, then nodded. Her hands, meanwhile, had broken five eggs by cracking them against the edge of the bowl. She got some butter out of the refrigerator and knifed a portion of it into a pan waiting on the stove. The butter hissed. Her temples shone in the light. On her feet were the kind of ankle-high fleece-lined slippers grandmothers buy their grandchildren for Christmas.

Then Craig was in the kitchen with Davida; Alicia had not seen him come in. He stood behind her; Davida heard or sensed him and turned. She put out her hand to touch his shoulder; he jumped back as if burned.

"Hey, Craig," she said, "don't worry, I left my pigsticker at home."

"I don't know that," Craig said. It wasn't a voice Alicia recognized. It was dark, dark; it shocked the hair on the back of her neck.

"Come on, honey-pot," Davida said, flashing a strained sort of smile. "I'm just joking. You're getting so sensitive, can't you tell when I'm joking?"

"Oh, we all know about jokes," said Craig. "Especially you writers, you know how that old unconscious works: in jokework, veritas." His body made Alicia think of a sculpture where the proportions have been deliberately messed around with: shoulders too wide, hips too narrow, legs too short, the backbone seeming to occupy more space than it needed. A hulk. A gorilla. He stood there staring at her; the menace from his torso fairly breathed.

"But you know I love you," Davida said. Alicia recognized uncertainty on Davida's face and in her voice. She figured Craig probably saw it too. She knew what was coming; why were they making her watch it? She shook her head, trying to get rid of this tableau but in response to the shake the room seemed even more saturated with reality. The colors throbbed.

"Bullshit," Craig said.

"You're not kidding, are you?" Davida said in a new tone. She dipped her body slightly as she asked this; the shirttails lapped at her thighs.

Craig frowned with his entire face. Then he brought up his right hand, making an arc with his arm; his fist brushed Davida's nose and landed against her cheek with a crunch Alicia moaned and whispered, "Stop, oh stop." Beside her in bed Barney rumbled but did not wake.

"Craig!" Davida cried. "Don't. Stop, you're hurting me. What are you doing?" Her hand flew to her cheek where it tried to comfort her flesh. A dab of blood hit her upper lip. Her tongue licked at it.

"And how many times have you hurt me?" he said, beginning to sound normal again. Alicia's mouth was dry, then it filled with nasty-tasting saliva. "For instance," Craig continued, "I know for a fact you fucked that kid I saw you wiggling your ass at outside the B.P.L. The two of you had stars in your eyes. I know that let's-fuck look, the two of you . . Craig tested his legs, bouncing up and down like a boxer.

"What the hell are you talking about?" Davida hugged herself. The blood under her nose looked like a dot of red paint. "That was six months ago, he was just a kid who started talking to me in the reading room, for chrissake, he recognized me from a jacket picture. He wanted to talk to a novelist. A groupie. And anyway, what were you doing—spying on me? What's happening to you, Craig, you've been weird the last couple of days. Are you taking something again? What are you on?"

"Nothing," he said. "I'm not taking anything. And I don't believe it about that kid. You've been bullshitting me all along, you tell a lousy lie, I can tell every time."

"I'm not lying, Craig. I'm telling you the truth. I never saw him again. This is crazy!"

Again, Craig brought his right hand up, hitting the bowl on the counter, overturning it. The eggs dripped, ran over the side of the counter. When they reached the floor Craig stepped in them, smearing his shoe.

"You're acting crazy," Davida told him. "Please, let's go in the other room and sit down and we can talk about what's really bothering you. Please, Craig!"

"Get away from me," he said. "You're no good. You've got a fancy imagination all right, but you can't tell a good lie. I'm on to you."

Davida started to move like someone in the wrong place, covertly. The house was isolated. Alicia had the sense that it was set somewhere in a clearing ringed by trees or wide gray fields, out of shouting distance from everything but crows and frogs.

"I'll bet you're going to use me in one of your books. Aren't you? Say something, don't just stand there like a dummy, open your lying cunt mouth."

"You're crazy," Davida said. Alicia desperately wanted to shut her up, but this inflammatory word crazy kept escaping from her mouth.

"Don't call me crazy, Davida, I'm warning you, don't say that again." And Craig banged his fist on the counter, forks and a tin measuring cup hopped and clattered. Davida began to back out of the room. Her face, except for the blood, was white.

"Freeze!" he shouted. "Where do you think you're going?"

"Anywhere away from you. You're on drugs again and it's making you . . ." She hesitated. "Sick." Davida tried a desperate dash and nearly made it, but Craig grabbed her arm in time. His warning then turned into a murderous notion, the notion took hold and exploded inside his head. He began to behave like an animal. He growled, showed his teeth, his body vibrated. Davida, poised between fury and terror, stared at

Craig, unbelieving. Then she turned her head as if expecting someone to come in and rescue her. For a split second Alicia thought that Davida was looking at *her,* waiting for *her.* She shuddered, opened and shut her eyes several times but could not erase the scene; the projector kept right on rolling. Davida pulled, Craig held on. Davida screamed. The bandanna slipped from her head; her hair looked pasted down.

The noises from Davida's throat broke the reel. Alicia threw herself out of bed and rushed to the window, pressing her head against the glass, which was surprisingly cold. Then the picture returned. She was being punished; why were they making her watch the whole thing?

Davida moved awkwardly, half turning, half ducking. Craig made a desperate grab for her and caught her just above the wrist and gave her arm a fearful twist. The look on her face said he had probably broken a bone. She screamed and screamed; it sounded like a gull or a hawk; it hurt Alicia's ears, it pierced her breast. Davida screamed and screamed, stopping only long enough to draw enough breath to continue screaming. She scrambled as if trying to crawl up a bank of mud. Alicia's own heart pumped furiously; under her breasts two lines of sweat formed.

"Davida!" she shrieked, waking Barney.

"Alicia," he said, "What's the matter? What are you doing over there?" His voice was thick with phlegm. He cleared his throat a couple of times.

"I saw Davida being killed," Alicia said, not turning around.

"What do you mean you saw it?" Barney turned on his reading light. The brightness stabbed Alicia in the eyes. She blinked. The scene inside the kitchen was gone. "You mean you had a nightmare."

"No, I mean I *saw* it."

"Alicia—" Barney began but Alicia interrupted him. "I saw exactly what happened," she said. "Craig came up behind her, acting crazy, paranoid, accusing her of things. Then he grabbed her. He was taking some awful drug, I guess. She was screaming and screaming. . . . It was terrible."

"A nightmare," Barney said.

"Barney. I just told you. It *wasn't* a dream." She watched him pulling himself out of bed and moving toward her. His legs seemed stiff.

"All right, whatever you say, it wasn't a dream." He reached out an arm.

"You don't believe me," she said, almost in tears. "How can I make you believe me?"

"I *do* believe you, Alicia. Please now, come back to bed. It's three A.M."

"Not for Davida it isn't," she said.

"Please come back to bed," Barney said. It seemed to Alicia that he didn't know what to do with her. He began to pull her by the arm.

"It wasn't a dream," she repeated again. "I know, because I got up and went to the window and still saw it, it just kept going. Craig was just about to kill her when you woke up."

"And I stopped it, didn't I?" Barney said. Alicia, an obedient child, climbed back into bed. The sheets were still warm.

"I guess so," Alicia said. "I'm terribly upset, I feel as if I was losing my mind. Help me, Barney."

"There're too many things at once. Davida, the New York job, your work, these . . . well, whatever you call them, these 'episodes' of yours." She heard the quotation marks.

"Too many things," she said.

"You're trembling," Barney told her. "I'll hold you."

He didn't try to make love to her but fell asleep again almost immediately. Gently she pushed him over and away.

And then the reel started up again. It started with a kind of crashing noise. Craig was howling, Davida pounded his sides with balled fists, weapons about as effective as feathers. She began to slide now, her knees having bent under and her heels taking off as if the floor was greased. He brought his right fist down over Davida's left eye. She cried out but more softly; she knew she hadn't a prayer. Blood ran down over her jaw. Craig pulled his leg back like a punter on the field and kicked Davida's pelvis. This produced the loudest scream yet, a noise that seemed to galvanize Craig. He put his hand beneath her turtleneck, from the bottom, raising it. The gold rope lay against her chest, a warm snake. The pendant winked its eye. Under her bra Davida's chest rose and fell like a bellows. Her eyelids fluttered quickly, dying wings. Alicia guessed she was about to pass out. Now Craig straddled her, left and right legs, one on either side. He reached down and with his paw tore at her bra, which for a moment or two was stronger than he was, then it gave with a popping sound. He began to punch her breasts while Davida moaned.

"You must go," he said. "Go!" Then he grabbed the chain he had given Davida and began to twist it, tighter and tighter against her throat. Her face turned pink, then violet, then blue. Her tongue emerged from between her lips. Briefly her eyes opened but only white showed. Her feet jerked several times, the heels lifting slightly off the floor, then they flopped sideways. Craig held on for dear life, still twisting and grunting and twisting. Under each arm two crescents of sweat darkened his shirt.

Can't you see she's dead, Alicia said to him. Let her go now, she's dead. You didn't have to do that, you could have told her to get out, said you never wanted to see her again, she wouldn't have bothered you. How do you know what's going to happen? Didn't you know, Davida, didn't he give you any warnings, any signs?

The reel ended and the scene went blank. Alicia moaned and rolled over onto her stomach, pressing her face against the pillowcase, which smelled faintly of soap. What Craig did after killing Davida mattered as much as what happened to the eggs on the floor, the butter, the lit stove. Alicia continued to weep, hearing the sounds in her house: the hum of the clock-radio, the furnace two floors below, Barney's uniform, gentle breathing. The tears drying on her cheeks, she lay in bed mourning her friend so dead, finished, ashes in a cookie jar.

The crying actually had not helped at all; it had merely peeled the scab again, exposing her wound to the sick air.

CHAPTER Twelve

"CAPTIVE on Cape Cod," Alicia said. The smell of dead clams went directly from the flats to her nose to her stomach; she thought she could probably get used to it if, God forbid, she lived here the year round.

Alicia Baer, along with the Griffin crew—editorial, Sales, Promotion, some business staff, Phyllis Vance—had been bused out to a spit of land just beyond the Sagamore Bridge and was quartered in an ugly spreading stain on the upper Cape landscape known as the Jolly Whaler Motel. It was to Mickey Eversharp that Alicia addressed her remark about being a captive.

"Sure," Mickey said, "I agree with you. But have you noticed how the bloodies here are twice the size of the ones you get in Boston? They want to make it up to you with booze."

"But they don't kill the jailhouse atmosphere," Alicia said. "At least not for me." Most of what Alicia had said since Davida's death emerged from one small tendril; the rest of her was steeped in grief. It was astonishing how normal she sounded, how resonant and upbeat the voice, how cheerful the eyes, how pulled together her general appearance. Inside, deep mourning; black, with tears.

Outside the Jolly Whaler it was cold and raw, several weeks, seasonally speaking, behind Boston. When Alicia started out on a solitary walk, the wind got underneath her coat and ran up her legs while the air bit into her cheeks and made her eyes run. The great out-of-doors was a letdown; it was vile and damp. Bare shrubs, whipped by an Atlantic wind, were tangles of dead snakes. She turned around and headed back to the Jolly Whaler.

During the conference, a semiannual three-day event designed to acquaint the Griffin travelers with the upcoming season's list of books (in this case the Fall List, that is, those books published between September and the following March), Alicia thought of herself as under house arrest, an important personage they couldn't afford to let out of their sight. She decided that, like other prisoners of note, she would put the time to good use and try to engage in some heavy thinking. She would try, for instance, to make up her mind about New York. Try.

There was little to do in the Jolly Whaler except drink and talk shop—which is exactly what Griffin's management had in mind. The motel had eight conference rooms, windowless affairs with accordion-type partitions for easy expansion and contraction, four bars, and seventy-five bedrooms with identical furniture.

"I hear that off-season the Cape is just one huge chapter of A.A. gone amok," Mickey said to Alicia, swigging. His eyes were getting red like the bloody Mary and he looked content.

"I can only drink so much," Alicia told him, "then I fall asleep. God's protecting me, I guess."

"Lucky you," Mickey said.

People had been looking at her oddly for the past few days, and not because she tended to fall asleep after two drinks. It was because they had heard rumors that Alicia would, would not, might, might not be leaving Griffin and going to a big fat job in New York—commonly referred to as "there." Alicia was certain the rumors had reached everyone at Griffin; after all, Margaret Bannister had heard them. Where had they started?

She could not recall having told anyone but Davida. No one. It was a secret, she thought, as well hidden as the love letters she had received from a man she had almost married and had buried in the basement in the side pocket of a suitcase slimy with cobwebs and mildew. In a sense, everyone at Griffin had read her letters. Alicia knew they looked at her with suspicion and some of them, with envy, but they avoided talking about it to her, as if she might have a distressing disease they didn't want to hear about. As for her invaders, they had followed her here to Barnstable County, in a pack; she could feel their breath on her neck and hear their whispering voices: "We *never* leave you alone, Alicia."

A man who looked more like a linebacker than a book salesman came up to the table—fashioned to resemble a hatch cover—shared by Mickey and Alicia in the Fo'c'sle Room. "Greetings," he said. "Mind if I join you two?"

"Hello, Jason," Mickey said. "You know Alicia Baer?"

"Sure," Jason said. "How ya doing?"

"Fine, thank you," Alicia said. Jason McHugh asked them if they'd tried the sauna. He complained about the continental breakfast; too skimpy. Then he said, "Too bad about your author, Davida Franklin. It's a damn shame. They caught the guy who did it, didn't they?"

"Yes, they did." Alicia tightened all her muscles.

"She was a very solid writer," McHugh continued. "It wasn't always that easy getting her books on the shelves but she had real class—I'll say that for her."

"She was classy, wasn't she?" Alicia said.

"I heard she was working on another book when she died," McHugh said. He wore a pale lavender shirt with amethyst-colored cuff links the size of robin's eggs. Alicia wondered if he was gay.

"They found her manuscript in the house where it happened," Mickey said. "We didn't expect that, did we, Alicia?" He looked at her with concern.

"It's her best book," Alicia managed to say. Davida had left her true legacy on a bureau in the bedroom of Craig's cabin: a manuscript that not only included a final chapter, but one that needed very little editing. A very nice piece of work, a complete and touching story. So Davida's agonized progress reports had either been invented or were sincere but wrong. She had been in excellent shape; her novel had passages in it that made the skin on the back of Alicia's neck contract and prickle. "I think this one is Davida's grapefruit book," Alicia said. It broke her heart to joke but what else could she do?

"What? Her grapefruit book? I don't get you," McHugh said. He scratched his head to underscore the bafflement.

"That's Alicia's way of saying her *break-through* book," Mickey said, supplying the translation. At the next table four Griffin folk erupted in the kind of laughter that follows only an extremely dirty story.

"Oh, I understand," McHugh said. "It's a joke. Grapefruit—breakthrough." He seemed uncomfortable; Alicia regretted the joke.

"Just a misguided attempt to be clever," she said, stumbling through an apology.

"That's okay," McHugh said. His neck was wrinkled, his eye sockets sagged; he was older than he looked. The life, Alicia thought, of a traveling book salesman can't be all beer and skittles. This must be one of the high points of his year. McHugh's tan jacket looked like cashmere but was probably a blend. "Are you two ready for another round?" he said, looking over his shoulder for their waitress. "This one's on me," which Alicia realized wasn't true, as it was all on Griffin.

"There's Peter Fairchild," Mickey said. "I thought he'd taken off for New York." Peter took a seat at the bar across the room.

"He came up to present his three books," Alicia said, trying to get Peter to notice them and failing. "He's doing it as a favor to their authors who'd be orphaned otherwise."

McHugh couldn't seem to stay off the subject of Davida

Franklin's novel. "I don't want to sound morbid or anything, but shouldn't we do something special for her?" he asked.

"Her novel won't be out for at least nine months, maybe even a year," Mickey said. Alicia could tell he was trying to deflect McHugh's prodding. She smiled at him weakly.

"That'll give us plenty of time," McHugh said.

"I think I know what you're driving at," Mickey Eversharp told the salesman, "and I'd be glad to talk to you about it—some other time." The last three words he underlined with heavy black lines.

Alicia sighed; her grief came back in a rush, filling her lungs with black soot. I should have known, she said to herself, all the signs said Davida was in trouble but I thought it was Toby. Even my E.S.P. is second-rate.

"What's the matter, hon?" Mickey said. "You look pale."

"I need a little air," she said.

"I'll go with you," Mickey said.

"In a minute," Alicia said. Her knees felt soft and she wasn't sure she could stand without their buckling.

"I hope I didn't say anything to upset you," McHugh said. He frowned and began to play with a book of matches.

"Of course not," Alicia said, her impulse to reassure anyone who seemed to need it carrying her along.

"I mean," he went on, "I think it would be a goddamn shame not to do whatever we can for the lady's last book—especially if it's as terrific as you say it is. I'll do everything I can for it, you have my word. It's a rotten shame . . ."

"Oh, shit," Alicia said. Without warning the tears that had been gathering for an offensive massed and went rolling over the slopes of her face. They were large and warm.

"Hey," McHugh said. "I didn't mean to make you cry. I'm sorry, I guess I shouldn't have brought up the subject with you here, I didn't know . . ." He looked at Mickey, who nodded solemnly.

"That's okay," Alicia said through her handkerchief. *"I'm* sorry."

Those lower in rank than editor were made to share a room; editors and above got singles. Alicia lay down before dinner. Her head ached and she felt puffy from too much food, too little exercise. Her phone rang. It was Peter Fairchild. "I'm in the next room," he said.

"Just like Doris Day and Rock Hudson," she said. "How's New York?"

"Filthy but filled with lovely things for those with the scratch."

"We miss you," she said. "No one has the nerve to get mouthy with Phyllis the way you did."

"What about Mickey?" Peter said.

"He doesn't count—she's not his boss."

"You coming to New York?" Peter said.

"You know, too?"

"Listen, honey child, there isn't much Peter Fairchild hasn't heard." Out in the hall the sounds of loud conversation, several people talking at once, filtered through the door. She said, "I have to make up my mind by next week. It's so hard, Peter, I don't seem to be getting closer to a decision." It was strange the way things kept balancing off, as if she were evening the legs of a table by sawing each in turn. "What do you think? Should I do it?"

"Hold on there," Peter said. "I stopped giving that kind of advice years ago. I don't want to be responsible for any disasters. Go on, say it, Allie, I'm some weird kind of friend."

"Well, you are, you know. And don't worry, I probably would discount what you said anyway. You've got a vested interest in New York." She hadn't noticed, but as they talked the sky had gone from gray to black and she was now lying in the dark. The room's smells intensified. Cigarette smoke clung to the blankets, clammy sea air drifted in through the slightly open window. Her own smells, the faintest trace of perfume on her wrist. She was tired and reluctant to get dressed again and be cheerful during dinner with the Griffin salesmen.

"Alicia, whatever you decide, you've got to trust yourself. You've got great instincts—didn't anyone ever tell you that?"

"Please, Peter," she said. "I'm going to cry."

"And if you come to New York I'm going to take you to lunch at the best delicatessen on Sixth Avenue and buy you some Cel Ray . . ."

"Peter . . . shut up, please."

Presenting a book to the sales force meant an inspirational talk designed to light fires under dampened souls. Some editors made of this an opportunity to show off, to be actors, to reveal oratorical talents kept under lock and key for most of their lives. Others found it an ordeal, comparable to parading naked in front of a thousand people inclined to jeer and shriek insults. Alicia, who had now been at it for eight years, had early accepted the advice of a Griffin editor long since retired, who had told her that all she had to do was pretend she was someone else, someone she didn't know and probably wouldn't like, better to choose someone like a politician or a movie star, with the tricks down pat. Alicia decided that she would be Florence Henderson, the woman who sold Wesson Oil on TV, because this Florence never stopped smiling no matter what, and was neither a spiller nor a person people spilled on. This Florence was the woman most people saw when they looked at Alicia, in a less pretty and slightly older version. Most people—those who knew her because they conducted business with her on the phone, ate lunch with her from time to time, cleaned her teeth, filled the tank of her Volvo with gas, delivered her mail, handed her change at the Puritan Deli—saw this neat package, a woman reasonably dressed, never in leather pants or headbands, with a reedy intelligent voice, sharp eyes and steady hands. Alicia was sure this Florence TV person was a fraud, a front, but in moments of self-analysis, she was aware she couldn't dismiss Florence by so simple an accusation as fraud. She was onstage too much of the time not to be taken seriously. She was, in fact, as "real" as the real Alicia, the one ridden with anxiety, indecision, and damned if she would do anything simple to please someone else. I am two people, she realized with a jolt each time Phyllis introduced her.

The next morning's session took place in the Chart Room around several folding tables with loosely pleated nylon skirts jammed together over an expanse of pale green, heavy-duty carpeting. The Chart Room filled rapidly with smoke. Wesley Moorehead, a senior editor, got unsteadily to his feet to talk about his several books. His first book was *Au Pair,* an epistolary novel which Alicia had read in manuscript, found very funny and endorsed in her report: "twenty thousand in hard cover, almost certain reprint sale, required reading for the *Preppy Handbook* crowd." *Au Pair*'s story was in the hands of a smart-ass teenager, via weekly letters to her best friend about the pretentious and wicked family she works for. As Wesley Moorehead rose, all blood seemed to drain from his head; his skin went ashy, his shoulders sagged. The paper he held clattered in a trembling hand. His teeth glistened, the whites of his eyes radiated panic. Alicia poked Mickey, sitting next to her, and whispered, "He's phobic about speaking in public; he's going to faint."

"Like last time?" Mickey said.

"Poor soul," Alicia whispered. As Wesley began to speak the words blurred; he started to sweat like a jogger. "The plot of this novel," he said, "concerns this—uh—baby-sitter, she's the eponymous *au pair* of the title. *Au pair,* you see, is a French expression meaning live-in baby-sitter, not exclusively for babies, but for any youngster . . ." Wesley Moorehead trailed off, looked up, hoping he'd said enough, and when it was clear that they needed more, sighed deeply, a shuddering sigh heard around the Chart Room, and continued. "The name of this baby-sitter is Lolly, the family who hire her for a summer on Martha's Vineyard, you see part of Lolly's difficulties arise from having nowhere to go on the one half-day a week they give her, the family that hires her is called Oakes."

"Who gives a damn what their name is," Mickey whispered to Alicia, "Just give us the high points."

Moorehead looked briefly up. One hundred and thirty-six eyes stared; his own eyes retreated to the paper in his palsied right hand. "The Oakes kids are Sonny, Mark and Susie. They are, respectively, ten, eight and five years old—quite a handful for anyone. Lolly, I forgot to say, comes from a large family, eight brothers and sisters, so she is up to these Oakes kids' tricks. Mother Oakes—Fanny—exploits Lolly unabashedly, makes her wet-mop the kitchen floor every day, take out all the garbage and clean up after the family dog, who has a vomiting problem. Meanwhile, Mike, the father, can't keep his hands off this delectable piece of goods who looks after his children."

Wesley's voice kept dropping. He took out a handkerchief and drew it across his brow; he was speaking now in just above a whisper.

"Can't hear you!" someone called out.

"Sorry," Wesley croaked. "I'll try to speak up."

"Give him the hook," Eversharp said. "He's killing his book."

"Oh, dear," Alicia said, "Why do they make him do it?"

"Why do they *let* him do it?" Eversharp asked.

Phyllis Vance had designed the program. She inserted herself between two editors so that she would seem more one of them. *Democratic,* thought Alicia, who mistrusted her boss at every turn. The fact was Phyllis was going to stick out and be singular whether she spoke first, last or never. Her presence there was sufficient. Her speaking style was polished, the words emerging discretely and flowing, the sentences rotund, varied, arching.

Her thoughts were coherent. She did wonderful things with her body, thrusting one hip, leg attached, forward, as if about to take a giant step into a bright future. Gracefully, she led her left arm through arcs, circles, figure eights, and other abstractions in the now stinging and fetid air of the Chart Room. Smoke had begun to mix with animal odors, armpits and crotch, scalp, and generalized boredom. The Vance chin was firm and uplifted, her voice clear and forceful. She wore a pale rust-colored dress that Alicia put in the three-to-five-hundred-dollar category and medium-heeled pumps of Italian origin.

"A commanding presence, wouldn't you say?" Mickey said softly to Alicia, leaning toward her. He smelled of cologne and something musky and animal. Her nose twitched.

"*Bien sûr,*" she said, wondering if she were going to adopt any more of Davida's habits for her own use.

Alicia watched two people light up cigarettes and puff as if they wished they were smoking joints instead of tobacco. Smoke hung over the table, a pale, dirty cloud. Alicia put her nose into her sleeve; it smelled like train upholstery. She wished she could get up and walk out. Then, tuning out, she recrossed her knees, which had somewhat stiffened from having been immobile so long, and wondered if Tolland and Lutwidge's sales conferences were any less awful than this one. She had heard that at Sales Conference time, the entire staff of T & L was transported by charter flight down to a warm island in the Caribbean.

Alicia drifted on, afloat, brushing Barney, who must have been sitting there, expecting her. The expression on his face was sad and resigned, as if he knew that whatever happened, whatever she decided, their life might still be cracked down the middle, irrevocably. Then she brushed Toby, once so robust and acquiescent, now skinny and covert. Oh, Toby, she thought, I'm losing you, aren't I? Tell me I'm not! She almost screamed this before she realized where she was.

Right now she would enjoy a visit to the New York

headquarters of Tolland and Lutwidge, all chrome and mirrors, with inky wall-high glass panels and dead ends. One out-of-town author—so the story went—had walked down a corridor, then turned to walk down its arm and discovered too late that what she thought was space was actually a mirror; she had put a split in her forehead that required eleven stitches to bring together.

Alicia was drawn to this shiny smoothness in spite of its hazards; it suggested that Tolland and Lutwidge knew how to operate, twentieth-century style, an assumption that was almost as useful as the six-foot panel of mirror behind the receptionist's desk (the better to arrange your features before that crucial appointment?). Alicia was afraid of getting musty, cobwebbed, cranky, constipated. The chairs in the Griffin waiting area looked as if they had been liberated from its president's grandmother's front parlor in Nahant. Alicia was afraid that if she stayed in Boston she would turn into granny's chair, she would never have the pleasures of chrome or cool glass tables or chairs whose arms were so cold they felt frosted.

At long last Phyllis wound up a stunning forty-five-minute show. Her books were steeped in commerce; she was a self-fulfilling prophecy: the most successful editor attracted the authors who wrote—or could be counted on to produce—the "biggest" books. Should one of Phyllis's authors produce a less than commercially successful book, it was nosed into the "prestige" category where it sat in red ink but with admirable critical notices, a book the Chairman of the Board could note with paternal "pride" (and hidden shame, like a son who has made his mark in choreography).

"And now, here is our intrepid Alicia Baer, with a lovely spring nosegay of books," Phyllis said.

"She's lost her marbles," Mickey said, giving Alicia a covert pat on the rump for encouragement, as she rose.

All at once Alicia became Florence Henderson, revealing teeth in a wide smile, nodding and enunciating clearly as a chorister. She told them about her first book, a history of New England sea towns—Salem, Portsmouth, Mystic, New Bedford—a book she had concocted herself out of articles by a local writer publishing in local magazines; about a biography of Willa Cather that she had been nursing along for six years—a "major" biography, which meant that no one else would attempt another one for at least another six years; and about a first novel sent by an agent, which had had to be rewritten four times and which almost sent both author and editor to a mental hospital for a short rest; and finally a book she thought of as inside out because it had been a television series first, albeit a series of intellectual content.

Then she said, "I'd like you all to know that Davida Franklin will have a novel on our next Spring List. It's a lovely story about a woman about to retire from a long career in civil service who finds herself inadvertently involved in international intrigue. No one can write like Davida Franklin, but I know you enjoy comparisons so I'll say that *Join the Dance* is a sort of combination Eric Ambler and Muriel Spark. It's short on polemic and long on the kind of narrative that hooks you immediately and keeps you going. Next time around, at our next conference, I'll tell you more about *Join the Dance.* Since it's her latest, and last, book, I hope you'll all do your very best with it—as a tribute to a really wonderful author." She was afraid, for a moment, that they were going to applaud, but they didn't, they sat quietly while she sat down herself. Death had subdued them.

The Sales Conference cruised in space, unanchored to any life near it, to Boston streets, MBTA schedules, the corruption leaking from the Massachusetts legislature, and to the daily needs of the family members of those held captive in the Jolly Whaler on Cape Cod.

Alicia stretched out diagonally across the king-sized mattress. Her feet were cold, she missed the bulk of her husband; he threw off heat when asleep. At eleven-forty Alicia was watching Johnny Carson fingering his chin, taking a swipe at his nose, bringing his hands together as if about to point them in prayer, when the phone on the bedside table rang softly.

"How are you?" Barney said.

"I'm fine," she answered. "Why are you calling, is something wrong?"

"No," Barney said. "Does something have to be wrong for me to call you?"

"Of course not, Barney, I'm sorry. How's Toby?"

"Toby who?"

"Come on, Barn, how *is* she?"

"She's fine, I guess. She's asleep." A stand-up comic with a blond mustache and a pair of rubber fins on his feet was making the audience laugh. Alicia heard only the noise, not the joke. The man with the fins wore a deadpan face and spit some water from his mouth in an arc.

"Did she eat her dinner?"

"How do I know?" Barney said. "Did you?"

Alicia laughed. "Steak," she said. "When it's on them I eat steak. It was overdone. How are you getting along?"

"All right, I guess. Is it okay for me to say I miss you?"

"Oh, Barney, of course it is, I miss you too." She did miss him, but that was beside the point. She had counted on this tiny separation to clear her head and bring her smack up against the right decision. His calling . . . well, perhaps it was fate's way of reminding her of what she might be leaving behind. But it wasn't just a matter of Barney versus New York. It had to do with the gradual closing of doors that once were open. When she was twenty there were hundreds; at thirty, there were a couple of dozen. Now at forty-three, maybe four or five, certainly not more than that. In another five years there might be two, maybe just one. Why did a decision, in order to be "important," have to involve this much pain?

"I'm relieved," Barney said. Their conversation was like that between two very young people on a second date who find they have committed themselves a little too far on the first. "I just wanted to know how things were going for you. Did you talk about Davida's book?"

"This morning," she said. "It went fine. I talked about it very briefly. They seemed interested, or maybe just ghoulish. It wouldn't surprise me if Mickey Eversharp promoted her book as the sensational new novel by the victim of the sensational murder."

"Like you say, his job is to move books."

"Mickey's the only thing that's keeping me sane. I hate these things."

"How's the weather?"

"Horrible. I wish I was home. I like you better than Johnny Carson. You don't have so many tics."

"Thanks," Barney said. "When are you coming back?"

"Tomorrow around five. Didn't I tell you?"

"You did but I forgot. Tell you what, we'll go out somewhere for dinner. Where would you like to go?"

"It doesn't matter," Alicia said. "Anywhere with you and Toby would be nice."

They hung up. She padded over to the television set and turned off Johnny. The quiet buzzed inside her ears. She got back into her cold bed and realized that when she went to New York the bed would always be half empty.

The next morning's session was a truncated one, with two short presentations, one a first novel about loneliness, the other a history of economics in Rumania, and then they broke for the final "social hour," an event in The Bridge, wrapping up the hellish midweek confinement in an ambience of jollity. Actually, Alicia reflected, more than half of them were dying to get away from the Whaler and were giddy with relief that the conference was finally over. Phyllis Vance had instructed her cadre of editors, via interoffice memo, not to be clannish during the final get-together but mix it up with the sales force. "Don't talk *at* them, talk *with* them," she wrote. "Poor souls, they spend four nights out of five in Best Westerns watching reruns of Carol Burnett all by their lonesome. They're starved for the sort of company you provide. Don't forget, folks, these men sell your books!"

Alicia wasn't so sure they all spent every night alone watching old sit-coms on TV but this question was as irrelevant as it was private; what they chose to do with their empty evenings was their own business.

The Bridge warmed up. Disoriented, Alicia grabbed a drink from a tray passed by a pubescent waiter. She took a swallow; it was bourbon and soda. She made a face. Across the room, Mickey was drawing laughter from five or six people with one of his vile jokes ("Why did God give women cunts? So men would talk to them"). She stood alone, then Jason McHugh was at her elbow. "I'm sorry for what I said yesterday," he told her. His mentioning it brought Davida back in full dress; Alicia had managed not to think about Davida for ten minutes.

"I wish you'd stop apologizing," Alicia said.

"I just wanted to make sure you knew that I really meant what I said when I said I was sorry. Boy, was I stupid."

Did he want her to deny it? "That's okay," she said. "I believe you."

He smiled. "What do you think of the Fall List?" he said.

"It's got its strong moments. Maybe too many of them," she said.

"This place is a garbage heap," McHugh said, startling Alicia, who looked at him hard to see if he was kidding. Apparently he was not; his face registered disgust.

"Well," she said, "that's a surprise, coming from you. I had you down as the ultimate company man."

"You had me down wrong," McHugh said. "I repeat, this outfit is publishing garbage. I've been trying to get me another job for over a year. I guess I have B.O. or something. I'm still here."

"I don't smell anything," Alicia said, smiling.

"And if you really want to know, book publishing is on its last legs." It began to dawn on Alicia that McHugh had been drinking for quite some time. He held his glass at an angle and his eyes were wet and blurred. "In a year or two they're going to put entire libraries on pins, not the heads but the pointed ends. Did you know that?"

"I've heard something to that effect," Alicia said. "But not right away, Jason, all that's somewhere down the pike. You'll be selling books between covers and inside jackets for a few more years."

"Not me, honey, I'm going into computer software." He dropped his empty glass on the soil of a potted fern and looked around for another to take its place. "This outfit is going downhill but fast." He mourned briefly. "Hey, old buddy," he said, brightening as another salesman brushed past on his way to the bar. "Let's you and me go find us another drinkee." And he swiveled away and was off before Alicia could say goodbye and wish him good luck.

The charter bus, its motor having been on for an hour, finally opened its doors; Griffin employees rushed to mount the steps and find seats for the hour-and-a-half ride back to Boston. Alicia stood with Mickey Eversharp in biting afternoon air. The sun was about to drop behind a line of spruce across a dusty field. Alicia said, "Well, thank God that's over. I'm almost looking forward to getting back to work." For a reason she couldn't identify, she felt as if a conspiracy against her had been dropped. Power had come back into paralyzed limbs; something that had held her spirit captive had, over the past few hours, released her. She switched her canvas bag from one arm to the other.

"Here comes the blue menace," Mickey said, nudging Alicia.

"Alicia," cried Phyllis. "Why don't you ride back to town in my car?"

"Ah . . ." Alicia was trapped.

"Come on," Phyllis urged. "We're just over there. You and I can have a nice little chat. I hate driving alone," she went on, swinging her blond cowhide case, "I keep thinking of things that need writing down and of course I can't do anything about it." For a moment Alicia was afraid Phyllis was going to ask her to take out a steno pad and pencil.

Phyllis's car was a maroon Mercedes, with seats upholstered with velours, the dashboard of polished wood, a radio, and a tape deck whose speakers were mounted behind the back seat.

"Sorry to take you away from Mickey," Phyllis said, "but I thought we could both profit from some time alone together." She drove with confidence and dash.

"I can see Mickey anytime," Alicia said. She rolled down her window three inches. The cold air hit her ear. Phyllis swung the car onto Route 3, leaving the charter bus behind, keeping the speedometer needle hovering over sixty-seven. Trying to get her shoulders to relax, Alicia wanted to guess what would happen next, while covertly studying the formidable Vance profile, its Roman nose, its full crimson lips, the jawline with its soft pads of flesh. She was determined not to make it easy for Phyllis; this was *her* idea, let her be the first to dive.

"There are a couple of things you and I should get straight," Phyllis said, finally breaking their silence. "Nothing I hate so much as barricades between me and my staff; if we don't have each other's trust, well then, we don't have much, do we?"

"What are you getting at?" Alicia said. Anonymous music—dentist's office music—poured out of the speakers.

"Just that I hear you're leaving us," Phyllis said. "Don't you think that's something I should have heard from you rather than from someone else?"

"Who did you hear it from?" Alicia said. "Because it's not

true. That is, I haven't made up my mind yet. I have had an offer, yes, but I haven't decided whether to accept it."

"It doesn't matter whom I heard it from," Phyllis said.

Firs and spruce flanked the road, which cut a path through the middle of a thick evergreen forest. The line of raw nature on either side of them was virtually unbroken. "Tell me about it," Phyllis said. "The offer. I'd like some specifics, please."

"I'll give you the short form," Alicia said.

"Have one," Phyllis said. She held out a small white paper bag. Murmuring thanks, Alicia dipped her hand in and pulled out a hard candy wrapped in brown cellophane. It turned out to be bitter coffee, coffee without milk or sugar. "They're German," Phyllis said. "My father used to bring them back for me when he went there on business after the war. I was an adult by then but he always came back with a little bag of these things. They keep you awake." Just like Phyllis, Alicia thought, to offer sweets that tasted like medicine. The bitter juice from the candy coated her tongue. "The short form then," Phyllis said. "I don't care what form so long as you don't leave out the essentials."

Alicia started through the history of the Tolland and Lutwidge affair, unhappily; it was like telling your high school teacher what happened beneath the stands at the football stadium. She was not obligated to tell Phyllis one word, let alone the whole thing, and here she was, confessing and making Phyllis a part of it by virtue of her ears alone. Phyllis made her do things she didn't want to do and so she was, consistently, Phyllis's creature.

"And I'd have the sort of autonomy at T and L," she went on, talking very fast, "that isn't the style here. Each editor there, if he or she feels strongly enough about a manuscript or an idea, can simply take it on; it doesn't have to go through eighty-seven readings and then a committee."

"We don't have eighty-seven people at Griffin," Phyllis said. She was getting angry, Alicia could tell by a crease of grimness next to her mouth. "I've heard about that sort of procedure," Phyllis said, "and believe me, Alicia, it doesn't guarantee success any more than our methods do."

"Maybe you're right," Alicia said. The last thing she wanted was to get into an argument with Phyllis. "I'm going to let Dick Freyburg know on Monday, and I promise to let you know what I've decided right after I speak to him."

"Aren't you afraid your position here will be compromised should you decide not to take that job in New York?" Phyllis asked. Clever woman, she mouthed what was on Alicia's mind.

"I'll have to take that chance, won't I?"

Phyllis made the closest thing to an animal snort Alicia had heard in a long time. It must have hurt her nose. They were approaching Boston now. An apartment complex loomed over a hillside, a carpet store in the middle of a field, a small shopping plaza, Howard Johnson's, and gray smog hanging over the horizon. "You said a *couple of things,*" Alicia said quietly. Suddenly she knew the invaders were in the car with her, riding in the back seat, smaller than life size so all five could sit together in a row. "I *am* mad," she thought. This thought no longer terrified her; it came as something of a relief.

"The other thing is about Davida Franklin's book," Phyllis said.

"Which one?"

"*Join the Dance*—the one you told the sales forces about yesterday. I thought we were going to scratch that book."

The traffic on Route 3 began to clot and Phyllis was forced to slow down. The muscles of her face grew ever tighter. She groped in the bag of candies, withdrawing one and unwrapping it with one hand.

"My God, Phyllis," Alicia said. "Even after what it's turned out to be? It's a marvelous book, it's the best parts of literary and commercial, an almost perfect balance."

One of the invaders—she did not know which one but it sounded like a man—sent her a message of encouragement.

"But you agreed, didn't you? You told me you would let her know we wouldn't publish," Phyllis said. Woman of principle, woman of decision, Phyllis turned Alicia's blood cold.

"You want us not to publish *Join the Dance* even though it's the book we've been counting on, waiting for all these years? I can't believe it!" The voice was rising. Alicia made a huge effort to control it, to pull it back down. "Phyllis, I want to know something—have you *read* it?"

"We made the decision."

"*You* did," Alicia said. She felt strength enter her soul through the bloodstream. She sat up straight. "You wanted me to and I couldn't do it when you asked me to—there was too much going on with the lawsuit and when I was ready, it was too late, Davida was dead. My God, Phyllis, I can't believe you don't want Griffin to publish her novel. How can you even think of not publishing it? It's a wonderful book, it's an original, it reads like a dream. If you had read it, you'd agree. Phyllis, this novel is as good as Spark's *Memento Mori*—and not so implausible. You'll be sorry if you don't change your mind."

It was the first warning Alicia had ever given Phyllis Vance; it made her feel as if she were in love.

"It's the principle," Phyllis said. "I can't have my editors going off and doing their own thing, especially when it's in direct opposition to my . . ." She hesitated; Alicia guessed she was trying to get around the word "orders." ". . . to my wishes," she finished. A lame word. "*I'm* the Managing Editor here, my dear, not you." The car inched past Grossman's mammoth lumber establishment; the skyline of Boston rose up like a thick piece of theatrical scenery. *Only ten more minutes,* Alicia thought. *Can I handle it?*

"Perhaps I'll take another look at it," Phyllis said, tight-lipped. A long pause followed, during which Phyllis seemed to be consolidating her categories, her principles.

She's going to make up to me, Alicia said to herself. *She wants me because I'm threatening to leave her. She can't stand it. She's mine.*

But it didn't come out quite that way; there was still a touch of the old wickedness in the newly exposed Phyllis, for she said, with some vehemence, "I'll tell you one thing, Alicia, if I change my mind and decide to take on this novel, I'm going to have Mickey promote hell out of it and in a way that will no doubt turn your pretty hair white. I'm going to do everything we can to tie in Davida's murder and anything else that seems relevant—"

"Or sensational," Alicia added.

"You've got it," Phyllis said. "I'm going to get my money's worth out of Davida Franklin. Damn," she went on, "at this rate I'm going to be late for dinner. The traffic's all going the wrong way. It should be going out, not in."

Just to tick you off, Phyllis, they've done it just to get under your milky skin, Alicia said to herself. She told Davida—she had already begun to hold regular conversations with her dead friend—not to mind too much; at least the higher-ups at Griffin would at last be paying her some serious attention.

CHAPTER
Thirteen

THE final name: Jared Koenig, M.D. It did not take genius to recognize that the M.D. was not embroidery; it had to have a specific meaning for Alicia, else it wouldn't be there. Alicia had saved Koenig, M.D., for last, as she was not, somehow, prepared to deal with it; it could only be bad news. Several times she reached for the phone and then withdrew her hand and did something else with it. Once she punched the first four numbers then recradled the receiver, her heart jumping.

Alicia asked Barney if he knew a Dr. Jared Koenig.

"The name sounds vaguely familiar," he said. "Internal medicine. Or maybe Gyn. Why?"

"Oh, one of the production people at Griffin has an appointment with him, her first, apparently. She asked me if I'd heard of him. People always think doctors' wives know all their husbands' colleagues and also all about medicine. We don't, of course. Someone asked me last week what she should do for her asthma. I told her to go see a doctor and she acted as if I were deliberately withholding information from her."

"Funny, no one ever asks me how to improve his book," Barney said. He unbuckled his belt and stepped out of his slacks. His legs were sinewy and spare; hers, on the other hand, were getting thick and lumpy, especially toward the top. He reached around for his pajamas hanging against the bathroom door. They were pale blue, like a little boy's. "I'll shower in the morning," he said. "To wake me up."

"I suppose that'll be five again?"

"Five-thirty." He pulled out the stopper of the alarm clock; it had a bell that, when it rang, went through Alicia like an ice pick. "I have to do a bowel resection ..."

"Spare me," Alicia said. Sometimes she thought her husband's work just like a plumber's. The only difference, it seemed, was that the pipes he worked on were softer and bled.

"What sort of name is Jared?" Barney asked, getting into bed.

"Fancy," Alicia said. "Good night, Barney."

He was silent. She figured he was trying to decide whether to make love. Herself, she was not at all in the mood, not body, not psyche; a small cube of fear had lodged in her abdomen. She put her hands over the place and pressed, hoping to melt it away. There was no way she could avoid calling the doctor with the fancy name; and she made up her mind to phone him in the morning, after Barney had gone off.

Alicia had three more days in which to come up with an answer for Dick Freyburg. It occurred to her that these two men, with their German names, knew each other. They both had designs, of one kind or another, on her life. Alicia let this paranoia do a wild solo number for a few minutes, then sent it packing. Barney shifted parts of his body; she was afraid he might reach over and start sliding his hand up her thigh until it reached the top and then nuzzle her cunt—which was now dry as any bone; it was astonishing what anxiety could do to the libido.

But Barney succumbed to fatigue rather than passion and was soon breathing audibly, a soft noise that calmed her. It reminded her of Toby as a baby when she would go into Toby's room and hang over the edge of the crib; the sounds of her breathing were the whispering of a ghost; she was always sure Toby would never make it to adult. Barney shifted and turned on his side, his face away from her. The snoring stopped. In the dimness (the streetlight glowed down to the sidewalk, very little of it rose to illuminate the house) Barney was a dark boulder, a big gray rock next to her in bed. He was absolutely still, she couldn't see the rise and fall of life. She caught her own breath and held it, then shifted to put him further into silhouette, closed one eye and focused the other on the ridge at the crest of the rock. Nothing, no motion. She touched his back, which seemed hard and cold. He must be dead.

"Barney!" Alicia punched her husband's back, her hand in a tight fist, and cried his name at the same moment. Terror fizzed her blood.

Barney moaned and said, "What's the matter, why are you hitting me? You woke me, Allie."

"Oh, God, Barney, I didn't see you moving, I couldn't see you breathe. I thought . . ."

"You thought I'd died in my sleep," he said, turning onto his back. "But you see I didn't. Here, feel." He took her hand and placed it on his chest, under the pajama top. She could feel his heart beating into her palm. "And here." He brought her hand to his mouth and blew on it.

"I don't know what happened," she said.

"Illusion. Don't worry so much, it happens to everybody."

"Not to me it doesn't," she said. "I could have sworn, you weren't breathing." Then: "I'm sorry I'm so jumpy."

"Listen, that's what I'm here for. I just wish you were happier."

"I'm all right, honestly I'm happy," she said. But her nerves were vibrating.

"Would you like some warm milk?" Barney said. "It'll help you sleep. I'll put some honey in it so it won't taste so awful. Hey, Allie, please don't cry, I'm alive. There's nothing wrong with me, I promise."

"Apnea," she said. "Except you didn't gasp or anything."

"Maybe," he said.

"Where are you going?"

"I'm going to heat up some milk."

"Thanks," Alicia said. How nice he was, how accommodating, going down like that to a drafty kitchen to fetch her a glass of warm milk. It was perfectly possible that, after she threatened to go to New York and crack their marriage down the middle, he had simply become a nicer person. Or, he might have been milk and honey all along and now, when it was probably too late, she was recognizing it for the first time since their third date, that time he had asked her to take off her blouse and had gaped at her breasts as if he had never seen a naked woman before. It was at that moment, seeing the twinkle of a tear in each eye, that she had succumbed to Barney, who, as she flirted with separation, seemed more and more the real thing, the answer to this woman's incipient loneliness. Because, in spite of how Davida had assured her about the pleasures of compromise, she could not have both, at least not in any form she was accustomed to.

It would have been so much easier if she could boil it down to the simple equation of Barney versus career, but that would have been as misleading as maintaining that all you need to write a book is something to say. It wasn't simple; it was as complicated as a marriage.

Davida would say—she knew how Davida would reduce it: "Your career, dummy, the world is swarming with so-called men. But there is only one job for you, cutie-pie, and that's where you can spread your wings and fly."

"Oh, Davida," she said, "You can do better than that."

The stale image Alicia had put into Davida's dead mouth seemed right somehow. Phyllis kept her wings clipped down to their stems. In New York they would spread, their spread would exceed a hundred feet.

And her mama, down at the edge of the swampland: "What are you thinking of? Marriage, your marriage, your husband, your little girl, how can you even *think* about anything else? You're more selfish now than you were when you were a child. I don't know what's happening to you, you're growing backwards, Alicia!"

"Mama, be quiet! I don't want to hear all that crap about how I was such a selfish child. I want to know what you think I should do now. No, I take that back; I already know what you think. You haven't opened your mind to anything new or different in fifty years. You're still wearing stockings and garters, for chrissake." She deleted her mother and lay there, agonizing.

Barney returned with a mug of warm milk. He hadn't bothered to put his slippers on; his feet were blue and chalky. She refrained from asking him what he'd done with the saucepan after heating the milk and then saw it, sitting in the sink, filled with water.

"Thank you," she said, accepting the mug. It warmed her hands first, then her lips, finally her throat. Barney got heavily back into bed. A man Barney's age no longer cared as much about grace as he did about sleep. Barney was a sleeper.

"Good night, Alicia," he said. He touched her flank through her nightgown. It was a touch of trust; the love that flowed from his heart came out through his fingers. He loved her still, even after she warned him she might leave their trusting bed.

"Night," she said softly. "The milk was lovely. I didn't know we had such good honey."

The next morning Alicia left the house at the same time as Toby and reached the Griffin Building just after Ham the custodian had opened up, unlocking the front door and turning up the thermostat. The building was still cool and the ancient radiators banged and clanked as if hit with hammers.

Alicia climbed up through the bowels of the building, climbed the swooping staircase quickly, her calves protesting as she reached the top floor. The second she walked into her office she realized it smelled like Alicia Baer; essence of Alicia, it was her perfume—Nostalgia—and dust and rubber cement. The air around her desk at home smelled the same. She tried to get a peek at the new occupant, pulled all her tricks, went limp, prayed, closed her eyes, tried to activate her Alpha waves, blinked, strained, went limp again and saw no one. Damn, she needed to see the woman—for she assumed it would be another female—using *her* phone, sitting in *her* chair, dictating letters for *her* Jenny to type. Alicia hated her. But what did she expect? Did she expect them to make a shrine of her office, to nail a plaque to the wall outside and seal it off? Alicia sat down and got out the address book.

Jared Koenig, M.D., and the number: 734–1220. With fingers she discovered to be trembling, she punched the number.

"Dr. Brand, Dr. Koenig's office."

"This is Alicia Baer, may I speak to Dr. Koenig, please?"

"Doctor isn't in yet," the meager voice said. "This is his answering service. His nurse is expected in at nine-thirty. Would you care to leave a message?"

"No. No, thanks. Thanks." Alicia hung up.

An hour and a half later Alicia, aware that her concentration was shot, focused on the manuscript page in front of her but her eyes left the words and crept slowly to the phone where they lit, refusing to budge.

"Fuck!" Alicia got up and closed the door to her office, startling Jenny.

She put through the second call. "May I speak to Dr. Koenig, please?"

"He's with a patient," the nurse said. "I can ask him to return your call when he's free."

"This is Alicia Baer. My phone number is . . ."

"Oh, Mrs. Baer," the nurse said, cutting her off, "I think I can interrupt the doctor, I know he wants to speak to you."

"Don't do that!"

But the person on the other end had already buzzed the doctor. Alicia heard a voice saying, "Is that you finally, Alicia?" It was not a voice she recognized. It was impersonal but compelling, like that of a lot of doctors she had run into, like a lot of the people Barney hung out with; it carried the same sinister tone of universal reassurance, reassurance in the face of anything and everything—"With good medical care," the doctor told Woody Allen in *Love and Death*, "I would say this patient has another ten minutes to live."

"It's me," she said. "And I'm not quite sure why I'm calling you."

"Not sure," Dr. Koenig repeated. "I can't believe what I'm hearing. I thought I had made it abundantly clear during your last office visit—and I thought you understood—that it was vitally important for you to come in at least once every quarter and let me have a look at you. When was your last visit?"

"I'm not quite sure," Alicia said.

"I'm going to be quite frank with you, Alicia," the voice of Jared Koenig said into her ear. "You don't at all strike me as one of those self-destructive females. On the contrary, you seem to have an excellent orientation toward your life. You appear to be remarkably conscious of how much you have to live for."

Dr. Koenig continued, implying death and destruction, but not saying precisely what it was that needed checking out. She closed her eyes and felt the room lift and spin. She gripped the edge of her desk.

"Dr. Koenig," she said, "I'll make an appointment to come see you. Okay?"

"Tell Moira I said to squeeze you in today or tomorrow. A condition like yours doesn't improve with age, you know." But instead of letting her tell Moira herself, he somehow got through to his nurse and with Alicia still on, said, "Mrs. Baer would like to come into the office for an examination today or tomorrow. Fit her in whenever you can, please." He clicked off and was gone.

"All rightee, then, Mrs. Baer," Moira began. "Can you make it at five-thirty today, you'll be Doctor's last patient?"

Alicia slammed down the receiver. She slammed it so hard it activated the buzzer inside the phone.

"Oh, no," she said, "You're not going to get *me* in there!" Alicia crushed an urge to cry and held out her hands, palms up. They were shiny and moist, crisscrossed with skin lines. "What's wrong with me?" she asked them. She was not going to keep this appointment with Dr. Koenig, his name meant sickness, not cure, not health; he would probably kill her. She would make an appointment with her own doctor, Tom Brainard. She'd have him check her out thoroughly in all the places it was possible to go without cutting into her flesh.

Her phone buzzed. "Well," Phyllis said. "At last."

"Sorry."

"That's okay. Look, Alicia, could you give me a report on the status of the Crater book? When do you expect a complete manuscript?"

"Geoffrey Crater?" Alicia said. "You know Geoffrey, every sentence has to be rewritten seventeen times. Give him another decade and he'll come up with a really good book."

"Oh, God, a decade. . . . Listen, Allie, would you mind very much calling him up and giving him a gentle goose? I know it's difficult but you can do it tactfully without scaring him. I've just been told by Chicago that we're going to have to start tightening the reins, be more hard-nosed about our long-range investments. Call him today, sweetie, will you?"

Don't sweetie me, Alicia told Phyllis silently. "Of course I'll call him if you ask me to, but Geoffrey's not going to like it. He'll panic, he'll go into a fugue state."

"Aren't you sick to death of touchy authors?" Phyllis said. "God knows *I* am. A pox on them. First Carlos Feeny doesn't see why we can't publish his first draft and now Geoffrey and his decade. How long *has* he been working on the book?"

"Five years?"

"Well, is it five or isn't it? You ought to know, you're his editor."

"Five years," Alicia said.

"That's long enough," Phyllis said. "Bug him."

"You're the boss," Alicia said.

It was not until dinner that Alicia's conversation with Dr. Koenig returned to her, elbowing its way through the crowd of domestic activity. She had not kept the appointment; she wondered if and how long he had waited for her.

"What sort of doctor did you say Jared Koenig was?"

"I said," Barney told her, "that I wasn't certain. Maybe he's in oncology. I really can't say for sure. Why, what's so important about him?" Barney sliced down into his pork chop; yellow juice oozed from the cut.

"This woman in my office keeps asking. Maybe she's frightened. I don't really know. Listen, Barney, is it possible to have a serious, maybe a terminal condition without knowing it, without having any overt symptoms?"

"What do you think? Is life a terminal condition?"

"You know that isn't what I mean."

"Okay." Barney patted his mouth with his napkin and looked at her steadily. Toby ate in teeny-tiny bites, delaying. "Yes, you can have hypertension without any overt symptoms. You can have a low-grade thyroid condition and think you're just irritable or in a lousy mood. And then there's cancer. You can have cancer in its early stage . . ."

Toby spoke as she mashed a green pea beetle between the tines of her fork. "Cancer again, can't you two ever talk about anything else?"

"We hardly ever talk about cancer," Alicia said.

"Mom just wanted to know about this Dr. Koenig," Barney said. Alicia heard apology in his voice.

"We won't talk about it anymore, Toby," she said.

"Good," said Toby.

Alicia was sure she had high blood pressure or cancer. She would choose the hypertension. Her throat closed down and the chewed-up meat inside her mouth had nowhere to go but out; she rejected spitting as too showy and waited for her muscles to relax, whereupon she swallowed the food and then stopped eating her dinner.

Toby retired to her room where, closing the door, she engaged in her history assignment or else in wide-awake dreaming.

Alicia, on edge, took a shower, turned on the television set instead of applying herself to the manuscript she should have been reading. She got into bed and let the eight-inch people inside the Hitachi hop around, trying to entertain her. Lou Grant, transformed overnight from an amiable clown to Mr. Moral Duty, came on with shirt-sleeves rolled up and tie askew, and began to talk to the young reporter with the long upper lip. Oh, God, he's sending him out on a carcinogen story. Alicia sprang out of bed and punched in the on-off button.

Downstairs, Barney's Smith-Corona office machine thumped, coming up through the bedroom floor as muffled humming, the nonwriter lingering over finishing touches on an article. Alicia drifted dizzily at the edge of sleep, with the thick noise of Barney's typewriter filling the spaces in the bedroom.

Alicia found herself in a huge examining room, an operating theater, like the one in the Eakins painting. Above her—she lay flat on her back on a hard surface—was a slanting skylight and beyond the window the dark of a moonless and starless night. Uninterrupted black stared down on her. She was naked and covered up over her neck (the edge of the sheet, or whatever it was, was as hard and rough as canvas and scraped her chin).

Things clicked and clanked and hissed beyond her range of vision; they sounded like autoclaves filled with instruments. She looked down her white length at the mound of her breasts, her knees and her bare left foot, its toes sticking up in a slanting row; she was overcome with pity for her foot.

Gradually the room came into focus. Men in frock coats—the Eakins picture again—stood over or near her, murmuring, some frowning, all with exceedingly serious expressions on their faces.

"Alicia, my dear, I see you are awake," one of the frowning men said. He was wearing a light blue apron like those available in kitchenware shops; it looped around his neck and tied around his waist. She could not see his mouth, as it was obliterated by a wide beard of crinkly brown and gray hair. This man drew closer and closer, bending so that his face nearly touched hers. She could feel the moisture of his breath against her cheek, on her nose. "I'm delighted that you're awake at last because we're counting on you to assist us in this examination."

"This isn't real," Alicia told the man earnestly. "This is my dream." Then she noticed a knife that looked more like a straight razor than a scalpel, being hinged and having a wooden handle. The doctor held it loosely, limply in his right hand. This object threw Alicia into a frenzy of fear. "This is a dream," she cried.

He moved his head slowly from side to side, and said, "I think not. Wouldn't I know if I were dreaming? And all my colleagues and associates here with me today?" He swept the hand without the knife around the amphitheater. There was a hum of agreement from the other men. Some of them nodded. "Not dreaming, not dreaming, not a dream."

"Are you Dr. Koenig?" Alicia said, with tears in the back of her throat.

"You know I am. Why should you doubt the evidence of

your own eyes? I want you to relax now, Alicia, the procedure will go far more easily if you take some nice deep breaths and try to relax your muscles—make them obey!"

In fact, his words served to tighten every fiber in her body; she felt her arms and legs, her neck, her fingers being stretched like taffy. She started to scream, then improvised a mad scheme and tried to get off the table and run. But when she attempted to raise her arms she found she could not move them; they were strapped down with leather bands as wide as a horse's girth. She strained hard and managed to lift only her head and part of her neck. "Let me up!" she screamed.

"Now, Alicia, you know how important it is that you allow us to have a good look at you."

"No," she said, "you're not my doctor. I have my own doctor at home." But she could not remember his name.

"These gentlemen have come here at considerable expense to themselves," Dr. Koenig said, beginning to sound severe, if not impatient. There were nods again, from the spectators, who were now sitting against what seemed to be a slanting wall. All wore gray or dark brown or black suits and looked down intently and with a sense of anticipation, as if impatient for the play to begin. "We are not going to disappoint them, are we, Alicia? You can't tell me that this all comes as a surprise. We did talk about it, you and I, in my office."

"Yes, it *is* a surprise," she cried. "I don't know anything about this. I swear. What are you going to do?" She was so frightened now that she began to urinate; it flowed out of her, forming a damp, warm spot underneath her buttocks, which immediately turned icy. She did not want Dr. Koenig to see or smell it. She had the sensation that she was growing younger and younger. Now she was no more than seven or eight. "Stop," she shrieked, "I want to go home. I want my mommy."

"Here, darling," she heard her mother's voice. "I'm here. Please lie still. Dr. Koenig isn't going to hurt you."

"Yes, he is. Tell him to stop!"

"Quiet," snapped Dr. Koenig, all business now. "Nurse, will you please help the patient assume the lithotomy position."

A young woman in a brittle blue and white uniform and no visible bosom appeared, and, unstrapping Alicia's right leg, bent it smartly and thrust her heel into a metal stirrup so cold it felt as if it had been buried in ice. Then she did the same thing with Alicia's left leg. She looked only at Alicia's body parts, not once at her face. Alicia wanted to cry but when she tried she found she was mute, nothing came from her throat.

"Now move down towards the end of the table," he told Alicia. "More, please, you're not down far enough." He put his hand on her hip and shoved. She inched down; her knees flopped sideways. She could feel the tenseness in her thighs. "That's better," he said, looking down on her as if he owned her and was appraising her value in dollars.

Alicia closed her eyes. "Save me, get me out of this," she prayed. The spectators began to sing softly in practiced unison, a tune she did not recognize. It seemed to hover around several notes, never going more than one or two in each direction. Then Alicia felt Dr. Koenig's ungloved, gritty fingers part her lips roughly. He shoved a cold metal speculum inside her vagina, an invasion that broke her silence; she screamed.

"Hush, darling," her mother said from in back of her. "You'll distract Dr. Koenig."

"Help me," she cried.

Dr. Koenig tucked a large white napkin under the collar of his shirt and held up an instrument that looked like a fork with two tines and, disappearing behind the hill of her legs, pulled out the speculum and inserted the fork in its place. He dragged this along the walls of her vagina. Pain shot through Alicia's body like an explosion. She screamed and screamed.

Her mother moaned.

The doctor pulled out the fork. A piece of flesh, the size of an artichoke leaf, dark pink and torn, was impaled on the end of it. He ate it. The spectators applauded; their applause was muffled as if they wore thick cotton gloves.

Alicia thought she was going to throw up. She tried, but could not keep the blob of food from backtracking out of her stomach. It came bitterly into her mouth. The pain cramped and held on tightly. She attempted to thrash loose once more, pulled one leg out of its stirrup and was just about to free the other when the nurse grabbed her around the calf and said, "*Schweige!*"

"Alicia." Her mother was weeping now in sad, guilty-sounding gulps.

Dr. Koenig said, "And now for the cautery." He turned to a young boy to accept a bunch of dry twigs bound together with a yellow bulb of flame at the top. He approached Alicia with it.

Terrified, Alicia gathered all her strength and wrenched herself free of restraints, snapping them; she heard the buckles clang against the steel legs of the examining table. She threw herself off the table and hurtled through a set of swinging red leather doors and out of her dream. "Aah," she cried, sitting bolt upright in her bed. Her nightgown clung to her skin wetly. "Barney, where are you?"

"Here. Here I am," Barney said, emerging from the bathroom and clicking off the light behind him. "Another nightmare?"

"*This* one was a dream. The other wasn't."

"Want to tell me?"

"No, not now, maybe tomorrow. It was too awful. I was being tortured. Oh, God, Barney, what's happening to me?"

"I'd say you're having one hell of a time making up your mind over this job thing. I'd say the sooner you get over this indecision the better you'll sleep."

"Would you say I was possessed?"

"Yes," Barney said in the dark. "But your demons are your own creation. They don't come from outer space." He paused.

"It might not be such a bad idea for you to see someone," he said.

"We've been this route, Barney. I'm not going to see a shrink. A shrink can't help me."

"You're so special? What makes you immune to help? Jesus fucking Christ, even Nixon went to a shrink!" It was not the best time for Barney to be rebuking her; she was too vulnerable now. The smell of the bad dream filled her nostrils and mouth like smoke. Alicia ground her fingernails into her palms and tightened her throat muscles.

"Barney," she began, "I sound as if I think I'm entitled, don't I?"

"You said it, not me." He paused. "There's almost no one who can't be helped," he went on, as her eyes adjusted to the dark, as black went gray and shapes—of chair and desk and chair and bureau—formed. The huge metal wastebaskets beneath her desk blinked. "It's just a question of whether you're prepared to accept it. Being neurotic is a little like being an addict; you enjoy it and want to get rid of it at the same time."

"Thanks, perfesser," she said, knowing this would hurt his feelings; still, she couldn't bear his pedantry. If she had, a moment earlier, been prepared to tell him about the invaders of the book, she now drew back; his tone killed her confession. Quite unexpectedly, however, the invaders clamored loudly, but all together so that they were blurred crowd noise.

"Damn," she said. But she was relieved because she could not have found the words to describe Jeannette, Wilma, Roger . . . "Well, you see, I've recently met these people, they're most of them perfectly ordinary men and women, the only thing is they insist they know me and I've never laid eyes on any of them and it's really very very upsetting. You might say I'm going a little mad, if you know what I mean, I mean it doesn't make any sort of sense. Barney, I know what you're thinking . . ." And the face of Pearl Withers, like pudding, like trouble, swam into Alicia's plane of vision, staring horribly and then faded, drowned in thin air and was gone again; all the invaders receded the way pain does when it's over, and she lay there in the dark bedroom next to her husband and wondered why she felt so terrible, so alone, and why there was a hole, a raw space, where her heart should be.

CHAPTER
Fourteen

EVERY other Saturday Barney went into his office on Beacon Street where he was consulted by patients too anxious to tell him what was really on their minds. This saved time but it kept them hidden beyond their physical symptoms. Barney complained to Alicia that they were zombies—"Doesn't anyone know how to communicate anymore. I thought that was the big thing—communication." Alicia said, "They're probably too scared. Either they think they've got cancer or they're terrified of an operation."

"That's really primitive, isn't it? Dark ages. I haven't lost anyone in the O.R. in months."

"It's true, though," Alicia said. "They're too frightened to talk to you."

The day after Alicia's nightmare about Dr. Koenig was one of Barney's office-hours Saturdays. At seven-thirty he stirred and kicked off the covers, waking Alicia.

He turned and looked at her. "You don't look so hot. Are you okay?" He hoisted himself out and stood over her in his wrinkled pajamas. The skin of his cheeks was punctured through by tiny hairs, some of them white.

"That dream," she said. "I can still feel it. It was incredibly vivid, not just the faces but the pain, I actually felt the pain inside me; it was like fire."

"I'm not going to repeat what I said last night. You know what I think you should do."

"If you're not going to repeat it, then don't," she said through her teeth. Alicia turned away from her husband and curled up under the covers. A tear for Davida slipped from her left eye, another slipped from her right; they met on the pillowcase. I'm pointed at something, she said to herself. What am I pointed at?

Barney had not moved away. Alicia read his hesitation as concern.

"Barney," she began. She wanted him to get back under the covers with her.

"I have to get going," he said. "I've got a woman coming in at nine, another at nine-thirty, *und so weiter.*"

Alicia sighed, heard Toby in her room, a bureau drawer pulled out, a window shut. You could always tell when someone was in the house, even when they weren't moving. Alicia thought about asking Toby to spend the day with her, mother and daughter together. She might try to bribe her with yet another pair of running shoes. Red ones, with arrows.

Barney went into the bathroom and shut the door after him. Alicia heard him turn on the shower, and pull the curtain across its rod and start humming.

"Ah," Alicia sighed again. Toby came into the room, in jeans and a turtleneck, clogs on her feet. "Where's Dad?"

"He's in the shower." Alicia pulled herself up and put Barney's pillow behind her neck.

"I need to ask him something," Toby said.

"Ask me."

"I'd rather ask him."

"Suit yourself," Alicia said. If the kid was going to be nasty to her, she was going to be nasty right back. Toby got the message and withdrew, went downstairs, her clogs like hammers on the steps.

During breakfast Barney said, "I'll be through seeing patients at one-thirty or so. Do you want to meet me for lunch?"

"What have you got up your sleeve, Barney?" Alicia said. Her mouth tasted as if she had been sucking the front-door key. She bit into a piece of buttered toast. The dream adhered to her like a bad name—"collaborator," "whore," "shameful one," "hypocrite."

"No, Alicia, I just thought, since it's spring, since you need some cheering up . . ."

"You mean maybe I'll have a famous decisive moment, maybe I'll get off the pot." Alicia showed him her teeth in the parody of a smile.

"If you two are going to fight, I'm going to leave," Toby said.

A thinness seemed to spread inside Alicia; there was nothing she could do to stop it. "Didn't you have something you wanted to ask your father?" she said, giving Toby a dark look. Whatever it was that Toby had kept baffled all her life was seeping out of her now; it seemed about to spill over. But at least she was eating her eggs and toast, Alicia was sure of that.

"I need some money," Toby said.

"I gave you your allowance on Thursday," Alicia said.

"I'll pay you back."

"How much do you need?" Barney asked.

"Why don't you ask her what she wants it for?" Alicia said.

"Okay. What do you want it for, Toots?"

"I don't have to tell you."

"And I don't have to give it to you," Barney said. Toby scowled and stood up. "Don't worry, Daddy, I won't ask you again!" she said. She ran out of the dining room.

Alicia's eyes stung.

Barney got up, still holding his coffee mug with its Harvard seal visible but faded from many sessions with the dishwasher. "She's upset," he said. "Also rude. You shouldn't let her talk that way."

"*I* shouldn't let her?" Alicia said. "You're blaming me."

"I didn't say it was your fault," he said. He put the mug down. "You're upset. Toby's no dummy, she can tell you're going through something unpleasant, she loves you, she's catching it. That's all I meant."

"Please don't blame me, Barney, I don't think I can handle it." Alicia felt vulnerable in her bathrobe; she was back to housewife.

"I'm not blaming you. Honestly, Allie, I'm not." But it was obvious to her that he was. Everything in a family bounced off one member and hit another, you couldn't speak or move or sigh or do anything in a family and not have it touch someone else in some small way. Nothing in a family was absorbed quietly, without rippling.

"I *will* meet you for lunch," Alicia said, getting up and gathering the breakfast things.

"One-thirty, then," Barney said. "The Union Oyster House, is that all right? I'll leave you the car."

"Sure," she said. "Maybe I'll go down to Quincy Market and buy some artificial flowers."

They heard Toby banging down the stairs once more, then opening and shutting the front door. "God, I hope she's not doing drugs," Alicia said.

"It's a nasty world," Barney said.

Alicia spent a long time getting dressed. She wanted so badly to talk to Davida that her words pushed past the silence and came out in whispers.

"I'm going to meet Barney for lunch, Davey. I think he's going to force me to make up my mind."

"You can't futz around any longer, Alicia, you're coming apart at the seams," Davida said.

"I want to ask you what it's like there."

"Better not."

"I should have warned you about Craig," Alicia said softly. "I knew he was rotten. He has wicked little eyes, a bad, thin mouth."

"I wouldn't have listened, you know that. I was madly in love with him."

Alicia drew up a gray flannel skirt, then put on a blue silk blouse with a Chinese collar. She looked at herself in the mirror, saw Alicia staring back, not too bad for a woman forty-three. She half expected to see Davida peering over her shoulder.

"I should have been worried about you, Davey," she said. "But I was only worried about Toby, I thought something terrible was going to happen to her. She's straightening out, I guess, getting tougher, though it's fucking hard on her old mum and dad. It's about time, I suppose, that she got a little mouthy. She's outgrowing me, Davey, and I can't stand it, she has no use for me anymore."

"You know that's not true. She's just an adolescent. I remember when I was her age, I thought I was going crazy."

"What's true is what I see," Alicia said. She decided against wearing a jacket over the blouse; it was getting warm.

"Toby's okay," Davida said.

"And you're dead," Alicia said. "So much for my extrasensory perception. It's good so long as it works but it doesn't work all the time, it's faulty, it breaks down. I can't count on it. I was so worried about Toby and I should have worried about you and now it's too late and I miss you so much that sometimes I can't see straight." The mirrored Alicia blurred and swam.

"Enough!" she cried. The noise of the word flew around the room. She stepped into a pair of low-heeled pumps, got her trench coat out of the hall closet, and, leaving a note for Toby, slid into the front seat of the Volvo and backed it out of the driveway and headed for Boston.

Alicia felt lightweight. I'm high, she thought. It's fake. She recognized the signs. This floating feeling would be replaced by a lethargy that would make each arm and leg feel like a hundred pounds and put her brain to sleep. Her blood tingled, her ears widened to every sound. Although it was not yet noon, hundreds of men, women and children had come to Quincy Market to gorge themselves. It was a palace of food—green fudge, raw clams and oysters, huge muffins studded with raisins, shiny orange barbecued ribs, pineapple quarters on sticks, lollipop-style, potato skins stuffed with chili and topped with mashed avocado, hot dogs, Greek salad, and more, much more, vats of nuts and dried fruit, shish kabob, fried rice, pastrami sandwiches. Each establishment—The Brown Derby Deli, The Potato Peel, The Ming Tree, The Walrus and the Carpenter, and dozens more—was not much larger than a booth at a country fair; each dispensed food to people who lined up, handed over their money and took their fodder off to devour it either standing at what looked to Alicia like the high counters in the bank where you write out your check or sitting at bare wooden tables. Above, an enormous dome poured daylight down in a cool pale circle. People ate with deadly intent; this eating had as much to do with simple nourishment as illicit sex with procreation. Alicia saw almost no one smiling.

Escaping the crowd inside the hall, Alicia left it and went outside, to South Market. April air bathed the crowd there with a warmth not felt since the previous October, but spring seemed a novel blessing rather than something inevitable. Alicia took a deep breath. Everyone here too appeared to be eating: triangles of pizza, Greek salad in clear plastic boxes, sausages in bulkie rolls, Syrian pockets. Mouths chomped and throats swallowed. Beer was guzzled, soft drinks were sent down to drown the food inside distended stomachs. A trash can overflowed with pink-stained paper plates, cups with daisies crawling over on them, uneaten crusts, plastic forks, paper napkins. Alicia, not a bit hungry but revolted by so much food, sat down on a bench next to a woman who looked like a teenager but had a baby of a year or so next to her. The baby wore a yellow jacket too small for her—little wrists stuck out three inches beyond the cuffs—and next to her, a bearded father. Both mother and father fed the child from a paper container of french fries. The child grabbed a fry in a fist and shoved it at her mouth. Alicia watched this family covertly. Then she became aware, gradually, that she was being stared at. Across the way, some yards off, was a woman sitting on a bench, a woman dressed in an open gray cardigan sweater over a long dark skirt whose hem was coming down. On her head she wore a knitted cap and her hair stuck out beneath it like quills. Alicia recognized the woman as Pearl Withers. She turned her head sharply, knowing it was too late: she had been seen. Alicia looked again. Pearl leaned over a dirty canvas bag, chin down, and, rummaging in it, withdrew a sandwich on dark bread. Pearl began to eat it. Her eyes behind the glasses settled once more on Alicia.

"I'm for it," Alicia said aloud. The young woman next to her snapped her head around and stared.

"Oh," said Alicia, "I guess I must be talking to myself."

The woman barely glanced at her. Alicia got up. She did not want to—her mind pulled her backward and away—but she walked over to where Pearl sat eating her sandwich.

"Pearl?"

"It's you, Alicia, is it. I thought so."

Alicia nodded. She wasn't going to initiate anything. "My doctor," Pearl went on, "says I have glaucoma. I may go blind."

"How terrible. I'm so sorry," Alicia said.

"Don't waste your pity on me, my dear. Why don't you sit down with me?" Alicia squeezed herself in the space beside Pearl and her neighbor. Pearl hitched at her sweater. "You mustn't waste your pity on me; you would be far better off indulging in a little self-pity."

Alicia thought Pearl was bullying her again. She didn't like it. Their meeting, which had been swallowed, returned as a full-blown, articulated memory.

Pearl continued: "The doctor informed me that had I

submitted to a simple test a year or so ago, they might have caught this condition and halted its progress. How easy for him to tell me that! It costs money to have one's eyes examined." Pearl's face screwed up in disgust.

Alicia wanted to avoid a discussion of money with Pearl. She began to devise ways of escaping as soon as possible.

"I understand," Pearl said, "that you are thinking of changing positions."

"How did you know that?"

"One hears, my dear, one hears these things. I suspect you are having great difficulty making up your mind."

"No more than anyone would under the circumstances," Alicia said.

"I doubt that very much," Pearl told her. "I know you extremely well, perhaps better than you know yourself."

"And *I* doubt *that.*"

"You won't leave," Pearl said. "Mark my words."

The crowd surged and flowed around them like a soft wave on the bay side. The heat of the sun grew stronger and spread.

"I can't stay here, Pearl," Alicia said. "I have to meet my husband." She consulted her watch in a conspicuous gesture.

"You are *so* transparent, Alicia," Pearl said. "You cannot bear to sit next to me. You believe I have become what is commonly referred to as a bag lady."

"Oh, no," Alicia said. She felt herself flush.

"Do me the courtesy of being candid. It is the least you owe me after what we have been through together."

Alicia got up. "I really have to be going," she said.

"You won't go," the woman said. "You won't leave. You will never go to New York; you are hopelessly tied to your job and your family." Phlegm caught in Pearl's throat. She scraped it up with a cough, took out a scrap of paper napkin and spat into it. Alicia's stomach jolted.

"You must leave me alone," Alicia said.

"We shall see," Pearl told her.

"I don't want to see you again, Pearl," Alicia said, feeling braver by the moment.

Pearl said, "You won't leave me." Alicia fled.

The shop called Crabtree & Evelyn smelled like a meadow in July, sweet and spicy. Tiny pale bits of dried herbs, shriveled leaves curled like shrimp, and desiccated flowers filled dozens and dozens of jars ranging in size from finger-length to knee-high. This store contained nothing but scent.

A woman behind the counter said, "Are you interested in anything in particular?" The way she said it made Alicia think she was being taken for a non-buyer.

"No thanks," she said. "I'm just looking. Or rather smelling." The woman did not react.

"Is that you, Alicia?" Alicia turned and saw Jeannette Ashburton, huge in a wool coat from the 1960s, with large flat round buttons and a too-short skirt. She held up a jar of dried flowers with a ribbon around its throat.

"What are you doing here?" Alicia asked.

"The same thing you are, I imagine. I come here a lot. I love this little shop; it reminds me of the house I grew up in. My mother always kept a bowl of this stuff in the front hall. It loses its strength after a few weeks, don't you know?"

"How are you feeling these days?" Alicia asked, as the lunch with Jeannette returned to her in detail for the first time since it had taken place.

"Same as ever," Jeannette said, sighing. "Though I must say I haven't had an attack for almost two weeks now. I had to let Paulie go—she was stealing from me. Little things, a belt with a brass buckle I was rather fond of, a small silver salt cellar. I can't imagine what she wanted with these things. I confronted her and she denied it, of course, but it couldn't have been anyone else."

"I'm sorry to hear that," Alicia said.

"The way of the world, is the way I see it. Our little

deceptions." Jeannette took a deep breath. "Cousin Thornton tells me you may be leaving Boston for another job—New York City, is it? Toiling in one of those gigantic book mills. What a pity. . . ." She put down the jar and started off down the row of shelves, looking, fingering, sniffing. Alicia trailed after her.

"What's a pity?"

"That you gave up writing. That you turned your back on a natural gift and settled for working on other people's work instead."

"Jeannette, I've told you that I love my work. I get a tremendous amount of satisfaction from editing. My God, I wouldn't do it if I didn't enjoy it. God knows I don't do it for the money. I do it because I want to!"

"Methinks she doth protest too much," Jeannette said crisply. She opened a huge jar labeled "Savannah Gardens" and leaned over it, sniffing. "Now that's what I call intoxicating. Smell it!"

"I can smell it from here," Alicia said.

"I'm going to tell you something you may not want to hear," Jeannette said. "If you do go to New York and leave your family behind or whatever curious arrangement you work out, you may just start writing again. Stranger things have been known to happen."

"What nonsense!" Alicia cried. "I don't want to write."

Jeannette looked startled. The woman behind the counter glanced at them. Alicia realized she had said this more loudly than she had intended.

"I think you should go anyway," Jeannette said, straightening up. "I don't believe people should allow themselves to stagnate. That was one of the things I tried to tell you girls at Carey. Change, constant change, that's the ticket."

"Look who's talking," Alicia said. "Your apartment is nothing but a museum. You haven't moved an inch out of your own past."

"You can hardly expect me to throw away those valuable

furnishings, can you? That would be ludicrous. Forgive me, Alicia, but you're growing more difficult by the day . . ."

"You don't want me to forgive you, you don't care what you say to me." She stared hard at Jeannette Ashburton, who picked up a plastic envelope filled with potpourri and marched to the counter with it.

"A conventional phrase," Jeannette said coldly. "I don't see any reason to beat around the bush. You gave up something precious. Don't make a second mistake of this magnitude. Change your life—you're being drowned in domesticity."

"Forgive *me,*" Alicia said. "But I don't know what gives you the right to be so blunt—and so bossy. You're nothing but a sad old busybody."

Jeannette stared at Alicia with cold wide eyes. "You're making a fatal error," she said. "But I've had my say in this matter." And turning to the saleswoman, she said in the prettiest, politest voice Alicia had ever heard, "And how much is this, please?"

Shuddering, Alicia bolted from the store and stood breathing hard by the door. Then, so as not to have to see Jeannette again when she came out, Alicia walked hurriedly past the shops bordering the mall. Their names repelled her—The Barefoot Eagle, The Sandpiper, Bear Necessities, Crate and Barrel—so cute. What on earth did they sell in The Barefoot Eagle? The editor in Alicia said that birds don't have feet and don't wear shoes in *any* case and why did everything here have to be so cute? Humorless and pedantic over these deliberate imprecisions and the attempt to be adorable, Alicia shook her head and went back into the great hall, not wanting to at all but aware now of the design: she'd seen two; there were still three to go.

Alicia stood by The Walrus and the Carpenter watching a husky youth opening clams as easily as if they were fortune cookies, when she heard a voice in her ear, breath on her neck, "Alicia."

She whirled. Roger Tucker laid his palm on her upper arm. "I knew you'd be here this morning," he said. "I'm showing some Spanish architects around the market. They want to know why everyone appears to be on the edge of starvation. They thought we had plenty to eat here in America, no one starving. I say, 'Look at that archway, regard this amazing use of space,' and all they want is to have their pictures taken wearing Victorian clothes. . . . Dearest woman, just seeing you again makes my knees go soft. Come and sit down with me for a minute . . ."

"Where are your architects?"

"They're having their pictures taken in costume." The afternoon she had spent with Roger came back to Alicia bathed in pastels and accompanied by lydian music and the throb of sex. Roger led Alicia to a table under the dome. He sat, she sat. He said, "My obsession with you is as strong as ever. Your beautiful face, your lovely body superimpose themselves when I'm doing a drawing. I dream about you, about us, almost every night."

"Roger, please, you've got to stop this. There's no future in it. Please be reasonable."

"Reason has no meaning for me," he said. "It doesn't enter the equation."

Two boys in Red Sox jackets sat down at the table. Their paper plates were piled with Chinese noodles crowned with chicken wings. Roger looked at Alicia hungrily; she saw his eyes moisten. "Would you like to sit somewhere else," he said.

"No," she said, "and I can't stay here much longer either."

"Are you going to New York?" He sounded so bleak he might have been saying *New Zealand* or *The Moon*.

"You too?" she said, not really surprised. Music came at them but the noise made by the people was so great it swallowed the connections; Alicia could not even tell whether the music was classical or rock. "How do you know about New York?"

"I know everything about you, ' Roger said. "I know you're

worried about your daughter—needlessly. I know your closest friend was killed, I know about you and your husband."

One of the boys stopped tearing at his chicken wing and smiled at Alicia. She winced.

"I don't want to hear this, Roger," she said as quietly as she could.

"I can't help it."

"You've got to."

"And what about New York? Are you going?"

"I'm not sure."

"Don't go," he pleaded. "I couldn't bear it."

"If I stay I won't see you anymore," she said. "So what difference does it make?"

"Just knowing you're in the same city, that I might catch a glimpse of you on Commonwealth Avenue."

"You're a fantasist," she said. "Let's get out of this place, it's making me claustrophobic." She got up and began moving away.

"Let me make love to you one last time," Roger said, following her. He grasped her arm.

"You've got to leave me alone," Alicia said. "I'm not up to an affair, Roger, I can't lie to Barney, he trusts me, God knows why, I'm wicked enough, but he trusts me. I'm not built to go sneaking around motel lobbies. Other women do it, it doesn't seem to bother them, not at all, they can lead double lives and be happy as clams at high tide. They put the husband in one slot, the lover in another and that's that, all neat, no messy edges. I can't do it. It would drive me crazy. The only way I could meet you would be to leave my husband and I'm not going to do it. I love Barney."

"You can't. I don't believe you."

"I do, Roger."

"That means you're not going to New York, then, doesn't it?" His lips trembled.

"I just told you, I don't know yet."

"You can leave your husband for a half-assed job but not for me!" Roger squeezed her arm, hard. Alicia let out a noise of hurt and annoyance. "Leave me alone, Roger, you're scaring me."

"Lord knows I don't mean to," he said, practically in tears. He let go and put his palm over his eyes. "I'd rather die than cause you distress."

"Then don't have anything more to do with me," Alicia said. "Because you *do* distress me, I can't handle your ardor. I'm too weak."

"You weak? You're not weak, you're as strong as—"

"A horse?" she asked, smiling.

"I can't compare you to a horse," he said, refusing to share the humor. A heavyset man in a long leather coat jostled her; she fell against Roger. She was immediately aroused, hating herself for it.

"I'm asking you again, Roger, I want you to let me go. Now."

"I can't live without you. I don't want to live without you."

"You'll just have to," she said and forced herself to leave his side. She thrust herself into a clot of people moving slowly in the glass-covered corridor between hall and mall. Her legs were warm and soft. She thought of what Roger's fingers felt like on their journey over her bare flesh.

Once more outside, trying to regain her equilibrium—what was left of it—Alicia looked at her watch. More than half an hour's time before she was to meet Barney. She deliberately searched the crowd for a familiar face and caught sight of Wilma Fearing sitting on the same bench that Pearl, now gone, had occupied. Wilma held a large pad on her lap and was scratching on it with a fine pen.

"I've taken up art again," Wilma said as Alicia drew near. "I know I'm not good enough to sell anything but it keeps me out of trouble." Wilma looked thinner and more nervous than ever.

Alicia peered at Wilma's pad. The drawing was nothing more

than a tangle of lines; Alicia was not certain of the true shape of anything pictured there.

"I'm trying to do the crowds," Wilma explained. "You know, chaos rendered in black and white?"

"I see," said Alicia.

"I've joined a class in adult ed in Boston," Wilma said. "My teacher says I have talent but then she needs to keep her job, doesn't she?" Wilma seemed to be pleading with Alicia to corroborate the teacher's evaluation.

"It's a little hard to say, when you're more or less a beginner," Alicia said.

"I'm hardly a beginner," Wilma said. "I've been a dabbler all my life."

Alicia thought: Wilma doesn't like me. Fine—I don't like her either.

"Can I ask you a question?" Alicia said. Wilma nodded. "Why are you here?"

"Do you mean today or generally?" Wilma said.

"Right now. Today."

"To talk to you," Wilma said. "Though I don't know why. It always makes me jumpy when I talk to you."

Alicia laughed. Wilma looked cross. "I want to tell you," she said, "that it doesn't matter one way or the other whether you go to New York or not. You always land on your feet no matter what you do. You're steeped in luck. Always were."

"That's not true at all," Alicia said, not aware until this moment of how angry Wilma made her. "I've landed on my bottom enough times so that I'm permanently bruised."

Wilma eyed Alicia with obvious disbelief on her face: the thin lips spread in a tight little smile, her brows shot upward. "No, Alicia, you're definitely one of the lucky ones. Things have a way of turning out right for you whatever the circumstances. As for me, well, I guess I don't have to tell you that rotten doesn't begin to describe my luck, it's as if there were a curse on me. I never, like some people, had anything to begin with. . . ."

Alicia felt a rush of adrenaline in her legs. "I work terribly hard for what I get," she said. "You think it's easy because you don't see the work. What I have didn't just happen, like some accident, like winning a lottery or stumbling across the Pharaoh's tomb. Just because it doesn't look hard to someone on the outside doesn't mean that I didn't put in a huge effort . . ."

"For chrissake, Alicia, stop patting yourself on the back. Whatever you say isn't going to convince me you're not lucky." Wilma bent over her drawing again. "Damn," she said, "I've run out of ink." She stabbed the air with her pen.

Alicia was stunned by Wilma's accusation; she couldn't say anything. The urge to hit Wilma was so strong that she squeezed her hands together into a single fist. . . .

"I'm not going to let you lay your grief on me any more," Alicia said in a steady voice.

"You're a bad listener," Wilma said. "I don't know how you can be so lucky and be such a lousy listener." Wilma raised her head and looked out in the noontime crowd. "There's a man staring at you," she said. "A man with a beard. Looks nasty to me."

"Dr. Koenig," Alicia said softly, forcing herself not to look at him. "I'm going to meet my husband," she said to Wilma. "I don't want to see you again, Wilma. I thought maybe we could be friends but not now."

Wilma shrugged. "Face it; you never did have any use for me."

Having made certain that Dr. Koenig was not following her, Alicia walked more slowly, under the late April sun. A plane sliced diagonally into the sky, making a slow path upward, trailing its long gray tail which separated and puffed in the invisible currents of air.

It was only a few blocks from the market to the restaurant where Alicia met Barney; he was there first, sitting at a table where he could keep an eye on the front door. He waved when he saw her. She smiled across at him.

"This is the first place I ever ate oysters in," he told her after she was settled. He squeezed a shower of lemon juice over a plate of them.

"I'm sorry I'm late," Alicia said.

"That's all right," said Barney. "Where are the flowers?"

"What flowers?"

"The artificial flowers you said you were going to buy."

"I didn't buy anything."

"What were you doing? Wasn't it crowded?"

"It was very crowded," she said. "Mobbed, in fact. I don't know why I stayed there so long. It's really unbelievable; they're going to have to make another circle of hell for places like the Market on Saturday. Though I suppose there are some people who actually enjoy being squashed."

Their waiter came over and took Alicia's order. "Who brought you here?" she asked Barney.

"My cousin, Frank Lieber. He thought I ought to have oysters and a girl. I was seventeen and severely retarded, I guess. I think Frank regarded the oysters as a sort of rite of passage." Barney had removed his glasses; they lay beside his water glass like a prop in an advertisement for beer.

"You never told me that before," she said.

"There's a lot I haven't told you," Barney said.

"Is that so?"

"Aren't you going to eat that?" he said, pointing to the chowder the waiter had brought her. He picked up some oyster crackers and dropped them into her bowl.

She smiled. "I feel pretty good," she said. "I don't know why."

"I'm glad to hear that," Barney said. She realized that no matter how hard she tried to make it otherwise, he would never shed his incipient caution; he wore it like an eccentric wears an overcoat in August. Alicia took a spoonful of soup. She was suddenly ravenous.

"Did you have the oysters and the girl on the same day? I should think you would have."

"I did. I did," Barney said. "Her name was Elaine. She was a friend of Frank's sister. She couldn't stop talking the whole time."

Alicia said, "Do you think we ought to tell each other all? Would that be a good idea?"

"I like it this way," Barney said. "It's worked so far and as I always say, if it's not broken don't fix it."

"I never heard you say that before," Alicia said.

"Don't you have something you do have to tell me?" Barney asked.

The invaders of the address book—Wilma, Jeannette, Roger, Pearl, Dr. Koenig—let her know then that they were right there in Boston's Oldest Restaurant with her, yammering for her attention but instead of growing loud, they grew fainter, as if they were being dragged off in a cart. Their sounds receded, they seemed to be fading into the back of the picture, they dissolved into the vanishing point. And as this occurred, Alicia Baer's two lives, reality one and reality two, merged and were swallowed by the mist at the end of the world.

"Please listen to me now, Barney," she said. "I've decided to stay here and not take the job in New York. It may mean that I have to murder Phyllis Vance, but I'm going to keep my job and stay here with you and Toby."

"Are you sure this is what you want?"

Alicia dropped her spoon. It struck the side of her bowl, ringing. "Why are you asking me that? Don't you suppose I know what I'm doing?"

"I'm sorry," he said. "I didn't mean to suggest that you hadn't thought about it carefully."

"You did, Barney, you don't realize what that question makes me feel like. Accept my decision as I offer it. Trust me."

"You're angry," he said. "I hope this isn't the way it's going to be: you angry because you never tried the other way. Angry at me."

"I won't be, Barney," she said. "But you have to act as if you believe I know what I'm doing."

"It's a bad habit, isn't it?"

"You do the same thing to your nurse," Alicia said. "You talk to her as if she were a dummy. Marcia's quite smart, you know, she should have been a doctor."

Barney said, "I'll try not to do it anymore." He lowered his eyes like a child after a scolding. "I'm a rat," he said.

"No, you're not," Alicia said. "And I don't want to play that game either."

"I have to tell you, Allie—well, I can't tell you, you'll just have to understand somehow—that I'm terribly relieved you're not going to New York. I've been distracted myself. I didn't want you to go, I couldn't bear the idea that you might take the job. I guess I'm used to you. It wouldn't have worked out, you commuting, it might have worked mechanically but that's all. You know, there were nights when I didn't sleep more than a couple of hours, worrying that you might leave me. Ha!" he said. "I sound like a baby, don't I?"

"Why didn't you tell me? Sometimes I felt you really didn't care one way or the other, that you'd forgotten all about it," she said.

"Not for a second," Barney said. "And I did tell you, I swear I did. That night you lost your address book, when you first told me you might go to New York, I asked you if you loved me."

"That's not quite the same thing."

"I'm going to order us some champagne," he said brightly. "To celebrate."

"Another rite of passage," she said. She didn't see any point in telling Barney that the last few times she had drunk champagne it had given her a terrible headache.